The DOG PARK Detectives
Paw and Order

Blake Mara is a pseudonym of Mara Timon, author of Second World War thrillers *City of Spies* and *Resistance*. She started writing as a child; mostly short stories, but when an idea caught her imagination, she followed one 'what if' after another until her first (and second, and third ...) novel emerged.

Mara is a native New Yorker who moved to the UK about twenty years ago. When Covid hit, she went cliché and got a pandemic puppy – a miniature dachshund with a massive personality. This opened her eyes to the canine-loving community that blossomed around the local dog park, and who became the inspiration for *The Dog Park Detectives*, the first book in her cosy crime series. But while her dog park pack have tackled some local crimes, they haven't found a dead body in the park ... yet.

For more information, follow Mara at her website or on social media:

www.blakemara.com
X @TheBlakeMara
f BlakeMaraAuthor
@TheBlakeMara

Writing as Mara Timon:	*As Blake Mara:*
City of Spies	The Dog Park Detectives
Resistance	Bone of Contention

The DOG PARK Detectives
Paw and Order

Blake Mara

SIMON & SCHUSTER

London · New York · Amsterdam/Antwerp · Sydney/Melbourne · Toronto · New Delhi

First published in Great Britain by Simon & Schuster UK Ltd, 2026

Copyright © Blake Mara, 2026

The right of Blake Mara to be identified as author of this work has been asserted in accordance with the Copyright, Designs and Patents Act, 1988.

1 3 5 7 9 10 8 6 4 2

Simon & Schuster UK Ltd, 1st Floor
222 Gray's Inn Road, London WC1X 8HB

For more than 100 years, Simon & Schuster has championed authors and the stories they create. By respecting the copyright of an author's intellectual property, you enable Simon & Schuster and the author to continue publishing exceptional books for years to come. We thank you for supporting the author's copyright by purchasing an authorised edition of this book.

No amount of this book may be reproduced or stored in any format, nor may it be uploaded to any website, database, language-learning model, or other repository, retrieval, or artificial intelligence system without express permission. All rights reserved. Enquiries may be directed to Simon & Schuster, 222 Gray's Inn Road, London WC1X 8HB or RightsMailbox@simonandschuster.co.uk

Simon & Schuster Australia, Sydney
Simon & Schuster India, New Delhi

www.simonandschuster.co.uk
www.simonandschuster.com.au
www.simonandschuster.co.in

The authorised representative in the EEA is Simon & Schuster Netherlands BV, Herculesplein 96, 3584 AA Utrecht, Netherlands. info@simonandschuster.nl

Simon & Schuster strongly believes in freedom of expression and stands against censorship in all its forms. For more information, visit BooksBelong.com

A CIP catalogue record for this book is available from the British Library

Paperback ISBN: 978-1-3985-5270-8
eBook ISBN: 978-1-3985-5271-5
Audio ISBN: 978-1-3985-5272-2

This book is a work of fiction. Names, characters, places and incidents are either a product of the author's imagination or are used fictitiously. Any resemblance to actual people living or dead, events or locales is entirely coincidental.

Typeset in Sabon by M Rules
Printed and Bound in the UK using 100% Renewable Electricity at CPI Group (UK) Ltd

For my niblings, Matthew and Alexandra. I love you, believe in you, and will always be here for you.

And for my beloved, borky Dude, without whom this book wouldn't happen and I would be a much lesser person. So very, very grateful to have you in my life.

Meet THE PACK

Louise Mallory and her miniature dachshund **Niklaus (Klaus)** moved to the neighbourhood after her divorce. Klaus is a pandemic puppy, and Louise's introduction to the dog park community. Klaus thinks he's a slightly short Rottweiler. Louise could be called the same. While stepping back from the company she founded, Louise has discovered a talent for sleuthing.

Irina Ivanova lives in the building next door to Louise. Despite working in law, her superpower is internet stalking. Her Scottish terrier, **Hamish**, is Klaus's best friend and a canine trash compactor who will eat anything (and then get sick).

Ex-convict **Gav MacAdams** looks older than he is, thanks to time in prison for GBH. He has a wonky hip but can still handle himself in a fight. So can his Affenpinscher, **Violet**. On a good day, Violet looks like a demented Pomeranian; on a bad day, she resembles Gru's dog from the Minions movies.

Jake Hathaway recently moved in across the canal from Louise with his grey-and-white Staffordshire terrier, **Luther**. Jake is a dark horse, with no online presence. Louise is attracted to him, but can't seem to find out much about him. He's continued to defy Irina's stalking skills, maintaining a consistent and (to Louise) frustrating air of mystery.

Ejiro is a soft-spoken gentle giant from Birmingham, who is often the voice of reason within the Pack. His smart-mouthed partner **Yasmin** is petite and energetic. They have a boxer, **Hercules**, who is ball-obsessed.

Fiona ('Fi') is an Australian redhead who doesn't take much seriously. Her cocker spaniel, **Nala**, is very fond of (and submissive to) Klaus.

Claire is a journalist for the local rag, *The Chronicle*. She's Irish and has a French bulldog ('Frenchie') called **Tank**. They both have a tendency to brazen their way through stuff, even if Tank sometimes does randomly barf (it's a Frenchie thing).

Meg is an IT programmer, working in nearby Canary Wharf. She has a brown dapple dachshund called **Tyrion**. Because, you know, what better name would you give a feisty and clever little fiend? All dogs love Meg; she's a goldmine for treats. She's dating **Ethan** (aka 'Cat boy'), who has a crotchety cat called **Marlowe**.

Local Lothario **Tim Aziz** has a Jack Russell called **Loki**. Tim has recently been dumped by his long-suffering girlfriend, who finally had enough of his infidelity.

Expats **Paul** and his partner **Ella**, are expecting their first child. Despite having good friends in the Pack, Ella's fearful of the neighbourhood and keen to return to France. They have two black Labrador retrievers: **Bark Vader** and **Jimmy Chew**. Jimmy is notorious for stealing other dogs' toys (and breaking the squeakers). Vader likes mud puddles.

Dr Indira ('Indy') Balasubramanian has a Romanian rescue called **Banjo**. Banjo looks to be part border collie, part corgi and 100 per cent street dog. He's come a long way since he was adopted, but isn't overly interested in engaging with the other dogs.

Kate Marcovici is an artist new to the area. She has two rescue beagles, Perseus (**Percy**) and Andromeda (**Andy**).

Outside the Pack (but still of note)

Andy Thompson and **Scott Williams** are detective constables with the Met Police, who met the Pack last June while investigating the murder of Phil Creasy. Andy is smart, ambitious and, despite her blowing hot and cold, fancies Irina. Scott thinks Irina's bonkers. Both, though, have a (sometimes grudging) respect for the Pack. They're part of a team that includes **Family Liaison Officer Nicole 'Nic' Saren** and **CCTV officer Doug 'Harry' Harriman**. They report into **DI Alf Badolato** and **DCS Richard Grieves**.

Gav's mates **Jono** and **Norma** own a café in Poplar and have a mastiff-cross called **Rocco**.

Barbara ('Babs') Lane is Louise's very capable second-in-command at the consultancy firm she founded.

Annabel Lindford-Swayne works for one of the property management companies developing the area around Partridge Park, thanks to her father **Robert Lindford-Swayne**'s connections. She's Louise's friend as well as her go-to person when Louise has questions about the official side of Partridge Park's gentrification.

Caren 'Not Karen' Hansen and **Benny Bryce** are local hairdressers at the Hands-On salon. Caren is now in police custody following her involvement in local crimes.

Mo is the owner/manager of the News-N-Booze off-licence, and a good friend of Gav's.

Angela is one of the local doggie daycare providers.

Hazel Carstairs has two Yorkshire terriers, **Bella** and **Meeky**. She often dresses them in animal print outfits that match her own.

Susan ('**Shih Tzu Sue**') has recently moved to the area with **Bonnie** the Shih Tzu. She's not overly social with the Pack.

Dave Najafi owns Cluckin' Good Chicken, the new chicken shop on the High Street as well as a string of cut-price perfume shops.

Sunday

Prologue

HAZEL CARSTAIRS

'Meeks, you little ratbag, what have you eaten?' Hazel Carstairs leaned over, wrenched open her Yorkshire terrier's mouth and fished around until her fingers closed around something soft and moist. She threw it into the bushes without looking at it. Absently wiping her hand on her trousers, she leaned over to shout in the little dog's face. 'Why do you eat crap off the street? You're gonna get sick. You're gonna get sick and people are gonna think I don't feed you.'

Meeky wagged his little tail and licked her hand, and Hazel felt herself melt. She had three grown children and a squad of grandchildren, but none of them held her heart the way her two Yorkies did. Unconditional love, given and returned, no matter what. That was the beauty of dogs, innit?

Hazel straightened Meeky's zebra-print coat and

frowned. There was no shortage of litter on the ground: a colourful assortment of discarded vapes, drinks cans, a few broken bottles and some chocolate wrappers. Chocolate, for heaven's sake. *Toxic enough to put a dog's liver out of commission for good, and it was left around like it were someone else's job to clean up after 'em.*

Meeky's sister, Bella, was eyeing up a discarded sarnie. 'Don't you dare,' Hazel growled and toed the sandwich out of reach. 'The people what leave this crap around, they're the first to whinge about the foxes an' the rats. Ain't like it's the rats' fault, mind. They go where the food is. Better 'em than the trash. At least they'll give you a chance to chase 'em.' *She looked at the two small dogs at her feet.* 'Bred to hunt 'em, your lot. Not like you'd know what to do if either of you actually caught one, though. Soft, you are. Both of you. And thank heavens for that. Last thing we need is for you to chase one of them rodents across a busy street.'

The idea of that scared the crap out of Hazel. Maybe the rats were more sensible than her Yorkies.

No, it wasn't just that the trash were unsightly. It were dangerous to the dogs. And the kids.

Cos the trash wasn't only on this side of the iron fence. The sea of rubbish flowed into the children's play area. The basket swing swayed in the morning breeze, a denim-clad leg draped over its side. Underneath it lay a couple of energy drinks cans and a foil packet of crisps.

Hazel had read somewhere about a dog that had got its snout stuck in a crisp bag. Poor thing couldn't get it off and suffocated. Fury began to pulse deep inside of her. Scooping a Yorkie under each arm, she strode towards the swing to give the young man a piece of her mind. She didn't expect it to make a huge difference to the park, didn't believe in that woo-woo crap her granddaughter spouted about 'ripple effects', whatever that meant. All she knew was that maybe one less person would be polluting her park.

One less person leaving crap that could endanger Meeky and Bella.

It wasn't just anger; it was *righteous* anger.

Hazel picked up speed along with decibels. 'Wot you think you're doing, leaving this garbage here? You so privileged you think it's someone else's job to clean up after you? You think you're too good to walk five farking steps to drop it in the bin?'

The leg continued to gently swing, but the opposite knee, resting against the side of the basket, didn't move. The young man's chin rested on his chest, like he was sleeping.

Sleepin' it off, or maybe pretending to sleep so that he didn't have to answer her.

Weren't the first time, prob'bly wouldn't be the last. Either way, he didn't take any notice of Hazel.

'Wot? You too stoned to listen to me?' With a Yorkie in each hand, she couldn't push the kid to wake him up. Not without putting one of the little scavengers down. Instead, she raised her foot and kicked the swing. 'Farking fool!'

The man's head lolled a little to one side, but otherwise

he didn't move. The energy drinks clearly weren't worth their money.

'Wake up and look at me when I'm talkin' to you!'

His head lolled a bit further, and a sick feeling spread through Hazel's belly; one that had little to do with the litter surrounding her. The man's sunglasses slid off, bouncing on the pavement.

'Oh no,' *Hazel whispered. His head really shouldn't lean that far to the side. Not a' that angle, like.*

Her foot nudged the swing again, this time more gently. 'Wake up, you clod. You can't be dead.'

She looked away from him – those cloudy, staring eyes; the gaping mouth; the thin red line across his neck – to her dogs, but they were focused on a half-eaten Mars bar a few metres away.

'Please don't be dead,' *she implored, knowing it was already too late. She did a quick scan of the area. Maybe she could leave him there for someone else to find?*

Wi' all the dead bodies around here, there's gonna be someone, some CCTV, that puts you right here right now, Hazel, *she told herself.* You don't do the right thing, someone's gonna think you was involved.

Instead of the 'why me' that she intended, the words that erupted from her throat were 'Jesus farkin' Christ Almighty!'

The echo faded, and Hazel wondered if she could get away with one more angry kick to the swing. Deciding it wasn't a great idea, she shifted Bella to her other side, pulled her mobile out and dialled 999.

1

LOUISE

Sarah the Trainer

> Hey, we've moved from Vicky Park to Wells St Common, just behind the People's Pub. It's a bit quieter, less distractions for the dogs.

> Running late – sorry! Be there in 5.

Once upon a time, I was pathologically early. 'To be on time was to be late', and all that. Then I got a dog, and not just any dog: a dachshund. 6.5 kgs of shouty stubbornness.

His legs might be little, but they were like emergency breaks. No matter how much time I left to get somewhere, I always ended up skidding in late.

Five of my friends were already at the Common, standing with their dogs in a loose circle, laughing with Sarah the Trainer. Today she sported a bright parka over leggings that had her Pomeranian dog's face on them and a headband with cat ears. Her long dark hair was tied back from her face with a string of green poo bags. While I had issues with chicken bones left on the street, her bone of contention was the dog poop that people couldn't be bothered to clean up. She'd even written and recorded a song called 'Pick it Up'.

She was also a cracking good trainer and had been a massive help when Klaus was a pup and I didn't have a clue what I was doing so it made sense to call her about running a scent training class.

I slid my rucksack off my shoulder and stepped in front of a contraption that looked like a lopsided flower pot. Klaus gave it a suspicious sniff, and readied himself to raise his leg on it.

'Sorry I'm late,' I said, holding him back. 'Thanks for waiting, and for running this special session for us, Sarah.'

'It's not like our dogs don't already know how to sniff out a dead body,' Irina drawled. She wasn't wrong; this past June, Klaus and Hamish, Irina's Scottish terrier, had found a dead body in our local park, then a few months later our friend Yaz had stumbled on another one, posed on the canal path with a box of chicken wings. She'd credited the find to her Boxer, Hercules, but knowing Herc, he'd been more interested in the chicken than the dead man.

'I don't want to find a dead body, but I'd be happy if Tyrion could find me a few truffles,' Meg said. 'I read somewhere that dachshunds are the second-best sniffers out of all the dogs.' Meg was the understated one in our group: petite and wide eyed, she gave out a little-girl-meets-Goth vibe, but if you were in a tight spot, she'd be the one you'd want in your corner.

'That's right,' Sarah said, pointing at Meg and smiling. 'Just after bloodhounds.' If she saw Irina roll her eyes, she ignored it. 'Here are some more fun facts. Your dog has up to *three hundred million* olfactory receptors compared to your six million. The part of their brain that is responsible for interpreting these is forty per cent larger than ours.'

I looked down at Klaus, wondering how all that could fit into such a small package.

'They can smell a hundred thousand times better than us. Their noses are so sensitive that they could detect half a teaspoon of sugar in an Olympic-sized swimming pool.'

'Yeah, and Hammy would try to eat it.' Irina's throaty Russian accent carried on the cold December air. 'And then end up in Doggie A&E.'

'Again,' I pointed out.

She tucked a strand of fair hair back behind an ear. Where most of us were bundled up for the tundra, Irina's jacket was open at the neck; this weather was nothing to her. She inclined her head toward me. 'True.'

Sarah let the sidebar slide, and I felt like the kid in class who was not only late, but who then got caught goofing around. I would have blushed, but my face was already red from the hike to Vicky Park. 'Dogs smell in 3D, just as we see in 3D,' Sarah went on. 'Our eyes see two slightly different pictures and our brain puts them together to make one picture. Dogs' nostrils can work independently and their brain puts the scents together to help them figure out where the smelly stuff is.'

'Cool, hey?' Across the circle from me, Fiona was giving her cocker spaniel, Nala, an impressed look. 'You're more than just a pretty face.'

'A dog's nose can separate air so that one portion goes to the olfactory sensing area, which is responsible for distinguishing scents, and the other goes to the respiratory system for breathing. Also nifty: dogs can inhale and exhale simultaneously. Pretty useful for when they're sniffing around. You'll be unsurprised to know that we humans can only do one at a time.'

'Next-level multitasking.' Claire pulled her beanie hat off, refastened her blonde curls under it, grimacing at her French bulldog. She'd made no secret of her low expectations for Tank. *He has, like, three brain cells, Lou. One is focused on food, one on humping and one, maybe, is on me. Maybe. And let's face it, with a half-hidden nose, he'd have to get right up to something to find anything.*

Tank was finding Nala just fine, and that second brain cell was definitely firing up as he edged closer to the pretty spaniel.

Who obligingly rolled onto her back.

And stayed there, despite Fi's irritated hiss. 'As much of a tart as her mam,' Claire joked.

Sarah pretended not to hear the aside. 'Dogs have an extra olfactory organ. This is called the vomeronasal organ – and don't ask me to say that three times, fast. It's also called the Jacobson's organ and is responsible for detecting pheromones. This organ has helped dogs survive for thousands of years. It can help them identify suitable mates, discern between friendly animals and potential predators, recognise emotional states, notice when someone is pregnant, detect illnesses.'

A couple of kids, one holding a football, edged close to our group.

'Some dogs are even being trained to detect cancer. If you were to roll out a human's olfactory region it would be the size of an A4 piece of paper. If we rolled out your dog's, it would be the size of a football pitch.'

Herc planted his feet and began to bark at the children. In short order, the daxies had joined in the fun. *Got your back, bro!*

The kids bolted. Which set off the remaining dogs.

'Sorry,' I said, aware of how often I was apologising. 'They're all bark, no bite.' Which was true, but I wasn't going to lie: Klaus always looked pleased with himself when he chased off stranger danger.

'No problem. It happens in every class.' Sarah gave us a few minutes to get our dogs under control before continuing. 'I know this is the boring part. I'm just trying to give you a bit of background so you know what we're going to be working with.'

'It's not boring at all,' Meg protested. 'We're sorry. Please continue.'

Sarah reached into her pocket and pulled out a red rubber bobble toy. 'Okay, so you're probably wondering why I told you all to get one of these?' Hercules took that moment to circle a few times, then squatted.

'Jesus, Herc. You didn't want to poop on the walk here, but you need to do it right now?' Yaz fished a poo bag out of her pocket and knelt beside her dog. She made a gagging sound. 'I don't know what treats Daddy's been sneaking you. It's about the size of Tyrion.'

We all stared at Meg's little dappled dachshund. 'She's not wrong,' Meg said. 'Sorry, Sarah.'

'She's not wrong indeed,' Sarah said with an affable smile. If she was irked, she wasn't showing it, thank heavens. 'Now then.' She held up the red bobble, waggled it from side to side and repeated, 'Anyone want to guess why I asked you to start getting your dogs used to these?'

'Because there's some sort of statistic that they're into sex toys as well as chew toys?' Irina asked.

Yaz opened her mouth to respond.

'Enough!' I snapped before Sarah did. 'Enough already.'

Yaz stifled a giggle, and turned to toss the poo bag into a nearby bin.

Sarah's expression was a mix of amusement and gratitude. Irina's observation wasn't wrong, but it was out of place. I mouthed *Sorry* to Sarah and gestured for her to continue. Klaus gave me the side-eye, no doubt hoping I'd be distracted enough to miss him trying to wee on the wonky pot.

As a group, we'd agreed to do the training near Victoria

Park instead of our local 'Partridge Park' to minimise distractions for the dogs, but having their best friends in the same area was turning out to be as distracting for them as Irina's smart mouth was for us.

I didn't envy Sarah; this was going to be a long hour.

By the time Sarah was done with us, most of the dogs understood the basics of searching out the red toy, primarily because it was either stuffed with treats or because they'd get praise and, well, another treat when they did so. Their food obsession made training easier, but there was a long way to go until they'd be able to put any truffle pigs out of business.

'I didn't know that we were using red because dogs can't see that colour. Did you?' Fiona asked, falling into step beside me. A tall Australian with long auburn hair, red was her favourite colour. Today she wore a red parka with a matching red hat and gloves, and she had Nala on a red lead. Not for the first time, I wondered why she'd gone for a blonde cocker spaniel instead of a red one. 'I guess much of the stuff I buy Nala gets ignored because she doesn't see it.'

'Or see you when you're trying to call her,' Claire suggested, dragging Tank away from a picnic table as we walked home. There was a buzzing sound, and she dug around in her pocket to retrieve her phone. The others all pulled their own mobiles out and stared first at them, then at me, swearing softly.

'What?' I pulled out my own phone to see.

Partridge Bark

Paul (Bark Vader and Jimmy Chew's Dad)

@Louise is losing her touch – someone else found a dead body in the 'hood today.

Kate (Percy and Andy's Mum)

OMG – who?

Paul (Bark Vader and Jimmy Chew's Dad)

Who died or who found him?

Ella (Bark Vader and Jimmy Chew's Mum)

Arrête. Stop playing the fool, @Paul. We do not know who died. Not yet. Not who. Not how. Only that the old woman with the two Yorkies – I do not know her name – found him in the children's playground in the corner of Partridge Park. The

> police have cordoned off the area ... Again.

'You really have lost your touch, Lou. And now that Klausi's been all trained up on being a sniffer dog...' Fi's wink took the heat out of the statement.

'I'm with Meg on this.' I shrugged. 'I'm just as happy for Klaus to find me truffles.'

'Which explains exactly why you drag us up here on bloody freezing early Sunday morning, so the dogs can learn to search on command?' Irina said. 'Not many truffles growing in East London.'

'Not that I usually agree with the, ahh ... with Irina, but Lou,' Yaz said, catching herself before referring to Irina as 'the Tsarina', a nickname based more on Irina's attitude than her nationality. 'Our local crops seem to be weed and dead bodies.'

'Want to bet that it's one of the hounds that passed on today's session that finds the next body?' Claire paused to allow Tank to lift his leg for the 258,373,466th time on that street.

'That why you're here, Claire? Find a body and get the inside scoop?'

'If I'm a part of it, I can better report on it.' Claire winked. 'Although with Tank's nose, the chances aren't high. Speaking of which, anyone fancy taking the scenic route home past the kiddie park?'

Yaz shot Irina a look. 'Kill two birds with one stone?'

'What do you mean?'

Yaz grinned, unrepentant. 'Claire can get the scoop. And you can get another date with PC Andy. Assuming, of course, that he'll be working this case. He does tend to catch the ones that happen around here.'

'He's a detective, not a PC,' Irina snapped. Yaz knew that, of course. She just got a kick out of calling him that to wind Irina up. 'And he doesn't get to choose what cases he gets.'

'Well, we do get our fair share of crime.' Yaz drew out the last word. 'And I guess you haven't scared him bad enough to have him recuse himself from anything that happens in the neighbourhood.'

It was a valid question. There'd been an almost instant interest between Irina and Andy when we'd first met him, over the body of our murdered friend Phil Creasey, back in June. From there it had gone up, down, side-to-side and backwards, yet, as far as I could tell, not forwards.

'So, do you want to go then?' Yaz continued. 'We're almost there.'

'No.' Irina shrugged, pulling Hammy away from a half-eaten sandwich on the sidewalk. 'You go if you want to.'

'Great,' Yaz said. 'We'll give him your regards, shall we?'

I slowed down, studying Irina until she demanded, 'What?'

'Nothing,' I lied. Truth was, there was something off in her tone. Almost as if she didn't *need* to see Andy ... because she was seeing him later?

Or worse, had she reverted back to her situationship

with Tim Aziz? The local Lothario had been cut loose by his long-term, long-suffering girlfriend when she'd finally had enough of his cheating. Just because I hadn't seen the telltale signs – Tim's Jack Russell, Loki, keeping Hammy company on Irina's balcony while he 'entertained' her inside – didn't mean it wasn't happening.

'You're not back on with Tim are you?' I whispered at her.

Irina's eyes narrowed and she shook her head.

So, maybe there *was* something reprising with Andy. After her jerking him around for so long, he'd have to be nuts to have any sort of relationship with my crazy Russian friend, but stranger things had happened.

'Louise?'

I blinked at Meg. 'Sorry?'

'I live by the park anyway. Why not come over for a coffee? At least you can warm up.' *And see what the police were up to.*

The words were out of my mouth before I could stop them. 'Sure, why not.'

2

ANDY

Andy watched Mrs Carstairs walk away, clad in a zebra-print coat that matched her dogs' jackets. She'd tried to come across like an old-school moll, but he suspected that finding a dead body in the kiddie park hadn't just thrown her off her game, it had deflated her.

'All mouth, no trousers,' Detective Scott Williams said, agreeing with Andy's assessment. 'Kind of like her little dogs. Speaking of which, it's more than an hour in, and no sign of Marple and her Pack.'

Williams stood, arms crossed over his chest, while the coroner strapped the dead man to a gurney. Around them, the crime scene was being processed, fingerprinted, photographed. They'd check for witnesses and CCTV, but this neighbourhood was a black hole for both.

'Wrong.' Andy jerked his head behind Williams. 'No sign of Marple, but her Pack are watching from the balconies. I can see the French guy with the two black Labrador retrievers in the brick building, third floor. I'd bet that every move we make is being relayed to their group chat. Kind of surprised we haven't seen them, though. They usually walk their dogs here.'

'Want me to check? Far as I know, I'm still in the chat.'

Andy was unsuccessful in suppressing a grin. 'Irina hasn't kicked you out yet?'

'Hasn't found me. No reason to – I wasn't the idiot who gave her my number. Profile pic's a close-up of my neighbour's dog's snout. Has been for years, so that people can't find me if I don't want them to.'

Andy hummed a response, and Williams pushed his point. 'Not that I'm not glad that you managed to convince Irina to add you in in the first place.' He winked, knowing full well that Andy, worried about the danger the Pack might attract, had added himself and Williams to their group chat when Irina had left him with her unlocked phone. 'Shame that she kicked your skinny arse out.' He paused for effect. 'Of the chat, that is. As well.' His grin was unrepentant.

Andy shook his head, and stared at the sky. It was the red button that Williams kept pressing. And he wasn't done yet.

'Anyway, looks like you spoke too soon, Andy. Here comes the paw patrol.'

Andy turned, realising that he had to twist further than usual to see past the white paper hood he wore.

'Don't worry. There's no sign of your girl, or her little dog,' Williams cackled, and Andy wondered if his partner was *trying* to sound like the Wicked Witch of the West.

He craned his neck, watching a group of women coming down the canal path. They were bundled up for the cold, anonymous in their beanies and puffer jackets. What gave them away were the dogs in front of them: two miniature dachshunds wrapped up like floppy-eared burritos, a French bulldog that looked angry (even when he wasn't), a pretty cocker spaniel that flirted with everything they passed, human, canine or rubbish bin, and a black-and-brown boxer that was bigger than all the others put together, but who seemed to think he was the smallest.

Andy let his breath out slowly. There was no sign of the black Scottish terrier, though he knew that the women striding towards him were no less determined than its owner.

'Seriously, Andy. Keep the hood up. It suits you, and hides your fair form from the gentler sex.'

'You'd call that lot gentle?'

'Nope.' Williams grinned. 'Not a single one of them. But you got to admit: cases are never boring around here. Think that's why Grieves still goes all hands-on every time?'

'He's the DCS. I doubt he does it because he's bored,' Andy said.

The women were stopped by a uniformed officer outside the taped-off perimeter. 'Frank'll move them on,' Andy said, with a sliver of hope, all the while knowing that it was only a matter of time before his mobile phone began to buzz.

3

LOUISE

Partridge Bark

Paul (Bark Vader and Jimmy Chew's Dad)

> @Louise @Claire @Meg @Fiona @Yaz I saw you talking to the police. Any new intel on our latest dead body?

> Sadly no – they moved us on pretty quickly.

Claire (Tank's Mum)

> 'Nothing we can share with you at this point' yada yada. ☹

Claire put her phone down and reached for mine, reading aloud the news article I'd found in one of the national papers.

MAN AND DOG STABBED IN EAST LONDON PARK

A man and his dog were stabbed as fighting broke out over the weekend in Victoria Park.

Two men and a woman were arrested in the wake of a violent confrontation, which followed an incident involving two dogs in the popular, dog-friendly East London hotspot.

Police and paramedics were called to the Grove Road entrance of the park at just after 9:45 on Saturday morning and found a man in his forties with several stab wounds. A golden retriever was also found wounded, and another two individuals and an additional dog nearby had sustained dog bites. The man's injuries were deemed serious but not life-threatening, and he was taken to a nearby East London Accident & Emergency department while the dog was conducted to an emergency

> veterinarian clinic. A crime scene cordon has been put in place while the police continue to investigate.
>
> This comes just weeks after three young children and their fifty-six-year-old grandmother were rushed to hospital with life-threatening wounds after being mauled by an XL bully dog in South East London.
>
> A thirty-two-year-old man was arrested and taken into custody on suspicion of having dogs dangerously out of control.

'This to me proves that humans, not dogs, are the issue. I know I'm generalising here, but responsible dog owners would never put their dogs in dangerous situations,' Meg said, putting a tray of coffee mugs on the table. She'd changed into a unicorn onesie while the kettle boiled, and tied her hair – long black curls with a good six or eight inches of blues and purples at the bottom – into a ponytail. 'Hell, I'd rather put myself in danger than risk T. Any day.'

'Totes. I know I'm biased, what with being a journo, but speaking of getting a bad name for a few bad apples, can I say how much I dislike that random blurb at the bottom about some other dogs in some other location mauling children?' Claire said. 'There's no evidence that the cases are similar, and it's not even clear in the last paragraph if that man was arrested for today's incident in Vicky Park or the one in South East London.'

'True. But getting back to the point, nothing on our dead guy this morning?'

'Not yet,' I said and put my phone away. 'That's the only East-London-park-related crime I can find for this weekend.'

'Don't worry, Lou, there's still the rest of the day to get through. It is interesting though that the dog-related barney – which I'd bet started when the humans argued, then involved the dogs – gets national coverage but they were pretty much silent when that woman was killed there last week.'

We all turned to look at Fiona. 'What?'

'Yeah. I only found out because I was walking Nala up there not long after it happened. Silly, really – I forgot we'd changed the date for the training session. Anyway, that part of Vicky Park was cordoned off when I got there.'

I considered myself a news junkie, keeping an eye on the local as well as international apps, yet I hadn't heard about this. Glancing around the table, neither had most of my friends. 'Oh, didn't you hear about it?' Fi asked.

The rest of us looked at each other. At least I wasn't the only one to have missed it. 'What happened?' I asked.

'Yeah, see, this is my point. No one knows, but it didn't sound like suicide.' Fi took a mug of hot coffee and put it at her elbow. 'Let me try to find the police statement.' She fiddled a bit, then passed her phone around.

> **DEAD WOMAN FOUND IN VICTORIA PARK**
>
> Shortly before 10:00 a.m. on Sunday, police attended a wooded area inside Victoria Park, Tower Hamlets, finding the body of a deceased person at the scene.
>
> The identity of the woman is yet to be confirmed and next of kin located, but the Metropolitan Police have confirmed that the Homicide Command have opened an investigation into the death.
>
> The area has been cordoned off, and will remain so for several days to allow the forensics team to continue gathering evidence. The rest of the park remains open to the public and there will be increased police patrols in the area.
>
> Anyone with further information is encouraged to contact the police on 101, or Crimestoppers on 0800 555 111, giving the reference number listed below.

'Shit. Homicide?'

'Yeah. There wasn't much else in the news that I saw, but then I avoid the news these days.'

Claire and I exchanged a glance: we didn't. And yet we'd missed this. Victoria Park wasn't our local park, but it wasn't all that far away either.

Fi took a sip of coffee. Winced, added a spoonful of sugar and blew on it. 'Someone I bumped into at the scene was speculating that the dead woman was part of one of the homeless camps, but I don't think that was ever confirmed.'

'Homeless camps? In Victoria Park?'

'In any park, Lou,' Claire interjected.

'There was some talk of secret tunnels in the park too, but I think that's just a myth,' Fi went on.

'Secret tunnels?' I leaned back and looked at my friend, intrigued. It wasn't impossible that she was winding us up now, but how cool would that be?

Fi twisted her long red hair into a topknot, fastening it with a pencil, and stretched like a lean cat. 'Yeah, every so often, someone talks about secret tunnels under the park, but I'm pretty sure they're animal burrows or made up, to be honest.'

'Maybe the remains of an old World War Two Anderson shelter?' I guessed.

Claire stood, placing her empty mug in Meg's sink. 'I hate to be a downer, but do we think the dead woman or the dog-on-dog-on-human – or whatever it was – in Victoria Park have anything to do with the body in the Partridge kiddie park?' She reached for Tank's harness. The Frenchie was snoring by the radiator, his head resting on Nala's back, while the sausages had burrowed under blankets on the couch. He opened one eye as Claire approached, then quickly closed it.

You could almost hear him: *If she thinks I'm still sleeping, we won't go outside.*

If Tank thought that was true, he underestimated Claire's determination.

'Going back to the crime scene, Claire?' Meg asked.

She shrugged into her coat. 'Yeah, see what I can learn. Doubt they'll tell me anything, but a girl's gotta try. You want to come along, Lou?'

I was already shaking my head. 'No thanks.'

Three sets of eyes fixed on me, in varying degrees of shock and surprise. 'Seriously? That's not like you.'

'Not my circus, not my monkeys. I didn't find the man. Probably don't know him. And, last but never least, I'm not a cop.'

'But you're so *good* at hunting down murderers!' Fi laughed.

'So good that I paint a bullseye on my forehead?' I shook my head wryly. 'Don't forget: since June I've come close to being run down twice, my flat's been broken into and I've been attacked by a crazed killer on the towpath.' I settled back into my chair, hands firmly wrapped around my mug. 'No thank you. I'm sitting this one out.'

I hadn't expected them to laugh *quite* that hard.

'Bet you a tenner that Lou finds a way to get involved,' Fi said to Claire.

'You're on.'

'Let's make this more interesting,' Meg suggested, winking at me. 'Don't take this the wrong way, Lou, but whether you get involved is a foregone conclusion. How about we discuss the "when"?' She adjusted the neckline of her unicorn onesie like a man tightening his tie. 'I've got a tenner on it happening before the end of the week.'

'I'm in. I think it'll be before Wednesday.'

'Me too. I'll take Tuesday.'

I rolled my eyes. 'So good to know that my friends have faith in me.'

'Oh, we do, Louise. We do. That's why we're betting

on you getting involved.' Meg grinned. 'Oh, and I'll put another tenner on Irina worming her way back into Detective Andy's good graces, only to piss him off again. Any takers?'

4

CLAIRE

Chron Tom

> Hey Tom, I saw what looks like a murder scene in Partridge Park this morning. I'm going over there now to see what I can find out.

What is it about you and your local park, Claire? You're not a suspect in this one, are you?

> Not this time. Just a journo trying to get the scoop. And trying to give her editor the heads-up without catching any aggro.

> Haha, fair enough. Good luck – let me know what you find out.

'Berk,' Claire muttered, although that didn't feel strong enough. She'd known Tom wouldn't be able to resist the jibe, the little toerag. Yeah, she'd been questioned by the police in October: she'd been seen on CCTV with her friend Jonny Tang not long before he'd been murdered. They'd done their job by asking her their questions – she would have done the same – but while they'd caught the murderer eventually (okay, the Pack had caught the murderer), she still missed Jonny.

Every. Single. Day.

She scowled at the message again. 'You'll find out when I submit the text, ass hat.'

Tank looked up at her, blinking into the sun.

'That's what *The Chronicle* gets for going cheap,' she explained. 'Sure, go ahead and recruit an external editor, instead of hiring from within. Total incompetence. One of these days, we'll find out he's someone's nephew or something.'

He wasn't, though. Claire'd already checked. But a family friend? A godson? A secret toy boy? Nothing was impossible.

It was a short walk from Meg's flat to the children's playground, but the journey was delayed by Tank's insistence on stopping to wee on every rubbish bin, as well as every third blade of grass. 'Next time I'm getting a female dog,' she told him, not expecting him to believe her.

He locked eyes with her and lifted his leg, squeezing out a few drops at the base of a tree. *See? I can do what I want,* he seemed to be saying. *I know you wouldn't trade me for anything.*

He was right, of course.

It didn't matter. There was no rush – the Murder Investigation Team would be there for hours, even if the dead body wouldn't. And the chances of seeing the victim were pretty slim anyway. The police had already set up a tent over him when they'd passed earlier.

What was she after? Claire didn't know. Maybe someone would find something interesting. Maybe she'd be able to overhear one cop sharing a theory with another? Slipping and calling the dead man by name?

Tank let out a challenging bark, and Claire followed his gaze towards a pretty young woman with mousey blonde hair walking a grey-and-white Shih Tzu, both of them wedged into too-small pink puffer jackets. The last time she'd seen the other woman around the park, the dog, Bonnie, had been in season. Tank, still intact, was interested, but the young woman had been fierce about maintaining a safe perimeter around her girl.

Claire didn't blame her; as hard as it was having an unneutered male dog when a female was in season, it had to be a thousand times worse having that female and trying to keep hopeful suitors away. That said, the young woman was a little standoffish. It wasn't personal, Claire knew. She kept the rest of the Pack at arms-length too; not unfriendly, per se, just not overly interested in engaging. She pretended she didn't see Claire. Kept her head down and walked away.

'Huh,' Claire said to Tank. 'Did you do something to offend her?'

Tank didn't have an answer.

Claire watched the woman go, then readjusted her scarf, pulled her beanie further over her forehead, and plotted a course towards the crime scene.

5

ANDY

'They're coming back,' Williams said.

Andy felt his blood run cold. 'Already?'

'It's been a couple of hours. Guessing they're keen.'

'Which ones?' The small hairs at the back of Andy's neck prickled.

'Relax, just the journalist.' Williams's smile grew a little. 'By herself. The one we brought in for the Tang murder right before Halloween?'

'Yeah, I know who she is.' Andy hoped his relief didn't show. Claire was single-minded, but didn't seem the sort to hold a grudge.

'Detectives,' she said by way of greeting, ignoring the PC's attempts to move her on. 'I heard there was a dead body found here this morning. Anything you can share?'

'You know we can't, Ms Dougherty.'

Claire nodded and smiled politely. 'Right. Well, I know you're part of the Murder Investigation Team. And I can see you've got blue police tape here, around the play area, but red around the swing. Guessing that's where the body was found?'

'Ms Dougherty . . .'

'Can you tell me if it was male or female? I heard it was a youngish male.' She gestured towards the buildings overlooking the park and Andy stifled a groan. The Frenchman with the black Labs was still out on his balcony, wrapped in a blanket, binoculars pressed against his face. Andy hoped he couldn't read lips.

'You know I can't.'

'That's okay. I'm sure I can ask Mrs Carstairs. I heard she was the one who found him.'

Andy struggled not to grit his teeth. 'Is there anything you'd like to share with us?'

Claire blinked. 'Why would I? I wasn't here. And, as far as I know, I don't know the victim. This time.' She tilted her head to the side, looking genuinely horrified. 'Or do I?'

'I have no idea. But the last time we found a body in the park, your dog people were able to help us narrow down the time it was dumped there.'

Claire shook her head. 'Can't help you. That time it was summer, so the windows and balcony doors were open. The dogs could hear everything. They went nuts, so we could pinpoint when it happened.'

Their sense of smell wasn't the only edge they had on humans; they could probably hear everything now, they just couldn't be bothered to go outside in the cold.

'Isn't establishing that sort of thing the coroner's job, anyway?' Claire asked.

'Nooo!' The shriek split the air. A woman in her fifties raced towards them, dragging two brown mongrels in her wake. Claire tightened Tank's lead before he could challenge them.

'Christ,' Williams murmured, not without sympathy.

Claire watched the flailing juggernaut approach.

'It's Eddie, isn't it?' The woman halted in front of them, eyes wide, chest heaving. She was average in height, with a long thin nose, stubborn chin and bits of lavender dye jazzing up her blonde-and-grey hair. One of the mongrels snarled at Tank. Claire moved him to her other side, but stood her ground. 'Edward Morley. Is that him? Is that my boy?' The woman craned her neck to see, and Andy stepped in front of her, trusting Williams to get Claire out of the way. This was the part of the job he hated most.

'No formal identification has been made yet, Mrs . . . ?'

'Carr. Caroline Carr. Let me see my son.'

'The coroner has already taken the, ah, victim away, ma'am.'

Caroline fumbled in her pocket for her phone. With shaking fingers, she opened her Photos app. Scrolled back, and back further. Andy's heart clenched. He'd seen this sort of thing before: a parent who had lost touch with their child, only to find out they were dead. Too late for goodbyes. Too late for any chance of reconciliation. All that lingered were memories of angry words and slammed doors. Andy didn't know what it would take to get to that point. He didn't see much of his own son, but he did everything he possibly could to keep the relationship good. Not only with the boy, but also with his mum. Andy's ex. Not because of any residual feelings, but because it made it easier to be a good parent.

Tears streaked down the woman's face. He didn't have it in him to tell her to stop scrolling, that he couldn't tell her whether it was her son or not. Not yet, at least.

Finally she stopped and presented the phone to him. The picture filling the screen was from summertime, although whether it was this past summer or years before, Andy wasn't sure. The young man in the picture was in his late teens, with brown hair and light blue eyes. The same long nose. But where Caroline's cheeks were red, flushed from the cold, the boy's were sallow, and his chin was more sulky than strong.

Andy handed the phone back. 'I'm sorry ma'am, I can't confirm anything – a yes or a no – at this point. But if you give me your details, I'll contact you know once we know more.'

From the corner of his eye, he saw Claire, head down, walking towards the canal path. If he could have, he'd have breathed a sigh of relief.

Only, some intuition pitted deep in his belly told him that he'd be hearing from her again. Soon.

6

CLAIRE

Partridge Bark

> Anyone know the woman with the two brown cross-breeds?

Paul (Bark Vader and Jimmy Chew's Dad)

> The one talking to the police now?

> Yeah. Is she in this group? I haven't seen her before. I can't seem to find her name/details?

Paul (Bark Vader and Jimmy Chew's Dad)

> Don't know. I have not seen her either.

Claire checked the group's participants again. There were more than a hundred, although it seemed like it was the same few people that posted. The Pack.

There was no one listed as Caroline, Caroline Carr, Caro, Caz, Carsky or anything similar. No one whose picture sported the woman's sharp features, or the two brown dogs. That didn't mean that she wasn't in there though. Maybe with a nickname and a butterfly profile pic or something. Claire made a mental note to be careful what she posted.

Partridge Bark

Paul (Bark Vader and Jimmy Chew's Dad)

> Is she connected to what happened? And, you know, what did happen?

> Other than a man being killed, you mean? I don't know. And I don't know if she's connected. Seems to think the man might

> have been her son, but the police weren't saying anything.

Meg (Tyrion's Mum)

> Bless – my heart goes out to them. I can't imagine what that'd be like …

Neither could Claire, but her thoughts were whirring. It was hard enough losing a friend. Jonny'd been murdered because he'd wanted to make the neighbourhood a better place. Why had Eddie Morley been killed, assuming that it was him? And who had done it?

She left a voice message for herself detailing his name and his mother's and what she wanted to check out, just in case, although she knew she wouldn't forget. The desperate look in Caroline Carr's eyes was already burned into her soul.

7

ANDY

'That lady was right. The dead man's prints are in the system.' Williams put his phone back in his pocket, tucked his hands into his armpits to warm them up and turned to face Andy. 'Edward John Morley. Twenty years old. Address is listed as Canning Town, same as Mrs Carr's, although from what she said, it sounds like he hasn't been there for a while.'

'What's he got a record for?' Andy asked.

Williams tossed him a wry look. 'What makes you think he's got a record? Could be a slew of reasons we've got his prints.'

'Okay, so why do we have them?'

'He's got a record.' Williams's grin faded when he remembered they were talking about a dead man, and a young one at that. 'Story's sad, and the record's long. In and out of Young Offender Institutions since he was about fifteen. Mostly drugs-related. I'm guessing he started using, then started selling, then moved on from there. Got involved with one of the gangs. Last time in YOI was knife-related. He was one of the kids put away after the Anthony Rowland stabbing. Doesn't look like he's had much to do with the gangs since then, but you know how it goes.'

Andy winced. It wasn't the first time he'd heard a story like that, but it still felt like an open wound.

'Coroner will check to see what he has in his system,' Williams continued, 'but based on the trauma around his neck, whatever it is, it probably isn't what killed him.'

'Or at least not directly, Scott. If he crossed a dealer, they wouldn't think twice about taking him out.'

Williams crossed his arms over his wide chest. 'It could be that simple, Andy.'

'But?'

'But if a dealer's about to take down a rival, they're going to go all showy, aren't they? Probably knife him in front of their crew, not strangle him. Probably wouldn't be solo, which would mean that someone, maybe even your dog park chums, would have heard something. Even with the balcony doors closed.'

'Still. No evidence to point to any of that yet.'

'No. Not yet,' Williams conceded. 'Look, I know how you hate seeing kids get hurt. And that kid's been through a lot. But we gotta take this one step at a time, mate, without making any assumptions. And do our best for him, which means finding whoever killed him. Because even though he isn't your son, and isn't my son, he's someone else's.'

Andy didn't need the reminder.

Edward Morley had been failed by 'the System'. Maybe even by his family too.

'Right. Do me a favour. Let Nic know what we've got and tell her to meet me at the mother's place.'

Something in his voice had Williams looking at him strangely. 'I'm sure Nic can handle it. You don't need to go yourself.'

'I'm the one who talked to her earlier. Feels right to be the one to break the news.' It wasn't his favourite part of the job, but at least he'd be able to give her some closure. He couldn't imagine what it must've been like for her in the couple of hours since . . .

Andy had already taken a few steps towards the park's gate, but turned back to Williams. 'Hey, Scott? The mother: Caroline Carr. Is she in the dog group?'

'If she is, it's under a different number than the one she gave us.'

'Okay, right. She's East London, but not that close to Partridge Park. How did she know where to go to find us? Before the body'd had a chance to make it to the mortuary?'

'A good question to ask her.' Williams paused. 'You sure you're ready for this?'

Andy looked away. 'Let me know if anything else comes up,' he said, intentionally not answering the question. Because he wasn't ready. Wasn't sure he'd ever be 'ready' to go and tell a mother about her son's death. Nic Saren, the Family Liaison Officer, was one of the best he'd ever worked with, and he was grateful that she'd be there to help him break the news.

Not that anything could soften the blow of a murdered child.

8

CLAIRE

Partridge Bark

Paul (Bark Vader and Jimmy Chew's Dad)

> The police are leaving the scene. Only two men in uniforms left behind.

The message flashed in the bottom corner of Claire's screen, then disappeared. She frowned, turning her attention back to the task at hand.

Getting information on Edward Morley was proving surprisingly difficult. He was a Gen Z; he had to have a tonne of social media accounts, but none were in his name – at least, none that Claire could find. Claire made a note to ask Irina for help. Despite being a lawyer, the

Tsarina's superpower was internet stalking. Maybe she'd have better luck tracking them down.

The only info she could find so far was that Eddie had been in and out of foster care and correctional institutions, although she couldn't find out the reasons why.

Thanks to Facebook, Claire had found a bit more on his mother. Caroline was younger than she appeared – only forty, with two sisters and a brother. The brother had moved out of the city, but her sisters listed 'London' as their locations, while Caroline had 'Canning Town' on her profile. She described herself as a mum of two: her other child was a daughter, Tracey, who was studying for her A levels. Most of Caroline's photos either featured Tracey, a series of girls' nights out (benders from the look of them) at the local 'Spoons or Kev Carr, her beardy husband.

Claire scrolled further back in time. There wasn't much in there about Eddie. 'I imagine having a son in a gang isn't great for the social media feed,' she commented to Tank.

Tank raised a leg and began to groom himself, uninterested.

Claire went back to Facebook, and clicked through to the first of Caroline's sisters. Amanda didn't post her address, but from the number of photographs taken from her flat with the iconic Olympic torch structure in the background, it was pretty likely she lived in the Stratford/Pudding Mill Lane area.

The other sister, Dorothy, lived in a pebble-dashed terraced house with a paved-over front garden slightly larger than a postage stamp. It was tidy, but unremarkable. She had a son, who barely featured on her feeds, and a Shiba Inu called Sushi, who dominated them. Several pics featured Sushi in a park that reminded her of the one near All Saints Church in Poplar.

'Closer to Partridge, but still not close enough to explain how Caroline found out about her son's murder so fast,' Claire muttered.

She checked the Partridge Bark messages again, but there was nothing there to hint at the dead man's identity.

'How the devil did she find out so fast?'

Tank farted and scrambled to his feet, wide-eyed and startled. He shook himself and padded over to the window. Flopped on the dog bed in front of it, and stared out at the traffic below.

'It isn't just the people with dogs that keep an eye on that park, is it?' Claire mused aloud. 'Maybe someone else, someone who knew Eddie, had seen him. Maybe just his body, or maybe his murder?'

Tank ignored her.

'Okay, so first things first: we have to find out who lives in that corner of the park who might be connected to Eddie or Caroline. Then we can figure out how to approach them. It won't rule out passers-by, but at least it's a place to start.' She closed her laptop, staring first at it and then at Tank. 'It's like hunting for a needle in a haystack, and don't take this the wrong way, but you're going to be no help whatsoever. You don't like fluffy dogs.' And the sentiment was usually returned.

She sighed and stared out of the window. It wasn't

much of a plan, but it was better than nothing. There was someone out there who'd seen more than they were letting on, she just knew it. Now all she had to do was find them.

9

ANDY

Nicole Saren, the Family Liaison Officer, was standing at the end of the street, huddled against a brick wall and blowing into her gloved hands. 'Colder than a witch's tit,' she commented. 'Where's Williams?'

'Checking in with Forensics,' Andy said as he reached her.

'Probably best,' she said, straightening. 'He means well, but he has the emotional IQ of an onion. Knack for saying the wrong things at the wrong time.'

Andy nodded, feeling disloyal for doing so, even though Williams would be the first to admit it. 'He updated you?'

'Yeah. Twenty-year-old boy, Edward Morley. In and out of foster care. In and out of trouble. Young Offenders, and all. Didn't make it onto our radars until after he ran away from home, though. I'm curious about the family dynamic.'

So was Andy. 'You okay to take the lead, Nic?'

'Sure.' Nic held herself straight, as if girding herself against the emotional barrage she knew would follow. Andy understood; no matter how many times you had to do this, it didn't get any easier.

Caroline Carr lived in a grey house halfway along a post-war terrace. There were no hedges, only a handful of plant pots, bare of leaves. Fake stalactite lights hung from the roof and a Christmas tree was set up in the front room next to the window. The lights were still on, although Andy was willing to bet the door to the parlour would be closed.

'She knows,' Nic murmured.

'She showed up at the scene,' Andy reminded her. 'I'd be interested to know *how* she knew.'

Her nod was almost imperceptible. 'Two-up two-down house. Not a lot of room for a son, if he ever came home,' she observed. 'Pretty clear message, that.'

'Maybe they have a loft or an extension on the other side?' Andy asked, holding out little hope. 'Besides, he was an adult, and from the number of times he ran away, he'd made it pretty clear that he didn't want to live with them.'

'Let's see what we find.' Nic raised her hand to the doorbell but the door opened before she could press it. The woman standing in front of them trembled. Dogs barked from somewhere in the house. It had to be the two mixed-breeds that she'd had with her that morning, Andy figured.

'Mrs Carr, I'm Detective Constable Andrew Thompson. We met earlier,' he said, holding up his warrant card. 'And this is Nicole Saren, our Family Liaison Officer.'

Caroline gave a quick glance at Nic, but her red-rimmed eyes were fixed on Andy. 'It's him, isn't it? The boy in the park is Eddie, right?'

'Can we please come in, ma'am?'

'Of course it is, that's why you're here,' she whispered. She bit her lip and for a few moments seemed lost in her own memories. 'Of course,' she said to them eventually, as if remembering they were there. 'Please come in.' She turned and led the way through the house, pausing at the kitchen door.

'You okay with dogs?' The barking was now interspersed with scratching, as if the hounds were trying to dig their way out through the door. 'They're friendly.'

'Yeah. We're good,' Andy said, slipping his hand into his jacket pocket, his fingers closing reassuringly around the half a pack of dog treats that he'd taken to carrying with him. Just in case.

Caroline pushed open the door and the two mongrels moved out, not lunging at the visitors, but positioning themselves between the officers and Caroline, trying to protect her. Andy felt a lump rise in his throat; the dogs, loyal as they were, couldn't save her from the hurt that the news would inflict.

Caroline absently pulled a couple of chews from a jar and gave one to each dog, patting their furry heads as she moved around them. 'Place,' she said, and both dogs moved to a large cushion behind the table, watching Nic and Andy with suspicion.

The kitchen was painted yellow, although the colour had faded and the walls were scuffed in places. A large water bowl was on the floor beside the dogs' cushion, along with a few toys in varying degrees of destruction.

Caroline poured water into a kettle and turned it on. Placed her hands on the counter and took a few breaths. They gave her the space to steady herself and then Nic guided her onto a chair and took over the tea-making.

'Tell me what happened,' Caroline demanded. Her voice was resolute, but her eyes pleaded for them to tell her it was all a big mistake; that it was someone else's son they'd found. That Eddie was alive. All right. Maybe even coming home.

'I'm so sorry, Mrs Carr,' Andy said. 'But between the hours of four and five o'clock this morning, your son, Edward Morley, was killed in Partridge Park.'

'Why?' She shook her head. 'Why Eddie?'

'That's one of the things we're going to do our best to find out, Mrs Carr. Nic and I will answer whatever we can right now, but I'll be honest with you: it's early stages and we have more questions than we have answers.'

'I get that,' she whispered.

'Okay, good,' Andy said. 'Is there anyone we can call to be here for you? Family? Friends? Vicar?'

She was already shaking her head. 'One of my sisters just left. The other will be over later.'

'Your husband?'

'Took my daughter to Winter Wonderland in Hyde Park.' She dropped her voice to a whisper. 'I didn't want to call them and ruin their day. Not until I knew for sure.'

Nic and Andy exchanged a glance. This was actually lucky for them: while Caroline was already aware of her son's death, Nic would be able to gauge the dynamic as Tracey and Kev learned and processed the news. A lot of people misunderstood the role of the FLO and thought it was primarily to support the family, but first and foremost, they were detectives, investigators.

And that meant starting with the family.

'What can you tell us about Eddie, Mrs Carr?' Nic asked. 'The more we know about how he lived, the better we can understand why he died.'

'So, you don't think it was just wrong time, wrong place? Maybe an accident?'

The hope in her voice hit Andy like a physical thing, but Nic's answer was gentle. 'It could have been, but we don't know for certain yet. Why don't you start by telling me what was Eddie like?'

Caroline's gaze strayed to a framed photo on the wall, showing a young boy in a West Ham football shirt, holding a football. 'He was a sweet boy. Thoughtful. Good student. Loved footie. Always taking care of his little sister. Even after he left, he'd come back sometimes to check in on her. Kev – my husband – was convinced he was only coming to ask for money, but he never did, you know.'

'Were they still close? Eddie and his sister?'

'No,' she said, deflating a little more. 'Not as far as I know, at least. You can ask her when she comes home.'

'We will,' Nic promised. 'You mentioned that he left. Do you know why?'

'Two alphas under the same roof, officer. He and Kev didn't much get along.'

'Any particular reason why?' Nic asked, her voice neutral.

Caroline's head twitched to the side. 'Eddie thought Kev was trying to be his dad an' wasn't having it. For Kev, it was "my house, my rules", but not like a taskmaster or anything. He just wanted to be head of his own household, you know?'

Andy nodded, his stomach clenching, wondering if his son was having the same sort of clashes with his mum's new boyfriend.

'He ran away from home that first time after an argument. Don't even remember what it was about. He was fourteen.' Caroline's lower lip began to tremble. 'That time, he went to a mate's. The mate's mum sent him home, and it happened again, and again, until Social Services got involved. They put him in a foster home.' That last sentence was whispered.

Nic nodded; she'd get in touch with the case worker.

'I should have done more.' Caroline's voice was tight, trying to hold back the tears. 'Should have tried harder.'

'What were his friends like?'

'Nice boys.' Her eyes were resolute. 'I know what you're asking, 'cos of him going to that Young Offenders place. He wasn't like that when he was living with me. He didn't have any friends in any gangs or anything like that.'

'And afterwards? After he was in the foster home?'

'I don't know.' She shook her head sadly. 'Even if he was involved in anything like that, I don't think he would have told me. Maybe when he was younger, but not then. Not at that point.' First one tear, and then another and another streamed down her face.

Nic's voice softened. 'Did he tell you anything about his friends? Maybe a romantic partner?'

'Last time I saw him, it wasn't that long ago, he said he had someone,' Caroline whispered. 'But he wouldn't tell me who. Just that I didn't know them. I was so relieved that he wasn't alone that I didn't press him.' She brushed at her face with the back of her hand, her chest heaving, not quite able to suppress the sobs. 'And now he's gone and it's too late to ask. Too late to tell him how much I loved him.'

10

LOUISE

Claire (Tank's Mum)

Hey Lou, fancy meeting up for the evening walk?

I'm about to meet Irina and Hammy – you're welcome to join us. Meet you at the bridge in 10?

Irina was waiting for me by the gate, wearing a green wool coat that matched Hammy's bandana. I leaned over. 'Jingle these bells, schnauzer boy?' I read. 'Seriously?'

She rolled her eyes.

'I mean, it's not like Hammy cares if someone confuses him with a schnauzer. Especially if they make it up to him with a treat or two.'

At the magic 'T' word, two sets of canine ears perked up. 'No. You two have to work for it.' They understood what that meant, and both sat down in a perfect sit. When Klaus didn't see my hand reach for the treat bag, he did a neat middle, looking up at me from between my feet with liquid eyes. I sighed and offered each a small piece of fish.

'We'll meet Claire and Tank over by the News-N-Booze,' I said, steering the way over the canal bridge. On either side, bright fairy lights lit balconies and windows. It was a small blessing in a country that started getting dark at four o'clock this time of year.

'So, you're getting yourself involved again? That was fast.'

'Nope. Just an evening walk.'

Irina laughed, full and throaty. 'Keep telling yourself that, Lou.'

'What's that supposed to mean?'

'You're bored at work. You're good at this. You're going to get involved, Lou. You won't be able to help yourself.'

I ignored her, but Irina wasn't done yet. 'Because, you know, it's not like Claire won't have the bit between her teeth.'

'She's a journalist,' I reminded her. 'Of course she's going to want to know what happened.'

Irina's laugh was more ironic than humorous. 'For heaven's sake, Lou. The dead guy was found a stone's throw from where her friend Jonnie Tang was killed only a couple of months ago. You think she's not – whether consciously or otherwise – gonna make a connection and go out for justice?'

I didn't need the reminder; I remembered exactly where Jonny had been found. Remembered more details than I wanted to. Yaz hadn't just called me when she'd found him; she'd asked me to wait with her for the police to show up.

Up ahead, Claire moved towards us with the momentum of a battleship at full speed, Tank in her wake (naked, bar his harness, as usual).

'Bloody cold,' she said by way of greeting. 'Where are we walking to?'

'I don't care as long as Klaus does his business,' I said.

As we were standing by the entrance to the canal path, we moved as one towards it – something we would never do alone and after dark. 'How was your day, Claire?' Irina asked, giving me a sly look.

Claire shot me a curious glance; Irina rarely bothered with polite banalities. 'You mean after we learnt of another murder in our neighbourhood?' she asked. 'I spent the rest of the day on my laptop, of course.'

'Of course,' Irina smirked.

'Learn anything?' I asked, as much in apology for Irina's barely rudimentary social skills as for my own curiosity.

'Started with the family, the same as the police probably do.'

'Okay?'

'I found the mother, Caroline, on social media. She's

got two sisters who still live in East London – she seems close with them – and a brother, who escaped. She has a daughter and a few years ago married Kevin Carr.' She paused. 'So, the dead man is called Eddie Morley, right?'

'I guess so,' I said, even though I had no clue.

'That was what his mum said when she showed up at the park.'

'How did she know to show up?' I asked.

'Million-dollar question, but hold on to it for a sec,' Claire said. 'The daughter's a coupla years younger than Eddie. Goes by Tracey Carr.'

'So? Maybe Caroline hooked up with Kev after having Eddie.'

'Not according to social media. Her timeline looks a bit scrubbed after the departure of Mr Morley. Or rather, before – guessing she got rid of any pics of him after he left.'

'Or died?'

'Don't think anyone'd get rid of pics of a beloved deceased. Maybe turn off the Memories On This Day function, but not bin the pics. I think he left her, and the two kids.'

'That sucks,' Irina said with genuine disgust. I didn't disagree.

'Yeah. She didn't stay single for long. Hooked up with Kev Carr at a night out with her sisters and moved him in right quick. Not long after, troubles start between him and Eddie, but he goes on to adopt Tracey. Did he actually adopt Eddie too? I don't know, but my gut says "No".'

'I don't have stats or anything, but I don't feel like it

would be that unusual that the guys would clash,' I said. 'It *is* possible that he adopted both kids but Eddie chose to keep his dad's name. Or reverted later. I don't know.'

'Neither do I,' Claire said, staring at the entrance to the park. 'Yet.'

'What about his social media?' I asked.

'Haven't found anything,' she admitted. She gave Irina a sideways glance. 'But I do know someone whose internet stalking prowess is even greater than mine that I hoped would help?'

'Not my job. My workload is already up to here,' Irina groused, raising her hand to her eyebrows. We didn't say anything but an uncomfortable silence grew between us until she relented. 'No guarantees. I'll see what I can do.'

I met Claire's eye behind Irina's back and flashed a discreet thumbs-up. It looked like Irina wouldn't be able to help herself either.

11

ADRIAN

Adrian Barlow closed the door to her bedroom with a soft click. She turned, leaning her back against it, and slowly sank to the floor. Tears ran unchecked down her face, but she bit her bottom lip, careful not to make a sound.

Eddie was dead.

She wouldn't have believed it had she not seen his body herself, lying on the swing as if it were any normal day. Only it wasn't. He didn't respond when she called his name. His eyes didn't light up when he saw her. There would be no more puckish smile from those blue lips; no more naughty jokes, usually at her expense.

She hadn't minded those jokes. She knew it was as close to a sign of affection as he would allow himself to give anyone.

We're two messed up peas in a rotten pod, he'd once said. Or had it been her? She didn't remember, but it didn't matter: it'd been true. And now there was only one messed up pea left in the pod.

She closed her eyes, and clasped her knees to her chest to stop herself from keening.

Murdered.

She had no doubt of that. The red line across his neck wasn't a sign of an overdose. She was under no illusions: for all intents and purposes, Eddie was homeless. That path was set the moment his mother moved Kev Carr in. The abuse had started subtly, then escalated. Eddie was fourteen when he reckoned he was big enough to defend himself. He was wrong, and was beaten for it. Had his mum stood up for him?

Had she bloody not. She told him to stop being jealous. And stop making stuff up.

When it was bad enough, he'd run away. Again and again. Social Services put him in foster care, but that was even worse. For him, at least. For Adrian, it had meant the sudden appearance of a kindred spirit. Broken, yeah. But she was too. She'd understood. She'd even understood when he'd had to run away from that home too.

She'd been devastated. Rick, their foster father, had told her she was too young to have her own phone then, although Adrian knew it had little to do with her, and more about what the phones could do. Putting it simply: Rick was as bad as Kev. He didn't want anything recorded. Not audio, and sure as hell not video.

And then Eddie was gone.

He'd finally learned to hide better and hadn't returned. It'd been the worst year of her life.

And then her foster care had imploded. Rick's missus'd accused her of trying to seduce Rick. Bloody ridiculous. The old bat probably couldn't accept that if there was any seducing happening, it was the other way around.

So Adrian was packed off to a new home near Partridge Park. The couple was older, and religious. Which meant a trip to church every Sunday, Grace before meals and more rules than she could remember, but at least there were no beatings. No need to keep her bedroom door locked, although she still did.

She couldn't believe her luck when she'd seen Eddie at the park. He was gaunt, his face grey, but when he grinned at her, it was the same Eddie. He got her a phone. It'd been 'recycled', he'd said, which meant that it was stolen. She didn't care. It meant that they could be together, even when they weren't.

He hadn't told her much about what happened in between him leaving and them meeting again. Just that he'd found a squat. She hadn't asked how he'd managed to survive. She didn't need to know the details: people like Eddie, they did whatever they had to do to make it.

Only he hadn't, had he? He was dead.

Adrian wasn't naïve. She knew what the cops saw when they looked at Eddie. They'd see the track marks; smell the skunk. It wouldn't be long before they learned that he had a record. That he might have drugs or alcohol in his system. Probably both.

'People like him' died every day, or at least too often to really bother the cops. What was another 'troubled youth' to them? If he was dead, it meant that he wasn't causing problems, right?

He was a soft target, an easy victim.

Only, he wasn't. He'd have fought like hell, because he'd had to fight every day of his life. There'd be defensive marks. Clues. Would they follow them, or would they take the easy way out?

Would they even be bothered to figure out his name? Much less, who killed him?

So Adrian made it easy for them. She'd waited until after the old woman'd stumbled across him. Masked her phone number and sent an anonymous message to Eddie's mum, telling her that he was dead. She hoped Eddie was right; that his mum wasn't a bad woman. The new husband was foul, he'd insisted, but his mum was all right, just weak. Couldn't stand up to her man for her kids. Who knew if she'd make sure the cops did right by Eddie? But he would have wanted her to know.

Adrian looked down at her arms. Pulled the sleeves further down to cover the scars on her wrists and hoped she hadn't made a grave mistake.

Monday

12

ANDY

The weather was freezing outside, but inside the station, it was arctic. Andy strode down the corridor, rubbing his hands together to try to keep them warm. From the other end, Detective Inspector Alf Badolato gestured that he'd be along in a minute. Badolato boasted about running a tight ship and didn't stand for people arriving after he did for the case updates, unless they had a good reason. Andy nodded and joined the rest of the team in the meeting room.

'Badolato's coming. With another wrongful death along one of the canals, I was expecting to see DCS Grieves.'

'He's in Malta,' Williams answered. 'A bit of winter sun and an excuse to avoid the in-laws for Christmas, if you ask me. He'll be disappointed to miss this one, I'm sure.'

'As if Badolato needed extra incentive to close a case before he returns.' Nic rolled her eyes. 'Any ideas why

Grieves is so keen on the area? Seems like every case we get along that stretch of canal, he shows up.'

Andy shrugged; it was as much a mystery to him.

'Morning,' Badolato announced, closing the door behind him. An uncapped marker was already in his hands. 'Let's start off with the new case. Edward Morley. Give me the 5WHs, Thompson.'

Andy cleared his throat and held up his index finger. 'The Who in this case is our victim, Edward John Morley. Twenty years old. Troubled past. In and out of foster care. In and out of juvie. No current gang affiliations, but given the neighbourhood and his past, it's not something we're ruling out.'

'Suspects?'

'No one clear at the moment.'

'Second "W": the What?' Badolato prompted.

'Death by strangulation. Straight across the front of his neck, rather than the U shape that you'd see if he hanged himself. They're running tox screens, but the smell of skunk clung to him like a second skin. Guessing he was high as a kite. Killer came up to him from behind, and Morley didn't see it coming.'

'Shit.'

'Yeah. Didn't see any defensive wounds but the coroner will give us more details, once the autopsy has been completed.'

Badolato nodded. Despite his Italian name, his face was startlingly pale, more Germanic than Latin. And unlike Grieves, who would often lean against the boards, getting marker-pen residue on the back of his clothes, Badolato was impeccable. Andy didn't need to listen to scuttlebutt to know that the DI was doing everything he could to get promoted.

Although Andy didn't know how much giving Grieves free rein over some of his cases had helped.

'The When?'

It was the usual staccato interrogation. 'It was a cold night, and the body cooled fast. Estimate is between four and five this morning.'

'Nothing more specific?' Badolato raised one white-blond brow. 'Your dog people couldn't give a better estimate?' He was referring to a case last summer, when the neighbourhood dogs' sudden barking in the early hours of the morning had allowed them to pinpoint the exact time the body of Phil Creasy was dumped in Partridge Park.

Andy waited for the sniggering to stop. He opened his mouth to confess to not having asked them the question, when Williams spoke. 'No, sir. We checked and there was nothing reported.'

'Reported?'

For a second, Andy wondered if Badolato had forgotten, then remembered that Grieves had run that case. 'They've got a WhatsApp, guv. Something happens, whether it's the dogs going nuts at fireworks, a set of plates found under a bush or some mutt's tummy issues, it goes in the chat. There was nothing in there last night or this morning to indicate anything amiss.'

'But he wasn't found until ten o'clock?'

'It's cold, guv,' Williams said. 'The kiddie park isn't

used as much in this weather. Coulda been even later if the old woman who found him didn't march in to have a "strong word" with him about littering.'

Badolato nodded. 'What else?'

'What'd you learn from the family, Nic?' Andy asked.

'Eddie was twenty, but he'd been in and out of foster care and Young Offenders for the last few years. Father left when he was fourteen, didn't get along with mum's new partner and things went south from there. He occasionally went back though, when he thought the stepdad, Kev Carr, wouldn't be around.'

'To get money from his mum?' Badolato asked.

'Strangely, no. She thinks it was to check in on his sister. Who claims she'd had nothing to do with him since he left the last time.'

'Can we verify that? Phone records?'

'Haven't found the phone yet, guv,' Andy reminded Badolato. 'But we have a number for him, thanks to his mum. Got in touch with the provider to request his records, but that'll still give us an incomplete picture if he lived on apps like WhatsApp to do his calls and messages.'

'Uniforms are still out, looking for the phone,' Williams added.

'His mum mentioned a new squeeze, but she didn't have a name. Uniforms asked around the park, but none of the other regulars there had seen him with anyone. They looked surprised at the thought that he had a partner. Maybe something will come up when we find the phone.'

'All right, keep on it. What else do we know about the sister?' Badolato asked.

'Tracey,' Nic supplied. 'Two years younger. She's a good student – she'll start uni in the autumn. Dotes on Kev. They were at Winter Wonderland together when Andy and I went to the house.'

'Together?' Badolato paused, eyebrows raised. 'I'd have thought that at her age, she'd want to go with her friends, not her stepdad.'

'I would have, at that age, but she struck me as a bit of a daddy's girl. Or stepdaddy's girl.'

'Your impression of the stepdad?' Badolato asked.

'All right, I guess. Seemed genuinely surprised to hear the news. Put an arm around the wife and her daughter and let them cry on his shoulders. Didn't get any red flags coming from him, guv.'

'His wife didn't call to let him know?'

'She said she didn't want to ruin their day,' Nic said.

'He was the reason Morley left the family home. Does he have motive to kill him?'

'Don't think so. He claimed he hadn't seen Eddie in years – something the wife and daughter were happy to confirm, although we all know that could be a front. I checked him out – no record. No complaints. He's worked for Transport for London since he was nineteen. I'll head back there after we're done here, see what else I can learn.'

She gestured for Andy to continue.

'The Where. Eddie's body was found in the basket swing in the kiddie area of Partridge Park. One leg in the basket, one out.'

'Is that where he died or just where he was found?'

'Evidence suggests both, sir,' Williams answered. 'As

Andy said, for the How he was garrotted from behind rather than strangled from the front.'

Badolato looked up from the notes he was taking. 'To confirm: garrotted, and not strangled by hand?'

'Thin line without the bruises you'd expect to see in manual strangulation. I expect the coroner'll confirm once the autopsy's complete.'

'You think the playground was incidental or intentional?'

'Don't know for certain yet, guv,' Williams answered. 'Little kids might play there during the day, but after dark, the teens take it over. I'd guess that he was there enjoying a spliff. Maybe sleeping it off, and our guy found him.'

'Crime of opportunity?'

'Can't confirm that yet.'

'Yeah? Well, find out for sure, one way or the other. I want to know *why* someone murdered Morley.'

Andy cleared his throat. 'Another interesting point: the mother showed up at the scene, not too long after we found the body. She lives in Canning Town, close enough to Partridge Park as the bird flies, but not so close that it'd be her regular dog park.' Three members of the team waggled their brows at him and he frowned. 'She has two dogs. Mongrels from the look of them. Doesn't mean that she's connected with the Partridge Pack.'

'But it doesn't mean she's not either,' Nic said. 'She received a text from an anonymous sender early yesterday morning. Could be Eddie's girlfriend, or maybe just a friend.' She beamed an image onto the ancient screen beside Badolato. In it were a series of messages on a phone clutched in a woman's hand, complete with green manicured nails at the edge of the screen.

Unknown Sender

> Eddie's dead. Murdered. Soz, but he'd want u to know.

> Who is this? U r not funny. He can't be dead – I only talked to him a few days ago.
> U r wrong. U have to be. He's not answering my calls! OMG, where is he?

> Partridge Park, the kids area.

> Who are you? How do you know? Did you kill my son?
> Who are you?

Nic flipped to the next screen and Andy looked away. He'd already seen the messages and didn't need another reminder of Caroline's anguish. She continued, 'The sender didn't give any more information and the number was withheld, but we're checking with the phone companies to see if we can find out who sent it.'

'Okay. So, any idea who might've killed him and why? Harriman? Anything on CCTV?'

'Not yet, Sir,' Harriman said. 'Still checking the area surrounding the park. Could take a couple of days.' His eye met Andy's. Unsaid were the words, *If we're lucky*.

Badolato sighed his disappointment. 'Right. The local rags will be expecting something. Release the basics but leave off any details, the kid's background, et cetera. Don't let on about the garotte. We have a lot of work to do here, and the last thing we need is an overexcited press.' He rolled his eyes. 'Or local sleuths.'

Andy knew the statement wasn't directed at him, but still, he kept his eyes forward and his expression bland.

'Okay,' Badolato said. 'Next up. Mr Wilkinson, his body found over at the Teviot estate. What can you tell me?'

13

CLAIRE

Fiona (Nala's Mum)

> Hey Fi, any chance we can do a dog swap?

> Nala's a little diva, but I wouldn't trade her for the world.

> I'm not suggesting we trade for good – you know what Tank means to me – just for a couple of hours around lunchtime, if that's OK? I'll walk the Chonk

> before getting to yours so you don't even have to take him outside.

< Why do I feel like this is a trick question?

> Not at all. It's just that Nala can be a bit friendlier than Tank. Sometimes.

< Haha, are you calling Nala a tart?

> That's kind of what I'm counting on.

< 🙄 Thank heavens she's been spayed! OK, fine – good luck to you!

'Thank heavens indeed,' Claire answered aloud. 'The last thing we need is for me to return Nala to you with puppies in her tum.'

Lying on his bed, Tank farted himself awake. He stared at his own bottom as if it were an alien creature, sniffed, made a disgusted face and padded towards her.

'Oh my god, you've grossed yourself out. Again.' Claire

looked at the ceiling and then back at her dog. 'Can there be any surprise that I'm recruiting Nala for this and not taking you?'

She'd just finished writing her story on the suspicious death for *The Chronicle*. The official statement from the Met Police was slim and sketchy, barely enough for a couple of paragraphs. She'd already found more out than what was provided, but opted to play nice in the sandbox. At least for now.

LOCAL MAN FOUND DEAD IN PARTRIDGE PARK

A man identified as twenty-year-old Edward John Morley, of no fixed address, was found dead on Sunday morning by a local dog walker in Partridge Park, East London.

His death is being treated as suspicious by the Metropolitan Police, who urge anyone with more information to contact them on their hotline, quoting the reference number listed below.

Mr Morley is survived by his mother, Caroline Carr, his stepfather, Kevin Carr, and his sister, Tracey Carr, resident in Canning Town. A vigil will be held in Partridge Park this Thursday, from 7:00 p.m.

Claire filed the story, knowing that it was only a placeholder. Yeah, the dead man might have been one of the miscreants who hung out in Partridge Park after dark, maybe one of the little toerags who kept setting off the fireworks that drove Tank nuts, but that didn't mean he'd deserved to die. And it didn't mean that his death should remain unsolved.

She might not have the same resources as the Met Police, but she had a bigger incentive: this had happened on *her turf*. The same place she walked Tank every day. She knew she couldn't stop all crime, but at least she could play her part in keeping her neighbourhood safe.

She slipped Tank's harness over his head, offering him a treat before clipping on the lead. 'Come on, Fart-boy. We're going to see Auntie Fi.'

14

LOUISE

Barbara Lane

> I saw Claire's article on the Chronicle about another dead man in your neighbourhood. Is it foolish of me to hope that you keep your nose out of this one?

> So far, said nose is clean. We passed by where it happened yesterday, but that's the extent of it. All I know about it was what Claire wrote.

> You're really not getting involved?

Nope. I don't know the man, but the Met are on the case. Hopefully they'll be able to get justice for him, poor kid. And his mum … Just before Christmas too.

> Seriously?

FWIW, I don't get involved in every crime here. 🙄

> Well, please keep it that way. Every time you get involved, the killer comes after you. I worry that sooner or later your luck's gonna run out.
> In other news, our friend in Gen Tech is playing silly buggers with contracts again. Moany Tony's asked, if you get a chance, can you swing by the Wharf this afternoon?

> You're not trying to keep me too busy to get involved in the murder, are you?

> The thought crossed my mind, but to be honest, he really did ask for you. Just do yourself a favour and don't stand under any mistletoe. Unless you want to take one for the team?☺

> I'd rather gnaw my arm off. But speaking of mistletoe, let's hope we don't see anything too questionable at the Xmas do on Friday. Everyone looking forward to it?

> 💯 I think they liked that you gave them the choice of what do to and where to go. Not really that surprised that they opted for money behind the bar

> at the Sipping Room over an escape room. They've had a busy year. They just want to wind down and have a laugh.

They did. Ours was a boutique consultancy company, that I founded with two friends years ago. Over time, I'd bought them out and had resisted the urge to allow the company to mushroom in size at the expense of the culture. We were small, niche and effective.

Not that we were so small that we'd escaped interest from some of the big consultancies, but I'd made a promise to Babs: I wouldn't sell up without giving the team a say in the decision. No one wanted our firm sold only to see it consumed. We talked to our clients about the importance of culture, and we practised what we preached.

The more difficult question wasn't what I wanted to do about the company, it was what I wanted to do about *me*. I wasn't stupid: I knew it was time for me to step back. Babs was the Operations Director, and damn good at her job. It was time to promote her to Managing Director, and to take one more step back.

The problem was how to step away from a company that I built, that I was proud of and emotionally invested in. It was almost as much a child to me as Klaus was.

I glanced down at him and he glanced back. *You still have me.*

'I know that,' I murmured, keeping my voice low so the people sitting at the tables on either side of me in the Nest, Partridge Park's café, didn't hear.

I *did* know that. The same way I knew that as owner, Chairperson and Chief Exec, I'd still be involved. Just not on a daily basis. So, what the devil was I going to do with all this 'spare time' to myself?

If I asked my friends, they'd roll their eyes and say 'Work the case!', but being bored was one thing, and stepping on the toes of the Met Police was another. Contrary to what half the neighbourhood thought, I had no aspirations to be a modern-day Miss Marple.

Lost in thought, I looked out of the window and watched Claire's distinctive walk – half stride, half stomp – pass by. She was bundled for the weather with a beanie and a heavy parka, but what was strange was that Tank wasn't leading the way. Instead, pretty Nala pranced at her side.

'Why on earth would Claire have Nala instead of Tank?' I asked aloud. Klaus's ears pricked up at his friends' names and he got to his feet, looking around. 'Want to go investigate? We can swing by Canary Wharf to see Moany Tony afterwards.'

Klaus didn't care about Tony Frater; he just wanted to play with his friends. He did try to get outside without putting on his coat, although by now he should have known that he didn't have a choice. Hell, if I had to wear a coat, so did he. He'd be grateful for it when we got a faceful of two-degree temperatures.

I shrugged into my own coat and slipped my laptop

into its rucksack, slinging it over my shoulder. Claire had a head start. I could have messaged her and asked if she wanted company, but from the way she was moving, she was on a mission. Best not to ask, when she'd only accuse us of slowing her down.

'No borking,' I warned Klaus. 'No point in giving the game up. Think of it this way: we're putting into practice what Sarah was teaching us yesterday. Only, instead of finding the red toy, we're seeing if we can sniff out Claire and Nala. Got it?'

He didn't look convinced, but was happy enough to be on the trail. Especially if there was the prospect of a bit of play time.

Claire wasn't taking the canal paths; instead she powered down the street, which made it trickier to keep up. She was around my height, about 164 cm, and the roads were getting busy as we neared lunchtime. A large shape materialised in the window of one of the cafés, and Klaus began to bark. It took me a second to register that the café in question was owned by Gav's mate Jono and that the massive dog inside was Rocco, a mastiff crossed with something that might just have been an American bulldog.

'I know that breed has a bad rap, Klaus, but don't take it out on Rocco. He's well trained and the most placid big dog I've ever met.'

I stepped up my pace, following Claire through Poplar to the recreation grounds. They weren't large, but managed to squeeze in a couple of tennis courts, a basketball court, a mosque and a church. We lingered behind a memorial to children killed during the First World War, where I threw down treats in piles of dead leaves, challenging Klaus to sniff them out. It was the best way to keep him occupied while I watched for Claire.

She emerged from the tennis courts to my left, which meant that she was doing laps around the little park. As soon they got close, Klaus perked up, the treats at my feet no longer interesting.

At first, he barked a greeting to Nala and Claire, but at about the same time, we realised that they were walking with a young man and a Shiba Inu. Klaus was fine with men – it was large fluffy dogs that sometimes set him off. Shibas weren't that big, but were big enough. His bark changed from the happy greeting to a deeper, 'stranger danger' warning.

Claire glanced our way and frowned.

'Oh my god, we've gate-crashed a date,' I said to Klaus, scooping him up.

Feeling like my foray into the world of espionage was about to end before it had even begun, I raised a hand in embarrassed greeting. 'Sorry, he's barky but friendly,' I explained as if they were strangers. Holding Klaus against my chest, we moved away from the park and towards the Wharf. Hopefully I'd have better luck with Tony.

And then, maybe, I might have a hunt around to see what I could find online. The dead homeless woman in Vicky Park last week, the young man yesterday 'of no fixed address' ... both sounded like 'soft' victims – the sort of people who get killed and no one notices.

Until the perpetrator targets the wrong person, and then someone does.

15

CLAIRE

Louise (Klaus's Mum)

> OMG – sorry about that! Klaus saw you and wanted to catch up. I hadn't realised you were on a date!

Claire studied the man beside her. He had dark hair, dark eyes and an olive complexion that spoke of tapas and sangria, but his face had the same bone structure his mother Dorothy shared with her sister Caroline.

She'd known she'd made the right decision to take Nala instead of Tank almost immediately after reaching Poplar

Park. The Shiba had pulled his guardian directly to her, and Nala had unsurprisingly rolled over with a coquettish look in her eye.

'Tart,' Claire muttered.

'Sorry about that. Sushi considers himself the alpha dog round here.'

'Is he?'

'I don't think your dog is disputing it.' The man grinned and stuck out a hand. 'Jeremy Silva.'

'Claire Dougherty.' Claire choked out her name from a suddenly dry mouth. He was *hot!* Younger than she was, but only by a few years.

Fast on the heels of that thought was the realisation that she'd given him her real name. Belatedly, she hoped he wasn't a regular reader of *The Chronicle* – most people weren't, even if they were local – who might recognise her. 'And the hussy down there is Nala.'

Nala turned her attention to Jeremy, curling around his legs, leaning her head on his knee and looking up at him with liquid eyes. He gave a surprised laugh. He rested one hand on the Shiba's head and leaned down to scratch Nala's neck with the other.

Claire now understood why Fi had more dates than a Hollywood starlet, and resolved to borrow Nala more often. 'I've never seen her do that with a stranger,' she said with complete honesty. And awe. Had Fi taught Nala that? Could Tank learn how to do it?

No. Tank would probably fart and then vomit on the guy's foot.

Jeremy smiled, eyes sparkling. 'Nice to meet you,

Claire Dougherty. And Nala, of course. I haven't seen you around here before.'

She blinked. *Does he know how sexy he is, surrounded by the dogs?*

She did her best to ignore the thought and waded in. 'We come here sometimes, but we live closer to Partridge Park. A young man was actually found dead there yesterday. I heard it was murder. Terrible stuff. Kind of makes you feel unsafe in your own neighbourhood. I thought it made sense to go a bit further afield today.'

'I don't blame you.' He looked away. 'Murder, you say?'

'I don't know, to be honest. I don't think the police released an official cause of death. Or any theories. At least, not as far as I know.'

'Some people are, like, doomed to be a statistic, you know?'

'Why? Did you know him?'

'You could say that.' Jeremy's face became stony.

They walked for a minute or two in a silence that was tense, but not as awkward as it should have felt. The dogs responded to the charged atmosphere, their playful wrestling settling down. They walked side by side, with Sushi occasionally leaning in to groom Nala's neck.

'I'm so sorry,' Claire said, 'for being so, well ... inconsiderate.'

'How could you have known?'

They passed through the shadows into dappled sunlight. It didn't do much to change the temperature, but it helped with the mood. 'I guess you're right.'

'Eddie – that was his name – Eddie Morley. He was an arse. Broken, you know? From the time he was a kid.'

'You knew him well?'

'Could say that,' he repeated. 'Our mums are sisters.'

'Oh shit – he was your cousin? I'm so sorry for your loss!' Claire felt a stab of genuine sadness for Jeremy. Her hand rose to touch his arm in comfort, but he froze and she let it fall before it could connect. *He has no reason to accept your touch,* she reminded herself. *It's not like he knows you. Or trusts you.*

And any trust would dissipate the moment he found out why she had sought him out under false pretences.

'We weren't close. His dad ditched when he was a kid. So, Eddie tried to step up. For a while, at least.'

'That's really sad.'

'Yeah, it is. But it happens a lot, right? Not everyone gets into drugs or gangs because of it. Then Aunt Caroline hooked up with a man who seemed pretty decent. Tried to be a good dad to her kids. But Eddie hated him on sight.'

'Because he wasn't his real father?'

Jeremy shrugged in a *don't know, don't care* sort of way. 'Not sure it matters why. Tracey – his sister – adored Kev from the start, but not Eddie. They clashed *all the bloody time*. When Eddie ran away, the house became normal. No shouting, no fights. Then someone returned him, like a lost dog, but he only ran away again. And again. Until he was put into foster care. Then he kind of fell off the map for a bit.'

For a bit.

Claire felt like she knew the answer but she asked the question anyway. 'What made them – him? – reconnect?'

'I guess he needed something. Probably money.'

Claire tried to hide a wince, but Jeremy saw it and nodded. 'Yeah. And Aunt Caro could never say no to him, could she? We'd heard he was involved in that Rowland stabbing a few years ago. Got sent to one of those youth offender prisons. Eddie was bad news.'

'May he rest in peace,' Claire murmured, because she couldn't think of anything else to say.

They walked in a comfortable silence for a bit. 'Not quite what you expected to hear on a dog walk, right?' Jeremy said eventually, shaking off the ghost of his cousin. He took a deep breath and shrugged deeper into his jacket, turning towards Claire. 'Christ, it's freezing out here. I have twenty minutes before I need to take Sushi back to Mum's and get back to the office.' He paused and gave her a tentative smile. 'Fancy a coffee?'

His eyes were tired, and seemed decades older than they had a few minutes ago. Something melted in Claire and she nodded. 'Yes. I'd really like that.'

16

LOUISE

Barbara Lane

> Finished the meeting and just got home. All's fine. Tony was being Tony and wanted to feel like he was the Big Man by summoning me to his lair. Have the team draw up the paperwork, usual Terms and Conditions. He said he'll sign.

Thanks, Lou. Bet Michelle and Sam loved watching

> Klaus while you were in there.

Didn't give them the option. If Tony's gonna summon me in to see him, then he can't be surprised to see Klaus with me.

> The security downstairs let him in?

He was tucked inside my coat. No one asked and I wasn't about to point him out.

> OMG, you're a legend, Lou. I would have loved to see that!

No you wouldn't. You'd have seen a softer side of Tony, which wouldn't work at all! I might be scarred for life.

> Moany Tony's a dog person? Who knew?

I set my phone aside, my attention returning to Eddie Morley. A few quick searches had yielded interesting results. On average there were about 110 to 125 homicides in London every year. I was surprised that while Tower Hamlets had a pretty high percentage of them, we were nowhere near the worst borough.

The majority of cases involved knives. As far as I knew, neither the dead woman in Victoria Park nor the young man in Partridge Park had been sliced or stabbed, but both press releases were pretty sketchy.

There were also several statistics relating to how many homeless people perished in the UK each year, but I wanted more: I wanted to know how many, in which boroughs of London and what their causes of death were, but the graphs I found didn't give me that level of granularity.

'I know a few Management Information specialists who could help sort out better dashboards with their eyes closed,' I grumbled, leaning back in my desk chair. 'Assuming you have the data, which the Met should have.'

By the window, Klaus ignored me, intent on barking at the delivery guy in the courtyard in front of my building. It would only be a matter of time before the other dogs in the complex joined in.

'Of course, whether you'd *want* that level of information in the public eye might be a different question.'

Klaus paused, giving me a querying look.

'Think Andy or Scott would tell me? I'll answer that for you. No. No, they wouldn't. All they'd tell me was to stay out of their investigation.' I rolled my eyes. 'For my own protection.'

Which left only one person to ask. My favourite cyber stalker.

Irina. Who would not appreciate me adding to her to-do list.

17

IRINA

Louise (Klaus's Mum)

> Do you have any idea how difficult it is to find meaningful crime statistics?

> Which stat are you after? I can check my inbox.

> Not helpful, Irina.

'Ask a stupid question, get a stupid answer,' Irina said aloud.

She frowned at the glowing screen in front of her. There was no sign of Eddie Morley on any of the social media sites. It wasn't the most uncommon name, but she'd still half-expected to find some older stuff; digital footprints from before he'd become homeless.

There was nothing. Not just on the bigger names – Insta, X, Facebook, Snapchat, TikTok, even LinkedIn (although she hadn't been holding out hope for the last one) – but the smaller and more niche platforms too. He must have deleted his pages, if he'd ever had them.

She checked a few more sites before leaning back in her chair with a frustrated sigh.

Eddie wasn't the only one who'd eluded her efforts. The difference was that he'd probably gone dark when he was still a minor, so it made sense that there would be nothing written about him, tagging him or mentioning him, until he'd been murdered.

Claire (Tank's Mum)

> Nothing I could find on Eddie Morley on the socials. Soz.

> NP. Thanks for trying!

> 👍

Irina opened a new browser window and entered the name of the other man who'd evaded her searches: her neighbour, Jake Hathaway.

Yeah, Lou was keen enough on him, but then she had a type. And based on what Irina knew of Lou's ex, it wasn't a good type. Probably best that she remained single. Not that Jake *seemed* that bad, but with no online presence, who knew who he was or what he was hiding?

She was doing Lou a favour by looking into him. What if he had a wife and platoon of kids stashed away somewhere? Or was every bit as dodgy as the chicken shop on the High Street?

Jake was good, she'd give him that. So far, despite six months of hunting, she'd turned up exactly zero.

'Damn man has to have a history. It's like he doesn't exist.'

She opened a bag of crisps and glared at the screen. 'You break her heart, and you'll have me to answer to. 'Coz I do not want to be the one to help her pick up the pieces. Again.' She crunched a few and then picked up the foil bag. 'What's wrong with people that they need their crisps to taste like a three course meal?'

18

BENNY

Benny Bryce stared at the object in the middle of his kitchen table. It reflected the lights from the small Christmas tree in the corner, but the flashing colours were anything but jolly; they were making him physically ill.

Danny was back.

Benny knew he'd returned back in October. He'd always been tight with Benny's boss Caren Hansen, but obviously not enough to keep her from being arrested and putting Benny's livelihood into jeopardy.

Would Danny have stopped her from blackmailing that hood, Dave Najafi or killing Jonny Tang? Would he have prevented her from breaking into Louise Mallory's flat, when she found evidence Caren lost?

Or had he encouraged her, maybe even helped her? That one thrived on chaos.

Benny didn't approve, but he'd learned to keep his

mouth shut. Caren was his friend and owned the salon he worked in, but Danny was ... well, Danny. Violent. Unpredictable. Terrifying.

He'd killed Eddie Morley.

Benny had no doubt of that: Danny had left Eddie's mobile on the table, like a grim electronic calling card. Or maybe, a challenge: *What'cha gonna do with this, Benny-boy? You gonna give it to the filth? You know what'll happen to you if you do ...*

Benny knew. And he knew he wasn't strong enough to stand up to Danny. He never had been. He rested his forehead against the cold glass window pane and tried to breathe. One by one, Danny was taking all options from him, but one thing was clear: he couldn't keep the phone here. The police would be looking for it. What if they searched his flat? What if they found it? What if Danny had managed to transfer his fingerprints onto it?

'Shit,' Benny muttered. He'd have to get rid of it.

He glanced out of the window, towards the park. There were gangs of kids who stole phones only to fence them for cash. Benny didn't trust them – if they recognised the phone, they might sic the cops on him.

No, he thought, stomach sinking even further. He had to get rid of it far enough away that no one would connect it to him.

Or to Danny.

Tuesday

19

LOUISE

Claire (Tank's Mum)

> Morning! Fancy a walk to Partridge Park? I could murder one of the Nest's apple fritters.

> Sadly not the only thing being murdered around the park, but yeah, we're just getting ready now.

> Great – meet you by the entrance to the canal path in about 10.

Klaus saw the coat in my hand and shot around the corner.

'You've got to be kidding me,' I muttered. 'Come on, Klaus. It's freezing outside and you don't like the cold.'

There was no sign of him.

'If I have to wear a coat, so you do.'

Logic didn't work on dogs; I didn't know why I bothered.

'I have treats!' I shook the treat bag. He came out from under the bed and padded towards me, stopping a couple of feet away. He rolled onto his back, tail wagging in a way that was heart-stoppingly cute. But not cute enough to get away with going outside without a coat.

I palmed a treat and stuck it through the neck opening. When he got close enough to eat it, I slipped the coat over his head and fastened it around him. Clipped his collar on while he was still chewing. Sneaky, but effective.

For the time it took for us to get from the flat to the building's front door, he seemed happy enough. But as I opened the door, he put the brakes on. *Nope. Not going out in this.*

'It's sunny.'

It's cold.

'Want to see Tank?'

He looked at me as if it were a trick question. 'Yes. Let's go see Tank!' My enthusiasm was met with suspicion. 'Yes! Tank!' Klaus's head cocked to the side and I knew I had him. 'Let's go see Tank!'

He gave me the stinky side-eye and followed me outside, every step making it clear that he considered this under duress.

Claire and Tank were waiting for us on the far side of the bridge over the canal. Claire was bundled up, but Tank only wore his harness. 'I was about to ask if you had to bribe Tank to go out in this weather, but I guess not.'

'Not sure if he feels the cold. Or if he's too dim to understand that he's cold.'

'That's not a very nice thing to say about your own dog.'

'No, but it's true. Three brain cells, remember?'

'And none of them are focused on body temperature,' I laughed. 'But whatever, he's sweet and we love him.' Tank and Klaus had finished their ritual of sniffing each other's butts and were happily walking side by side along the path.

'Did you know Sarah the Trainer was on *Britain's Got Talent*?' Claire asked.

'Yep. It was pretty heartbreaking. Her Pomeranian, Meatball, got stage fright on the day.' I was pretty sure she didn't want to catch up for either the pastries or to discuss Sarah. 'What's going on?'

She sighed. 'The more I find out about that dead kid, Eddie Morley, the more I want to cry. The dad did a runner. Eddie didn't get on with his mum's new partner and took off too. Got bounced around foster care, then ended up living on the streets until he turned up dead. Did you know he was only twenty?'

'That bit was in your article, but not the rest. Did the police release more information?' I asked.

'No.' Claire blushed. 'I ... ahhh ... I've been doing some digging.'

I nodded, expecting that. 'I've been following the news on this too. Sad as it is, his story isn't unique.'

'I know, but ...' She looked away, her gaze lingering on the bench that stood just ahead. 'I don't want him to be forgotten.'

For a moment I wondered if she was speaking about Jonny Tang, and my heart went out to her. His body had been found on that same bench less than two months ago.

'There's the vigil on Thursday,' I said gently.

'Eddie's mum is organising that. I'm more worried that the police won't prioritise him because he was homeless.'

'Fair point. From what I understand, they're already understaffed, and I read somewhere that case numbers always ramp up around Christmas. I could be wrong though. Anyway, what do you have in mind?'

'I don't know yet. So far all I've been able to find out is who he is, and a bit about his early life. As for now?' She shook her head. 'People only know him as they guy who's usually stoned somewhere around the park.'

'There's more than one stoned guy in the park at any point in time, Claire.'

'I know. Which makes it all the sadder.'

We were approaching The Nest. 'Let's change the subject. Tell me about your date yesterday. He was cute. Sorry I interrupted it.'

'You didn't. It wasn't a date,' Claire said, but her face had gone a deeper shade of pink. 'That was Eddie Morley's cousin. I was hoping he would give me some sort of clue about what happened. Or at least about how Eddie's mum found out so fast.'

So *that* was the digging about that she was referring to. 'So fast?' I echoed.

'She showed up at the park before the police could even ID him. She had to find out some way, and I thought he might know how.'

I opened the door to the café. Tank and Klaus led the way inside, with Klaus giving a relieved shake that started at his nose and ended at his tail. I gestured for Claire to enter first, and followed her to the back of the queue. 'Did he?'

'Nope. All he knew was that someone had texted her. He couldn't say who, or maybe he didn't want to.'

'What do you think?'

She frowned. 'Even if Caroline Carr knows, I don't think Jeremy does.'

We got to the counter and ordered two coffees, a cinnamon bun (my weakness) and an apple fritter.

'Jeremy, huh?' I glanced at my friend; her cheeks were flaming red. It could have been from the cold, but I didn't think so. 'When are you seeing him again?'

'Tomorrow.' She grinned shyly. 'We're going for dinner.'

'Why do I get the feeling that it's more than "taking one for the team" to get an in with a witness?' I teased. The red flush spread across her cheeks, giving me hope that she was finally getting over Jonny's death.

I only hoped that her determination to find Eddie's killer wouldn't get in the way.

20

MEG

Partridge Bark

> The shelter I volunteer at just rescued a MASSIVE number of dogs and pups. Really sad story – they're asking for any used but serviceable collars, harnesses, leads, etc. I'll be heading up there this evening if anyone has anything or wants to come along.

Ella (Jimmy Chew and Bark Vader's Mum)

I have got a lot of the boys' old things that I need to get rid of before we move back to France. I will try to get them to you before you leave for the shelter.

> Don't worry! Whenever you can drop them off is fine. They're at capacity, so it's all hands on deck. I suspect I'll be heading up there quite often until we can find homes for some of the poor babies.

Louise (Klaus's Mum)

I have a few old things too — and some warm jumpers that Klaus outgrew that might fit some of the puppies.

Paul (Jimmy Chew and Bark Vader's Dad)

@Ella – Do not pack up the Star Wars or Fortnite ones!

Ella (Jimmy Chew and Bark Vader's Mum)

Those are the first to go – they are horrible! 😊

Irina (Hamish's Mum)

Have you seen some of the designs @Louise makes Klaus wear?

Louise (Klaus's Mum)

Klaus is more offended by having to wear a coat than a lead with an alligator on it. @Meg, you're doing a good thing. I'm with @Claire and we'll both pack a bag for you. I'll throw in a few toys and a dog bed that Klaus doesn't like. I can't do

> tonight or Friday, but K and I can walk over with you tomorrow if you want.

'Fantastic,' Meg said aloud, moments before bumping into someone. She blinked, surprised that Tyrion had let anyone close enough. The man was tall, but hunched from life rather than the cold. He was forty-ish, Meg guessed, but these days, he looked older. He'd had a crap few months, since his boss was arrested for murder, attempted murder, attempted blackmail and, just to round out a full bingo card of awful, breaking into Louise's home.

'Last-minute Christmas shopping?' she asked.

'What?' Benny Bryce blinked at her, confused. She pointed to the bag of brightly wrapped boxes in his hands, and he offered her a weary smile. 'I went to Oxford Street this morning. So many people crammed in, no one was moving.'

'Brave man. I try to avoid it during December. Too many tourists.' Meg fell into step beside him. 'Are things at the salon going okay?'

Benny had been colouring her hair for years, and Meg considered him a friend. She was embarrassed to realise how unfair she'd been to avoid him, and the salon, for the last couple of months. It wasn't his fault that his boss was horrible.

'Caren asked me to keep it going while she's ... uhm ... gone. I've picked up the customers that haven't left since ... uhm ... October. And the admin is a killer.' He flushed at the word and his shoulders sagged. 'I still can't believe what she was up to. It's so stupid – the salon was doing well. Why try to turn it into a money laundering operation for a mob boss?'

Meg wasn't sure Dave Najafi was technically a 'mob boss', but from what she'd read, he was definitely dodgy. Trying to blackmail him was just plain *stupid*. And trying to hide blackmail with murder started a spiral that had one inevitable outcome.

'She's still being held without bail?' Meg asked.

'Yeah. Her case is coming before a judge in a few months, I think, but they have enough on her to put her away for a very long time.' Benny squinted at the sky. 'She could have been out on bail, but then she had to go and try to throw Louise into the canal.'

Meg was glad that Caren was still locked up, but seeing poor Benny run ragged saddened her. 'She didn't have to sell the salon?'

'No, but I might need to. Even with the big "Under New Management" sign in the window, people don't want to know. We're haemorrhaging customers, and the bills still need to be paid.' He shrugged. 'Can I blame them? Hell, I'd leave here in a shot if I could.'

'Well, don't you dare leave without telling me where you're going. No one gets my hair like you do.'

His smile didn't reach his eyes. 'This neighbourhood is hard, Meg. I don't know how much longer I can stay here. You heard there's another dead body down at the park?'

'I heard. In the kiddie playground.'

'Do you know anything about it? Who it was? Who did it?'

Meg shook her head. 'Nothing that hasn't been written in the news.'

'That surprises me. I was expecting you and your doggie friends to investigate it,' Benny said, his voice tired.

'Nope,' Meg said, careful about what she said on the street, even to her friends. You never knew who else might be listening in, right? 'Not this time.'

'Good.' He paused outside the salon, took off his beanie and ran his fingers through his shoulder-length hair. He glanced down the street at the Cluckin' Good Chicken shop that had recently re-opened after someone had set fire to the kitchen. It was only lunchtime, but the regulars were lurking outside.

'Good,' he repeated. 'It can be dangerous around here, Meg. I wouldn't want anything bad to happen to you.'

Meg nodded and watched him open the salon. She wished she could do something to help, but between her dog, her boyfriend, her job and her volunteering, she couldn't take on much more without breaking. Keeping her head down, she walked towards the Docklands Light Railway, hoping Benny didn't notice how quickly she moved away.

21

ELLA

Meg (Tyrion's Mum)

> Hey, Ella. Would you be free tonight to come with me to the shelter? I've managed to spook myself and would rather not be out late alone.

> Of course. But I do not want to take the boys – I think they might be traumatised by seeing the poor souls in the shelter. Tyrion is welcome to stay

> at ours with Paul. You know how much your boy likes to boss mine around.

> That sounds great – thank you!

Ella was glad for an excuse to get out of the house. From the moment Paul got home after work, he was either fussing over her and her five-month-old baby bump, or watching what was going on in Partridge Park. He loved the excitement of everything happening around there. Had bought binoculars and an electric blanket so he could stay out on the balcony on cold evenings and watch the action.

For a small-town boy, it was like being in the middle of some streaming service's latest crime series. Not only did he have front-row seats, but he was one of the *players*. It was exciting, something to brag about at the office.

Ella saw the flip side of that coin. Death was permanent. She didn't want to train the dogs to find drugs left in the park, or dead bodies in the long grass. Didn't want to be a part of that world. Ever.

She stood at the window and gazed out across the park. It was 4:00 p.m., but the sun had already set. The lamps along the pathways gave off a half-hearted light, and the Nest, on the far side, was already closed for the day, despite the Christmas lights blinking in the windows.

Christmas was coming, and now there was another dead body to be Paul's sole topic of conversation.

She sat down in the armchair by the balcony. Paul had started a journal in June, when the Pack found the first body, documenting what he thought was out of the ordinary on a daily basis. Each entry – and there was at least one every day that they were home – was neatly laid out in his small, precise script. Date, time, location. Even weather conditions. And then a description of what had happened and the individuals involved.

Some entries were trivial – a confrontation between two people, people littering or leaving their dog's poo on the paths. But some were more serious. Licence plates found in bushes. People mugged for their e-scooters and purses. The alarms from stolen Lime bikes, that reminded Ella of the theme from *Psycho*. 'Hackney birdsong,' she'd heard it called.

Despite herself, Ella flipped the pages back to the past weekend, wondering if Paul had seen something that might help the police. The usual group of kids that hung out in their corner of the park had been out, mostly smoking weed and letting off fireworks. On Saturday night, one of the boys had stolen a phone from a young Asian woman. She'd given chase, stopping every so often to catch her breath. Apparently the boy hadn't been in much better shape, constantly slowing down and looking over his shoulder.

Maybe it was hard to breathe in the balaclava he was wearing, or maybe it was the novelty – Ella knew this group was usually content to hang out and get stoned.

The woman had managed to catch the boy. He'd thrown her phone into the bushes and held up his hands. When she'd chosen to get her mobile instead of decking him, he bolted.

Paul had watched the woman walk away on shaking legs. There was no indication as to whether he'd phoned the police or not. But even if he had, the chances were good that both the thief and the victim would have been long gone by the time they'd arrived.

Ella wouldn't put it past Paul to buy himself a camera with a super-long lens for Christmas. For sure, she wasn't about to buy one for him. Hell, she couldn't wait to find a tenant so they could leave the area.

She flipped back a little further.

There was another group that was worse, despite being younger. Angela, the doggie daycare woman, once referred to them as 'the Baby Gang' because of their ages – whether that was what they called themselves or not, the name had stuck.

They usually operated on the other side of the park, closer to the dog enclosure, near where Yaz lived, but Paul had seen them up this way; a group of kids (girls as well as boys), mostly in their early teens, armed with knives.

He had caught them trying to break the CCTV camera mounted on a pole near the Nest a few months ago. They'd also broken the charging points for the electric cars on the street, although surely they'd known they wouldn't contain any cash to steal.

For them it was destruction for the sake of it.

As far as Ella knew, the dead man was too old to have

been *in* the Baby Gang, but that didn't mean they weren't involved. She'd heard rumours that he'd been strangled, not stabbed – was that their MO? She didn't know.

She closed the book and replaced it on the table. She rested her hand on top of it until her heartbeat slowed down.

All this talk of gangs: it made it sound like they lived in the roughest of estates, instead of a beautiful newbuild, a stone's throw from Canary Wharf.

Paul adored this strange mix of Southeast Asian communities, old East Londoner wide boys and the professionals like them, who'd moved here for bigger flats and better connections to the Wharf and the City. To him, every day was an adventure.

But it wasn't for Ella. She couldn't raise her child here, not with everything going on in this neighbourhood. She just couldn't.

And if they couldn't find a tenant, she'd leave Paul to sort it out and go home by herself. Only not to his family in Bergues, as was the plan. To her family in Paris. It wasn't the safest city in the world, but it was miles better than here.

22

ANDY

Scott Williams

Where're you at?

Down at the CCTV Monitoring Centre to check in with Harry. Why?

Mrs Carstairs is here to give her statement. She brought the little rats. Decked them out in cheetah-print parkas that match the one she's wearing. Greg at the

> reception desk told her that she can't bring them in. She's going a little mental.

Right. Tell Greg they're her emotional support dogs, the poor woman's had a rough 24 hours. Just make sure she cleans up after them if they do their business inside. I'll be there in 10.

> 👍 On your head, then.

Doug Harriman, the CCTV officer, was slumped in his chair. He didn't have the best posture on a good day – a downside of the job when what you're required to do is look at screens all day. He rolled his shoulders, trying to get rid of a crick in his neck. Rumour had it that his new girlfriend had bought him one of those Velcro braces to improve his posture. Andy made a mental note to tell Harriman to start using it, before that crick became chronic.

'Whatcha got, Harry?' Andy sank into the empty chair beside him.

Harriman didn't look up from the bank of screens in

front of him. 'No one showed up in the park between the hours of ten p.m. and six the next morning. The first person who appears to have come across the deceased was Mrs Hazel Carstairs with her little rat dogs just before ten a.m.'

'Okay.'

'However,' Harriman added, 'there are a number of blind spots in and around Partridge Park, which I'd bet most of the locals know about.'

'Yeah, that's true. When we consulted on the poles last summer, a local mums' group was quite vehement: no cameras anywhere near the kiddie area,' Andy said. 'Likewise, there are none on the street facing into the kids' corner.'

Harriman grunted. 'I get it, but it makes our job tougher. In the end, we put up two poles in the park. Not only do the locals know where they are, there's a gang of kids who keep trying to disable them.'

'So, nothing.'

'Any luck with the phone?

'Nope. Still missing. Nic come back with anything?'

'Not much more than she said in the briefing yesterday. Most of the family haven't seen Eddie in years. Foster care, juvie, the works. His sister and stepdad went no contact. His mum heard from him sporadically, but claimed she didn't know who he was spending time with or even where he was living.'

'You find anyone who might've been his friend that we can talk to?' Andy asked.

'There were people he seemed to know at the park,

mostly to nod hello to. One or two maybe a little better, but this time of year, everyone's bundled up to the eyebrows. I'm going back a bit further to see if I can identify anyone, but I'll be honest here, Andy. If he had a girlfriend or a boyfriend, then I can't find any evidence of it on the cameras.'

'Keep looking – there has to be something, somewhere.'

'Not necessarily, mate. He could've told his mum something to stop her from worrying. Sad, but it happens all the time.'

Andy nodded, trying not to wince at the number of times he'd done just that. 'Williams had a couple of uniforms asking around yesterday. The few people who admitted to knowing Morley described him as a good guy. Yeah, he smoked. Drank sometimes. But he tried to watch out for the others. Especially the younger ones. Apparently he wouldn't touch a weapon after being discharged that last time.'

'Consistent with what I'm seeing.'

'So, no ideas who he was tight with? Or who might have had a bone to pick with him?'

'If I find anything, Andy, you'll be the first to know.'

'Thanks.' Andy moved towards the door. 'And Harry? Put that back brace on.'

'Yeah, yeah.' Harriman waved him away, and Andy had a feeling that Harry was fobbing him off, but if his colleague wanted to look like Quasimodo, that was on him.

Andy took the stairs to the station's ground floor. He spotted Williams holding his phone, and headed over to him. 'Anything new?' he asked, watching Williams's thick fingers move in a blur across the screen.

'ME confirmed strangulation. No defensive wounds on Morley, and nothing appeared to have transferred to his clothing. Whoever did it was careful. Came up behind him, slipped a garotte over his head and *bam*.' Williams mimed pulling the weapon tight.

'Composition of the garotte?'

'She thinks it was a wire, consistent with a cheese wire.'

'Cheese?'

'Yeah. You can buy a wire cheese cutter with handles for about seventeen quid on Amazon. I say handles, but there's no evidence of that one way or the other. I just think it would be easier to hold on to. The alternative would have been for the killer to wrap the wire around their hands, and that would have left identifiable marks on them.'

Andy groaned. Trying to find something so easy to come by would be worse than looking for a needle in the proverbial haystack.

'Guessing no one found a cheese cutter in one of the rubbish bins?'

'Nope.'

'No, of course not.' Andy looked at the ceiling. 'Because getting fingerprints off nice wooden handles would be too easy.'

'Bone cold out there, Andy. They'd be wearing gloves,' Williams pointed out.

'All right. Where's Mrs Carstairs?'

'Interview Room One.' Williams waved towards it, down the hall. 'Gotta say, Andy, she might talk a good show, but she's never without those little rat dogs, with their ridiculous outfits. I can't see her having either the strength or inclination to kill someone. Especially not with the doglets running around.'

Doglets. That was a new one for him. He paused outside the door, listening to the dulcet sounds of two hyped-up Yorkies.

'She lawyered up?'

'Nope.' Williams shrugged. 'I explained that she had the right to, if she wanted, but this was more her telling us what happened when she found the body.'

Andy nodded and opened the door. The room had been painted bright white about two decades ago, and had since edged its way towards a dingy grey. It was a sharp contrast to Mrs Carstairs and her little dogs, all (as Williams had said) in matching animal print.

'Thanks for coming in, Mrs Carstairs.' Andy and Williams took their seats at the table, across from Mrs Carstairs.

'Better than having my neighbours see the fil— the police showin' up at my home,' she growled.

'Okay, let's go through the basics first. Can you repeat your full name and address?'

'You already have it.'

Andy sighed.

'Right. I'm Hazel Carstairs. This is Meeky.' She held up one Yorkie, then the other. 'And Bella.' She had a brash smile, but her hands were shaking. 'Because she's pretty, innit?' At Andy's unamused stare, she put the dogs down in her lap and mumbled her address.

'Can you tell us what happened?'

Mrs Carstairs scowled. 'Had a bit of a lie-in on Sunday. Walked the dogs to the park and saw a farkin' sea of trash in the kiddie area. I saw someone in there. Could smell the weed from the gate. I was gonna have a word about 'im leaving behind a feast for the foxes an' rats.'

'I'm sure he didn't leave all that there singlehandedly, even with a massive case of the munchies.'

'Yeah, especially if he were already dead,' she pointed out, burying her fingers in Yorkie fur.

'Yeah,' Williams echoed. 'Especially then. Did you see anyone else around?'

She shook her head. 'No.'

'Anyone on your way to or from the park?'

'Usual people in the main park. People with dogs, right? But mostly we stay out of the kiddie area an' it were too cold for the kids to want to play.' She tilted her head to the side, thinking. 'Or rather, too cold for the parents to take 'em there. Kids always want to go to the park. Mine did at least.'

'Can you give us names?'

'Well, there was Luna. Charlie. Baxter. I think we saw Loki. The Jack Russell, not the Malamute. Or the Chihuahua. Sorry, we got a lot of Lokis here.'

'Their *humans'* names?' Andy clarified, being careful not to look at Williams, who he knew would struggle to hold back his laughter.

'Christ, no. I don't know the *humans'* names. But Luna is a husky. Charlie's a golden. Loki is a Jack Russell, and Baxter is, well, only the Lord knows.'

One hour later and they were no closer to solving the murder. Andy and Williams thanked Mrs Carstairs for her time, and watched her shuffle out of the station, two tiny cheetahs yapping at her heels.

'You know any of those dogs?' Williams asked.

Andy had stopped asking why he'd become the go-to person for anything relating to the local dog community. 'We spoke with the owners when we arrived on the scene. They're local, but I haven't seen any of them – with the exception of Loki the Jack Russell – with any of the Pack dogs.'

'Who would have thunk that there were cliques even in the dog world.' Williams's brow furrowed. 'Loki the Jack Russell. Wasn't his owner hospitalised during that first case with the Pack? Back in June?'

'Yeah,' Andy responded, not keen on discussing Irina Ivanova's on-again/off-again bloke, unless the other man was under caution. 'I don't think Mrs Carstairs or the dog people had anything to do with it,' he continued. 'Littering isn't usually a reason to kill someone.'

'Not unless the rubbish killed someone's pet Fido. I'll check the Pack Chat just in case, but if you're gonna ask Louise about those other dog owners, see if any of 'em reported a dog getting sick from the litter?'

'Will do.'

'What next?'

'Let's go back to the park. Talk to the kids that hang out there. See if they "remember" anything new.'

23

LOUISE

DC Andrew Thompson

Hey Louise, what do you know about the people who own Luna the husky, Charlie the golden retriever, Loki the Jack Russell and Baxter the maybe-mixed-breed?

Why?

They were nearby when Mrs Carstairs found the body on Sunday. Just checking to see if they saw anything that she might have missed.

I would have thought you'd already have taken down their details. Not sure how much more I can add but tbh, I'd be surprised if any of them had anything to do with it. Luna is owned by a Canadian called Don. Travels for work a lot and has Luna board with Angela (who does daycare around here). Charlie and Baxter were rescued by a Thai couple, whose names I never caught and at this point I'm embarrassed to ask. Nice people though. Baxter and Luna scare the daylights out of Klaus (he's terrified of big fluffies), so we don't really see them that often. And Loki's dad you already know.

> Can you think of any one of them, or anyone else, who might have had motive to kill Mr Morley?

> No.

> OK. Have you heard about any more dog poisonings? Maybe related to something they ate off the street?

> More of a question for Irina, with the way Hammy scavenges, but no. Nothing I've heard about. Not since June anyway.

> OK, thx.

It felt like Andy was reaching. Mrs Carstairs had found Eddie Morley around 10:00 a.m., although heaven knew how long he'd been out there. The Met was seeking anyone with info, but I guessed that not many people had piped up.

My phone buzzed again, and I paused outside the dog

enclosure. Klaus, at my feet, was getting impatient, keen to play.

Partridge Bark

Yaz (Hercules's Mum)

> Anyone heading into the dog enclosure, be warned: someone (or maybe several someones) didn't clean up after their dogs. Lots of poo in there — like, elephant-sized, and some of it runny. Might be best to give it a wide berth until after a serious rainfall. Don't want anyone to get sick — or step in it.

> 😢🙀 Thanks for the heads-up.

Irina (Hamish's Mum)

> Honestly, is it that hard to pick up your own dog's poop? What's wrong with people?

PAW AND ORDER

Claire (Tank's Mum)

Where do you want me to start?

Yaz (Hercules's Mum)

@**Louise**, you might want to tell Sarah the Trainer to re-release her 'Pick Up The Poop' song on Insta. She is the one who went viral with that a couple of years ago, isn't she?

> Yep, that's her. Tell her yourself when we do Sniffer Dog Part 2 on Sunday.

Yaz (Hercules's Mum)

Speaking of which, if we're all out at The Hound on Saturday, do we really need an early start on Sunday?

> Nope – we changed the time to noon. The confirmation should be in your email.

I veered away from the enclosure and glanced around, hoping there was another dog for Klaus to play with. I smiled when I spotted Gav MacAdams in the main part of the park, reading a newspaper. His Affenpinscher, Violet, was resting under the bench, wrapped in a purple fleece.

I unclipped Klaus's lead. 'Where's Violet?' I said to him, and pointed. He didn't think twice, sprinting towards her, his hind legs working in unison, like a bunny's, in a way that never failed to make me smile.

On a good day, Violet looked demented – a snub-nosed bundle of fur and fury; the poster girl for 'what you see is what you get'. There weren't many dogs she liked, but Klaus was one of them. Not only could he deal with her temper, he'd actively provoke it.

It started with his 'I'm cute, you must love me' dance, as he pranced around in front of her. Within moments he'd pushed her with his front paws and she was chasing him, like a monster grape with fangs, making all sorts of gremlin-like sounds. He could have outrun her, but he stayed just out of range, his tail tucked in. Just in case.

'Hey, Gav, can we join you?' I called out.

'Suit yourself.' He didn't look up. Where Violet was dressed for the weather, Gav had conceded only by putting a padded gilet under his wool blazer. 'Although if you're gonna ask about the man they found in the park, I don't know anything about it.'

Gav was my go-to person when it came to the underbelly of the neighbourhood. An old-school East Londoner, he'd worked for one of the local crime bosses until he'd been put away for GBH. I wasn't sure how much of that was behind him, but he'd never been anything other than lovely to me.

'Okay.' I settled onto the seat beside him.

He was silent for a few seconds, flicking the corner of a page before clearing his throat gruffly. 'But if you want my opinion, the kid was homeless. A stoner. Me, I'd check with his dealer first.'

It was the same response everyone seemed to have, and I had nothing to prove otherwise; best to keep an open mind.

'Okay,' I repeated. 'Although to be honest, I was only coming over so that Klaus had someone to play with. Yaz said the enclosure is a mess.'

'It is.' Gav shook his head. 'Bloody disgraceful. Just because it's a dog park doesn't mean they don't have to pick up after their dogs.'

'The same people probably leave it on the street too.'

'Don't get me started.' He gave me a dark look. That was the thing about Gav: however rough his background, he was interesting, and always good company. 'How's the job, Lou? Heard a rumour that you were looking at early retirement?'

I laughed. 'I'm not even forty, Gav.'

'So?'

'So, I'm doing myself out of a job. I started a company. Trained a good second-in-command. Operationally, she can run things better than I can. Strategically? Probably that too. So, I keep taking a step back. I *should* be delighted to have all this free time, but ...' I held up my gloved hands, palms facing the sky.

Violet slowed down, her legs growing still but her chest heaving. As if she was disinclined to show her age in front of Klaus, she turned and sauntered back towards Gav, ignoring my sausage's pleas for one more run.

'But you're bored, and not looking forward to being even more bored. It's not that bad, in case you're asking.' Gav laughed, and then turned towards me. 'Something always comes up, doesn't it?' His eyes were hidden behind sunglasses, despite the weak late-afternoon sun, but I felt his sharp eyes studying me.

'Does it?'

'Is this why you throw yourself into solving every crime in the area?'

'I don't throw myself into every case,' I insisted, feeling like I was defending myself. 'Only the ones where it feels personal. Irina and I found Phil. He was our friend. What were we supposed to do? And then Yaz found Jonny, and Claire was brought in for questioning, and ...'

'Uh huh.'

'This guy that died the other day? I really hope the cops can find out who killed him. He deserves justice, and his mum deserves closure.' The truth, one that I wasn't ready to admit aloud yet, was that it felt good to be *able* to give the victim justice and their families that closure. 'But I'm not stupid, Gav. I know I don't have the resources or the training to do this on my own.'

'Not on your own, no.' Gav's voice held more than a trace of humour. 'You've got the rest of the Pack. You all seem to thrive on drama.'

It was less about the drama and more about doing the right thing, but Gav wasn't done. 'You're a lightning rod for this, Lou. Just be careful that you don't rattle the wrong snake.'

24

MEG

Partridge Bark

Paul (Jimmy Chew and Bark Vader's Dad)

> Is anyone going to The Nest's Xmas party on Friday?

Fiona (Nala's Mum)

> I can't do Friday, but I'm good to go for The Hound's bash on Saturday.

Louise (Klaus's Mum)

Sorry – I have my company's Xmas do on Friday. Klaus and I will see you on Saturday at The Hound.

Ella was tense as she and Meg walked down the High Street. It was only six o'clock, but the street lamps were losing the battle against the frigid December night. At the first sign of revving engines, Ella and Meg moved further away from the road.

Two cars blasted past in rapid succession, a white one and a blue one. 'I could swear the first driver had a balloon in his hand,' Ella said. 'As usual.'

'Nitrous oxide,' Meg replied, glad that Tyrion was safe with Paul. Not a lot of things triggered him, but he wasn't keen on the boy racers. Neither was she for that matter. 'It's like they know no one's going to stop them.'

'Yaz has been sending the police videos of the cars for years. With pics of the license plates. As far as I know, no one's been arrested or even fined.' Ella sighed. 'You know, if Tower Hamlets actually fined them, or fined people for littering, they would make a fortune.'

'I'd be happy if we could cross the road at a zebra crossing without worrying about becoming roadkill.' They walked in awkward silence, before Meg changed the subject. 'How's the search for new tenants?'

Ella grimaced. 'Grim. So far, no one who we both agree on, although we have more viewings scheduled this week. I would love to sell the flat instead of letting it, but Paul, he loves it. Loves the neighbourhood. He hopes that when the baby is old enough, we will come back.'

'I hope so too, Ella.'

She offered Meg a sad smile. 'If the neighbourhood changes for the better? We will see. But as it is now? I cannot.'

They passed the News-N-Booze on the corner. Then the little Tesco. As they reached the hair salon, Ella spoke again, this time hesitantly. 'I saw you talking to that man this morning,' she began.

'Benny? Yep. He does my hair.'

'And the woman who owns the salon? There is news of her?'

Meg understood Ella's concern. Two months ago, in her haste to attack Louise, Caren Hansen had pushed Ella into the canal. Irina, of all people, had saved the day, jumping into the icy water and getting her – and Jimmy Chew – back onto dry land and to the GP's for a couple of tetanus jabs.

'Don't worry – according to Benny, Caren is still behind bars. Given all the charges against her, I don't think she'll be out any time soon.'

'Bail?'

'Denied.'

'*Bon*. And they're still sure she was working alone?'

'If you had a partner in crime, would you go up against the Pack by yourself?' Meg joked.

'Probably not,' Ella admitted. 'Although Klaus is a far better guard dog than either Jim or Bark.'

'Ah, they're black Labs. They're bred to love everyone.' There was still an underlying tension which Meg was keen to break. She indicated the large shopping bag Ella was carrying. 'Did you put the boys' Star Wars kit in there?'

Ella grinned, the elfin smile that Meg hadn't seen in far too long. 'And the Fortnite one. They were cute when they were new, but they've been washed so many times the colours have faded to a dingy grey.'

'You know Paul will just buy new ones, right?'

Ella was about to reply when a skinny man with dark hair and pale skin approached them. 'Want some weed?' he asked.

'No thanks,' Meg said while Ella's jaw sagged.

'Sure?'

'Positive.'

He tilted his head to the side in a *no-harm-no-foul* sort of way and continued on, his stride unbroken.

'No one's ever asked me that, in all the years I've lived here,' Ella whispered.

'Seriously?' Meg laughed. 'I get asked all the time. And before you say anything, my drug of choice comes in a glass, in two colours.'

Ella relaxed enough to smile. 'Even more colours when Irina is mixing the cocktails.'

'Don't be daft. I don't let Irina mix my drinks anymore. I learnt my lesson years ago.' Meg felt the phone in her pocket vibrate and peeked at the screen.

Partridge Bark

Yaz (Hercules's Mum)

> @**Ella** @**Meg**, if you're still going to the shelter, @**Ejiro** will meet you there. We've got some of Herc's old stuff to donate. He should be there by 7, then he'll walk back with you, if that's OK?

> That'd be great – thanks @**Yaz**, thanks @**Ejiro**!

Ejiro (Hercules's Dad)

'We're in luck, Ella. We've got an escort home. And I'd like to see what'd happen if Pete the Pusher asks Ejiro if he wants to buy weed.'

25

LOUISE

Partridge Bark

Meg (Tyrion's Mum)

Thanks to everyone who's donated so far – the shelter is really grateful!

Meg (Tyrion's Mum)

Usually they don't accept open bags of food, but if they're from me and people I know, they'll make an exception. Does anyone have anything

> their pups have gone off that they'd be willing to donate?

Irina (Hamish's Mum)

> I've got a few bags. For all the crap he picks up off the street, you'd think Hammy was a good eater. But when it's served in a bowl, he's Gordon Bloody Ramsay.

Fiona (Nala's Mum)

> Same, same.

> I'm sure we've got something too. I'll pack it up with the leads and the spare bed and take it up tomorrow.

Jake Hathaway glanced at his phone and then at me. 'Luther and I will go with you tomorrow.'

I gaped; he rarely came to any Pack-related event. A dead-ringer for a forty-ish Hugh Jackman, Jake and I had become good friends since he moved in to the building across the canal last June.

Would I like more?

Sure. Yes. Absolutely. But as Irina was quick to point out, I hadn't (yet?) managed to charm my way out of the friend-zone, despite a drunken snog I'd attempted a couple of months ago. And while he remained a man of mystery in many ways – even evading Irina's cyber-stalking prowess – he'd proven himself to be a good friend.

I was grateful for his friendship, and for the regular Tuesday pizza-and-movie nights that had become our habit. We alternated flats and who chose the film. While I knew what sort of things he liked to watch, and witnessed his devotion to his Staffordshire Terrier, Luther, I still had no idea what he did for a living, who his family or friends were, what his goals and dreams were, or even where he was from. I guessed somewhere in Scotland, based on a soft burr that reared its head when he got agitated.

And yet, I still considered it a solid friendship. Bonkers, right?

But pizza, a glass of Pinot and Jake's company were exactly what I needed after a frustrating afternoon of trying to find a clue to who might have killed Eddie Morley, when even the Met seemed to be at a loss.

'Thanks but I don't need a nursemaid, Jake.' I glanced at the balcony door, where Klaus and Luther were curled up together. Both of them preferred that spot; it had the best vantage point for spying on (and barking at) whichever hapless souls entered the courtyard or ventured along the canal path. 'I'm perfectly capable of getting to and from the shelter with Meg.'

Jake laughed and took a swig from his bottle of Corona. 'Sure. How many times have you found yourself in trouble in the neighbourhood?'

'That's not fair, Jake.'

'Life isn't fair. Are you going to eat that?' He pointed at the last piece of pizza – mushroom and truffle. The meat-on-meat-on-meat one he'd ordered was long gone. He picked it up and took a bite. 'You're a magnet for trouble, Louise.'

I opened my mouth and then closed it. There was no way I could reasonably protest that point. And the fact was that I was giddy at the idea of having him walk us. Giddy to have more time with him, so if he was keen on playing the role of protector, I should just gracefully accept. Only, I didn't know how to be a damsel in distress.

Hell, I wasn't good at being vulnerable at all.

'I go out all the time on my own, you know,' I said, wanting to kick myself. 'I'm fine. I'll be fine.'

'Marple, you're like a cat, and you've got far less than nine lives left. If anything happened to you . . .' His dark blue eyes danced. 'I don't know what I would do . . .'

I held my breath, wondering if this was a signal.

'. . .on any given Tuesday.' He winked.

'Thanks,' I said, deadpan.

'Besides, I've got a ten-kilo bag of kibble that Luther turns his snout up at. You can take it if you're gonna take a cab there, but if you're walking or taking public transport – and it's, like, three buses to get there – it'd be a bit much to haul on top of Klaus's stuff.'

'Since you put it that way.'

'Good.' Jake finished his beer and stood up. He pulled another Corona from the fridge and leaned back against the countertop. 'You do good things, Marple.' His voice had softened and I felt heat suffuse my cheeks.

'I try.'

'You do. Even when it's best, or maybe easiest, not to.'

26

MEG

Louise (Klaus's Mum)

> Got another bag or two of stuff coming tomorrow. Jake has some of Luther's old food and will walk with us. I hope that's OK?

Meg put the phone back in her pocket and pretended to be interested in Ella's prospective tenants. The brothers who Ella was convinced would trash the flat. The young couple who'd arrived stinking of weed. Were they drug dealers? What would that mean for Paul and her, as the flat's owners, if they were busted? The older woman who'd had to leave her last flat because her unneutered cats were spraying everywhere and the neighbours complained about the smell. Nightmare.

Meg listened with one ear, making appropriate humming noises in the pauses. A sense of unease had crept over her; something felt wrong in the neighbourhood.

People assumed that because she dyed her hair funky colours and dressed in black that she was a Goth. Maybe even a Satanist. For sure, a witch. Meg never bothered to argue; if she had to explain herself to someone, then they weren't worth her time.

But what she *was,* was observant. And instinctive. She wasn't prone to overreacting, but if something felt off, it usually was. She zipped her pockets closed and looked around. She walked this way every week, sometimes with Tyrion, sometimes by herself, and she'd never had any trouble.

Meg missed T's presence tonight; he didn't let anyone close without a warning. Sometimes even after the warning.

She slowed down, her eyes scanning. For what? She didn't know. She didn't see anything amiss, but that didn't mean someone wasn't out there, hiding in the shadows. She could feel it; someone was watching them.

'So, what do you think?' Ella asked.

About what? Meg thought, but she didn't let on. Ella had been skittish enough since finding out she was pregnant. Being thrown into the canal only made things worse. There was no point in worrying her unnecessarily. 'Not sure. What does your gut feel say?'

Gut feel. Meg's said there was trouble ahead.

'My gut says sell the place and don't look back.' Ella sounded glum. 'I know that's horrible. I would miss our friends, and I know Paul and the boys would be devastated, but that's not a reason to stay. Which of the awful options do you think we should choose?'

They'd left the High Street minutes before, and the echoes of Ella's loafers on the sidewalk sounded eerie as they reverberated off the buildings. Meg glanced up, some of the flats above were lit from inside. People were home. If something happened, if she had to yell for help, people would hear.

But would they come?

She wasn't sure. That was why she took her kickboxing classes every Thursday. She could defend herself if she knew an attack was coming, but defending herself and her pregnant friend made it all the trickier.

Meg readjusted the bags in her hands, reminding herself to keep her body loose.

Hound's Haven wasn't far, maybe ten minutes away. Once they were there, they'd be safe. And if Ejiro was going to meet them, then they'd be safe coming home. She wanted to pick up their pace, but to do that would flag to whoever might be watching that she was scared, and a scared person almost always painted a target on their own forehead.

Not to mention, she'd have to explain herself to Ella, who would, to put it mildly, freak out.

There were lights, if not people. A newsagent's about halfway that they could duck into, if they had to.

Ethan. She should have taken him up on his offer to go with them. But her boyfriend had been working late all week, trying to meet a deadline, and she didn't need a man to protect her; she could do that perfectly well herself. To be honest, she'd put more money on Ella in a fight than Ethan. Sure, in an online game, he'd be ace, but in real life?

Something banged behind them. Meg dropped her bags as she turned, her back to the wall, her heart hammering, her hands up and knees bent in a defensive pose.

Nothing moved.

'Meg? Are you all right?' Ella said. 'There's no one there.'

Someone was, Meg was sure of it. Someone was watching them.

'What did you see?' Ella asked, looking at Meg nervously.

'See?' Meg echoed. 'Nothing. I guess the night just got me rattled.' It was a lie, but one that Ella seemed happy to accept.

They passed by the newsagent and an Asian man, standing outside, nodded to them. Meg forced a smile and nodded back, wondering if she should find an excuse to waste time inside. Maybe the person following them would give up and go away.

But the shelter might be closed by the time they arrived, and she didn't want to have to carry the bags home and back tomorrow.

'Let's go.'

Ella shrugged and lengthened her stride to match Meg's. What had they learned, whoever was following them?

That Meg was on high alert, that she could defend herself, maybe?

Did they know how often she came here?

Suddenly Meg was grateful for Ella's company. That Lou and Jake would come with her tomorrow. And she hated that. Hated being scared in her own neighbourhood. Scared to go where she wanted, when she wanted.

The sign above the entrance was dim. Hound's Haven. It was her haven too; she'd never felt so grateful to arrive *anywhere*.

And then a huge man stepped out of the shadows.

'Been waiting for you,' he said.

27

MEG

The man was enormous, close to two metres tall and looming over them both. His head was half-hidden under a knit cap and Meg couldn't see his face, just a huge silhouette against the dim lights.

'Shit,' she whispered.

He took a determined step towards them, moving like a panther.

Meg dropped the bags again, remembering what her self-defence instructor had told her.

Only Ella continued moving forward, without a care.

Meg opened her mouth to shout a warning, but no words came out.

Ella stopped in front of the big man. Put her own bags down and stretched up to give him a kiss on each cheek with her French elegance. 'It is good to see you, Ejiro.'

'Bloody freezing outside,' Ejiro said, taking up Ella's bags. 'Hey, Meg, good work you're doing, organising this.'

Ejiro. Of course it was Ejiro. Yaz had said he'd meet them here.

Meg's heart was still beating fast enough that she didn't trust her voice. She nodded and led the way into the shelter, relaxing only when Dolly, the shelter's welcome cockapoo, padded up to her for cuddles.

Meg sank to the floor, allowing Dolly to lick her face. 'How are they doing?' she asked the woman behind the desk.

'Still struggling to settle in. Confused. They might not have had the best home, but it was what they knew.' Annemarie heaved herself up from her chair and came around the desk. 'And while you or I might think they weren't responsible, the previous owners did do their best for the dogs. Those poor souls knew they were loved.'

'They'll find new homes – new families who will love them,' Meg said, glad that her hands had stopped shaking. 'Ones that will have the time and resources to take care of them properly.'

'God willing,' Annemarie answered. 'But until then, everything helps. Thank you all for your generosity.'

'You are welcome,' Ella said, blushing.

Meg slowly got to her feet, feeling angry that her jitters had made her contemplate not returning. This *was* important. More important than getting spooked by the dark. She forced a smile. 'Happy to help. I'll be back tomorrow.'

28

BENNY

Benny was exhausted. Not just physically – emotionally as well. He'd had enough problems on his plate even before Danny resurfaced, but now they were multiplying at a rate that terrified him.

He'd known as soon as he'd seen it that he should surrender Eddie's phone, the phone that Danny had left for him, to the police. Had known it might have something to help them find his murderer. But it was a test from Danny. If Benny gave Danny up to the police, Danny'd find a way to take him down with him. It'd happened before.

There'd been no other choice, really: Benny had gotten up early, put on gloves and wiped Eddie's phone down as best he could. Then tucked it into his back pocket and took the Tube into central London. Far enough away from Partridge Park that no one would be looking for it, or looking too closely at him.

Meg had been right when she'd said that Oxford Street in December was a nightmare. It was a sea of tourists and desperate, last-minute shoppers. As such, it was infamous as a pickpocket's dream.

Benny had bought himself a few things, had them wrapped as gifts, and blended into the crush. Within the first hour, he'd realised that someone had neatly picked his pocket; he hadn't felt a thing.

Except relief. Eddie's phone was gone, maybe on its way to China, if he was lucky. Or recycled to be sold off, with someone else's prints on it.

That relief was short-lived.

The problem hadn't gone away with the phone: the problem was very much still there. Along with a pervasive feeling that Danny wasn't done with him yet.

Wednesday

29

HAZEL CARSTAIRS

Hazel Carstairs wasn't having a great week.

It was still dark out when she left home, but it wasn't the trouble-makers Hazel was worried about. They'd've gone home hours ago – one of the few boons brought on by the farkin' Beast from the East cold snap.

Today she dressed Meeky and Bella in leopard coats that matched hers and pulled on a grey knit beret with a rhinestone brooch. Together they moved down the slope to the canal path. The Yorkies pulled left, towards Partridge Park, their normal morning walk, but Hazel couldn't bring herself to go back there. Not to that place what she found that dead man. Not yet.

'This way,' she directed, pulling the dogs with her. After a few steps, they were happy enough with the new direction, Meeky weeing on every blade of grass, while Bella scanned the area for anything edible.

They were beloved, but sometimes she had to question how clever they were.

In the cold early morning, the canal path shimmered with frost, and Hazel's boots crunched with each step. She made a note to order the dogs winter boots – the cold earth couldn't be good for their delicate paws.

The Bells pub was coming into sight. It had just reopened after some idiot had tried to firebomb it a couple of months ago. She'd been inside; it didn't look any different. 'Bet they used the insurance dosh on the ponies,' she muttered aloud. 'Miracle that place hasn't been condemned yet.'

Meeky and Bella didn't judge: there were usually crisps on the floor.

A man was sitting alone at one of the picnic tables outside, a baseball cap on his head and a takeaway coffee cup resting beside him. As she got closer, Hazel recognised him. People around here called him 'Pete the Pusher', but his name was Mike and she'd known him since he was a kid. Used to play footie with her son when they were small.

Figuring it'd be rude not to stop to say hello, she heaved her weight onto the seat beside him, careful to avoid the puddle of water left by the receding canal. 'Morning, Michael.'

The last thing she expected was to see him slide to the side and fall from the bench, his body splayed on the ground. 'Jesus, you still drunk?' she asked, only to notice the red tinge to the muddy puddle.

It *was* canal water, wasn't it? If it wasn't, then that wasn't mud on the dogs' paws . . .

Shock had Hazel counting her breaths, like the doctor told her to. Her gasps came fast, little white puffs in the air.

White puffs that weren't able to hide Mike's sightless eyes as they stared accusingly at her.

'Farkin' Jesus Farkin' Christ,' she shouted, gathering Meeky and Bella close. 'Not again!'

30

ANDY

'The pub put in CCTV a couple of months ago,' Harriman explained. 'Not that it was operational in time to stop the fire-bombing.'

Andy nodded. 'I remember.'

'Thing is, when they put in the CCTV, they only did the main entrance on the High Street, not the back entrance into the beer garden and canal path. Which was pretty stupid, if you ask me. Bigger risk from someone breaking in from the not-very-well-lit side.'

'Ever been in The Bells, Harry?'

'Nope. Saw it from the outside, and that was enough.'

'I can assure you, anyone going to the effort of breaking in would have a disappointing time of it. I'd bet they put the cameras in place in case there was some sort of confrontation between the punters here and the yobs at the chicken shop across the street.'

'Probably.'

Andy stood behind the bench where Mrs Carstairs had found the dead man, his back to the pub as he faced the canal. 'Any chance there's CCTV along the canal?'

'Lots of luck, mate,' Harriman replied. 'Best we can hope for is that one of the terraced houses further up has something pointing in that direction. If it was dark when our victim was killed – and I'm assuming it was – then the CCTV might capture a dark shape moving around, which might help us pinpoint the time, in case the coroner doesn't get it right, but won't have enough detail to make any sort of ID.'

Andy grunted.

'You're sure he was killed here? Never mind – the amount of blood there, of course he was.' Harriman answered his own question. 'But you're thinking that the killer entered and left via the canal path?'

Andy tucked his hands under his armpits to warm them up, wishing he had access to his pockets, but the paper boiler suits they wore at crime scenes prevented that. 'It's what I'd do. You've got gangs ranging about, and no threat of CCTV catching you.'

Williams, now finished questioning Mrs Carstairs, joined them. 'So, we've got a name. Mike James, aka Pete the Pusher.'

'You've got to be kidding?'

'Well, he's not going to use his real name is he?' Williams said. 'Mrs Carstairs knows the family. Saw him and thought it'd be rude to pass him without at least saying good morning. Moment she sat down, he tipped over. She called 999 and picked up the pooches, although both managed to get blood on their paws. Tracked it up a bit.'

Andy tried not to groan at how they'd compromised the site. 'What else could she tell us about the vic?'

'Michael James, thirty-five. Born and bred in Bow, moved this way about ten years ago. She wasn't sure what he had on him or what he was selling at the moment, but she figured it'd be "pretty much everything".'

'*Did* he have anything on him?'

'Nothing. I'd bet that whoever killed him took it.'

'Rival dealer?'

'Or a customer. Or an opportunist. The ME will confirm the cause of death, but I didn't see any defensive wounds. Just a single stab to his right side, just below the ribs. Had to be a pretty sharp blade to get through his parka.'

'Okay. Williams, talk to the Drug Squad. Get a list of dealers operating in the area. Harry, see what CCTV you can find. Ask a couple of uniforms to do the door-to-doors to see if anyone saw anything. And while they're at it, get them to check the bins near the canal path. In case the killer jettisoned the blade. I'll go with Nic to see the mother. See if she can tell us anything we don't already know.'

'Speaking of jettison, you wanna get divers in?' Williams suggested. 'In case he tossed the blade into the canal?'

Andy winced. 'I don't see Badolato signing off on that expense, but let's try anyway.'

31

LOUISE

Partridge Bark

Claire (Tyrion's Mum)

I spy with my little eye …

Fiona (Nala's Mum)

Someone doing a walk of shame?

Irina (Hamish's Mum)

The council replacing the bins on the canal path?

Yaz (Hercules's Mum)

One of the boy racers, either getting nicked or crashing into somewhere interesting? Cluckin' Good Chicken? The Bells?

Claire (Tank's Mum)

Not on that side of The Bells – whatever's going on is on the canal side. The police are back, and whatever's happening, you know it's bad when they bring in floodlights and a tent.

Claire (Tank's Mum)

OMG. I think I just saw DC Andy. And that can mean only one thing. ☹

Yaz (Hercules's Mum)

@**Irina**'s gonna get lucky? Or got unlucky and he bumped her off. 😲🐿️

Claire (Tank's Mum)

She messaged earlier, so probably not. But I'm on my way downstairs to see what I can find out.

Paul (Jimmy Chew and Bark Vader's Dad)

Oooh! Another dead body? I was just taking the boys down to Partridge – we'll meet you there in 10!

Ejiro (Hercules's Dad)

FFS, mate. You're becoming a ghoul.

Becoming? Paul was an ambulance chaser, keen to be in on any of the mayhem that happened around Partridge Park. And the more gung-ho he got, the more Ella veered away. As much as I'd miss them, I suspected that having a break from the neighbourhood would be good for their marriage.

Feeling a bit like an ambulance chaser myself, I messaged my friend Annabel. As a local property developer, she had waged a running battle with The Bells for years.

Annabel Lindford-Swayne

> Hey Annabel, if you haven't already heard, the police found a dead body behind The Bells this morning.

> Thank you, Santa! That's even better than having Idris Elba ask for my number!

> He what?

> Don't be daft. But if I'm going to ask Santa for a Christmas gift, a hot date with Idris, and The Bells shutting down are one and two on my list.

> You're as ghoulish as Paul. Someone died there. Have some respect.

> You're right, of course. And may he – or she – rest in peace. Any idea who it is? Was?

> No. Not yet. Claire is going down to have a look around, so keep an eye on *The Chron*'s site.

> Keep me in the loop. And let's hope that The Bells doesn't get a whole new tranche of new punters for the grim kicks of drinking where a dead man was found.

I looked over to the far side of the bed, where there was a lump under the duvet. Sticking out were two delicate little tan feet and a slim black tail. 'Fancy going for morning walkies?'

The tail began to wag, but otherwise the lump didn't move. Left to his own devices, Klaus would sleep until ten. Bad luck for him that I was a morning person.

'Come on, sleepyhead! We can go see Tank, Jimmy and Vader, if you like?'

The feet and tail disappeared under the duvet, but moments later, a perfect little black nose appeared like a lateral periscope.

I slid out of bed and made my way into the bathroom. Washed my face with cold water and brushed my teeth. Pulled on a sweatshirt and pair of jeans and headed for my front door. As I shrugged my jacket on I called out, 'I have treats!' and listened for the frantic patter of little feet. He didn't like mornings, but he was bribable.

We approached The Bells from the canal side. The pub was short and squat, a proud display of how little effort was needed to house a battalion of fruit machines. Paint flaked from the outside walls and the picnic tables were ancient and splintered. I'd only been inside once, and it wasn't a venue I'd voluntarily return to. Hell, it wasn't the sort of pub many people would choose to frequent.

I assessed the dilapidated area. What would I have done if I were the killer?

I didn't know the circumstances of the death, but getting to and from The Bells' beer garden was a piece of cake. There was no CCTV on the path, and not much more lighting. The killer could have walked, or (and maybe more sensibly) taken a bike.

The cordons were already up by the time Klaus and I arrived. There were a few people milling around, but Claire and Paul were easily visible, not to mention audible. Tank didn't bark much, but the same couldn't be said for Paul's black Labradors.

I sauntered up in time to hear Claire ask, 'Is this death connected to the one in Partridge Park last Sunday?'

The cop by the cordon wasn't going to give her an answer: both of them knew he wasn't allowed to, but as a journalist she still had to go through the motions.

What was interesting was that, regardless of his answer, Claire was connecting the two dead bodies. Tower Hamlets had more than its fair share of crime, but we didn't usually get two murders less than a kilometre from each other within a couple of days. At least, not if there wasn't an underlying thread linking them.

A white tent had already been erected, presumably around the body. Tiny red pawprints danced around its edges, stark against the frosted grass.

'Who was it?' I asked as we approached. Klaus was already straining to see his friends, and Paul, who wasn't that much taller than I was, struggled to get Bark Vader and Jimmy Chew back under control.

'The police aren't saying,' Claire said, then lowered her voice. 'But I heard Mrs Carstairs on the phone with someone. She said it was Pete the Pusher. The police went over and asked her – and us – not to say anything until they confirm his identity. My money is on them treating it as a homicide.'

A pair of Egyptian geese waddled along the embankment, their stoned-looking eyes taking in our Pack. The dogs were less unbothered, and another round of barking erupted.

The uniformed officer by the cordon gave us a filthy look.

Two murders. One victim, a homeless young man who smoked weed and had a troubled background, and the other, one of the local dealers. It did sound suspicious.

In my day job, one of the gifts I had was to be able to 'see' processes and patterns. On a whim, I opened one of my shopping apps and ordered a large-scale laminated map of the area and a pack of multicoloured star-shaped stickers, ticking the box for same-day delivery. I wasn't trying to solve the crime or anything, but my curiosity was piqued.

Partridge Bark

Fiona (Nala's Mum)

> What's going on? It's bloody cold outside. Don't make me walk down to The Bells to find out.

Paul (Jimmy Chew and Bark Vader's Dad)

> Madame Carstairs with the two Yorkies found another dead body this morning. The police teams are not letting anyone through.

Claire (Tank's Mum)

And not telling us much.

Yaz (Hercules's Mum)

Who was it?

Claire (Tank's Mum)

Unconfirmed.

'No point in pissing off the police in case they're still lurking around in our chat,' Claire said. 'I mean, it's not like Mrs Carstairs couldn't be wrong or anything.'

'Makes sense.' I picked Klaus up and held him close to my body for warmth. He wriggled, more interested in playing with his friends than being my hot water bottle. 'I don't blame Fi for not wanting to be out in this weather. You think they'll tell us anything?'

'No chance,' Claire sighed, giving the uniformed PC on the other side of the cordon a dark look. 'Not yet at least, and it's too cold to wait out here for long. I'll keep an eye out for the press release though. Fancy a coffee?'

'I need to go to work,' Paul said. His face was the picture of dejection. I was sure his shoulders would have drooped if he'd been able to control Vader and Jim from a slouch.

We walked back together along the path towards

Partridge Park. The police tape from Sunday had come loose: the remains of the outer cordon was blowing from the trees, the inner cordon from the children's swings, like a grisly maypole. 'Unearth anything new about Eddie Morley?' I asked Claire.

'Not really, but I can't ignore that we've got a homeless youth with a history of drug use and an overall troubled past murdered on Sunday, and then three days later a dealer is killed.'

'Same MO?' Paul asked.

'I don't think so. I didn't see any blood on Sunday and there was definitely blood at the scene today.'

'The pawprints?' I asked.

'Yeah – Mrs Carstairs's Yorkies got their paws dirty.'

'How's she coping? She found the man on Sunday too, right?'

'I don't know her well,' Claire said. 'But I'd say that she's not coping. At all. I think the council offers counselling. I hope she takes them up on it.'

'My money is on her self-medicating.' Paul mimed drinking out of a bottle.

'I wouldn't blame her for that either,' I said. 'Finding one body is bad, but two in a week? My God.' Unable to help myself, I glanced over my shoulder towards the kiddie park. 'I'm not sure I've seen so many fatalities in such a short period of time.'

'Murders, Lou. Don't sugar-coat it,' Claire said.

'You think they're connected?'

Claire shrugged. 'Maybe. Maybe not. But the question needs to be asked.'

32

LOUISE

Annabel Lindford-Swayne

It's a bit last minute, but fancy catching up for lunch today? I could do with a bit of fresh air.

You mean, catch up on the latest goss about the dead man outside The Bells?

Well, yeah. Obvs. Can you make lunch? I've got a few meetings your way.

> How about noon at The Hound?

When had everyone become so fixated on local crime?

June. When Hammy and Klaus found the first dead body.

I took a hot bath and worked my way through my inbox until it was time to leave. Klaus saw me getting ready and ran out of the room.

'Come on!' I shook my head, then changed tactics. I put on my own jacket and went to my front door. Unlocking it, I called out, 'You can stay here, where it's nice and warm.'

That option didn't seem to suit him either, and he came running. I was ready, and slipped the coat over his head before he knew what I'd done. Fastened the Velcro under his belly, and clipped on his collar and lead. 'You'll have fun,' I promised. 'You love Auntie Annabel.'

He did. He loved most women, canine Casanova that he was. He'd learned that young women make a fuss over him, and went all out to flirt. Pity he couldn't be bothered to make any effort with men for his single mama's sake.

The cold air hit me in the face with an almost physical force as we got outside. It was a good thing we didn't have far to travel.

The Partridge Park area boasted three pubs. Both The George and Dragon and The Bells were built post-World

War Two, when architects had gone for function over aesthetics. Both were low-rise and boxy, but where The Bells was decrepit, The George was tidy, and the preferred watering hole of the old East Londoners. My friend Gav fancied it, and while I was never told to leave, I never really felt welcomed there.

The Hound was technically furthest from my home, but had become my local. One half of the building retained its pre-war elegance, but the other half had fallen victim to a German doodlebug and been rebuilt in blockish Sixties style. Everything was mismatched, from the chairs that ranged from eighteenth-century knock-offs to wooden stools that looked straight out of a schoolroom, to the art-deco prints on the walls. It was a look that Annabel fondly called 'shabby chic', but the food was good, the wine list impressive and the atmosphere always warm.

Almost without me directing him, Klaus marched ahead of me, leading the way.

Annabel was already seated in a faux-Georgian armchair at a table by the windows, elegant as ever in cream cashmere and with her blonde hair styled in a French bob. The new 'do effectively hid the patch of hair that had to be shaved so the A&E doctors could stitch up the head wound she'd got last October, but regardless, it made her look like the lady of the manor.

Adding to that illusion, she greeted me, or rather Klaus, with her usual cut-glass accent. 'Hello, darling. Who's a good boy?' She fished around in her pocket and pulled out a meaty chew for him.

'And that's why Klaus loves women.'

'All women, or just me?'

'Most women, but especially you?' I compromised, and kissed her on both cheeks.

'I'll take it.' Annabel sat down and poured a glass of red wine for me. 'I hope Valpolicella is okay. I'm desperate for stodge and white doesn't seem right.'

If *I* drank red wine wearing pale cashmere, it wouldn't leave the pub unstained.

Then again, with a clingy little black-and-tan dog, not much remained pristine for long.

'That's fine. Stodge – and an Italian red – is perfect.'

Annabel raised her glass in a silent toast and relaxed back into her chair. 'I heard that Dave Najafi's shops around London are closing down one by one,' she drawled. Najafi was the owner of a chain of perfume shops. Last autumn he had diversified his portfolio by purchasing a fast-food chicken shop on the High Street for his nephew. Cluckin' Good Chicken was a beacon for trouble, importing its own gang of thugs 'for protection' and setting in motion the events that had landed Annabel in A&E.

'That's too bad,' I said, trying to find some sympathy. 'What happened?'

'Leases not being renewed and that sort of thing.' She shrugged. 'It's common enough, but I'd be willing to bet my father put in a few words with the landlords.'

'Ahh. Well, I wouldn't be upset if CGC closes. I'd love to have a good tapas restaurant there instead.' I closed my eyes and imagined it. 'Or poké. I love poké.'

'Right. Well, next time. Your choices today include good old-fashioned pub grub. Hurry up and order,' she demanded. 'I want to talk about The Bells.'

I sprinted to the bar, ordered my lunch and came back balancing a metal dog bowl, a couple of glasses, and a carafe of water. Poured water into the glasses and bowl, and set the latter on the floor.

'I don't know if The Bells actually had anything to do with the dead man, Annabel,' I said, straightening up. 'I think it was just an opportune place, with not a lot of CCTV.'

'It's right next to a high-rise block of flats.'

'Sure, but not a lot of people are going out onto their balconies in this cold, although I'm sure the police will check. And with everything that happens on the High Street, unless they made a lot of noise, I don't think people would have noticed.'

She frowned, and I continued. 'There's the usual traffic, although with the exception of the boy racers, that tends to slow down by ten in this weather. I don't know the details, but I'd guess that whatever it was happened after closing, or someone in the pub would definitely have noticed.'

'Did the dead man drink at The Bells?'

I made a face. 'I don't know, I don't tend to go there, but I heard he was a dealer, so he might well have.'

'I'll have a word with Pete.'

'Pete the Pusher?' My jaw sagged. How had she found out already?

'No, Pete the owner/bartender at The Bells, although I

wouldn't put it past him to be a pusher as well.' She shook her head. 'That pub can't be making much money from its clientele.'

That sounded consistent with what I remembered from my one time inside. 'There are more fruit machines than punters.'

'Always.'

'So, how *do* they make money? Money laundering? Drugs?'

She shrugged, and took a delicate sip of wine. 'Wish I could tell you, Louise. They've turned down every offer we've made them, and we've offered above the going rate for the place. Whatever's going on there, I'd be willing to bet isn't this side of legal.'

The sun was all but obscured with heavy grey clouds by the time we finished lunch. It wouldn't take long to walk home from the restaurant, but I didn't want to chance getting rained or sleeted on.

How long would it take to come up with a list of the local drug dealers or stoners?

A long time. And how the hell could I whittle it down to a decent subset of people to properly investigate?

Feeling slightly guilty for taking the DLR for only one stop, Klaus and I eased into an empty seat. Three young women, sixth-formers at a guess, sat around us, perfumed with Eau du Skunk. One was in the row beside me, a second sprawled behind her and the third slouched on the console the driver would use if we were moving in the other direction.

The girls wore school uniforms, but there was something hard about them that made them seem older than they were. It was their eyes, I decided. They were closed; shuttered.

The young woman behind me shuffled closer. ''Scuse me. Can I say hello to your dog?' she asked.

I blinked, surprised that she was engaging with me. 'If he's okay with that.'

'Consent,' she said, her mouth twisting into something tentative. She shifted a little closer and held out her hand for Klaus to sniff. 'I like that.'

So did he. I'd expected him to back away – he hated the smell of weed – but he was happy to allow her to gently stroke his ears. 'Do you have a dog?' I asked.

'No.' Her eyes were firmly on Klaus, but I had a feeling she was aware of everything happening all around her. 'But I'd love to have one. When I'm older.'

I nodded. 'I get that. I waited until the time was right, too. What type of dog would you get?'

'I don't know. Maybe a black Labrador. My mum had one, and he was lovely. Or maybe a German Shepherd, but I think maybe the Lab would be easier.'

'Both breeds are lovely,' I said. 'One of my closest friends has two black Labs. They're a lot of fun.'

'Waffle!' the girl beside me said to her friend. The one sitting backwards on the console nodded.

'I'm not waffling,' the first girl said, her voice unheated, her gaze still rapt on Klaus's. He was leaning into her hand as she gently scratched the side of his neck.

'You have the touch,' I told her. 'He's not like this with everyone.'

She blushed, pleased. 'I love dogs. I'd love to be a dog walker.' Her eyes met mine, and for a moment she let me see behind the shutters. 'Or even better, a dog trainer.'

'As if you could,' her backwards-sitting friend laughed. 'You're delulu.'

The girl flinched, and the shutters snapped back into place.

'That's amazing,' I told her, angry with her friends on her behalf. 'Dog training is important. And so's following your dreams.'

'Ain't no bad dogs,' she agreed. 'Just bad people. And to be fair, some just don't know to train their dogs.'

'So true,' I agreed, finding myself warming to her. Feeling a little embarrassed at how quick I was to write her off because of the way she looked or that she smelled of weed. Probably just trying to fit in with the other two girls.

It made me wonder, not for the first time, what I was missing about Eddie Morley. What were his goals? For sure, it wasn't getting murdered in a kiddie park. Hopefully Claire would be able to find out a bit more from Eddie's good-looking cousin.

The DLR slowed as we approached our stop. 'We need to get off here,' I said, apologetic. I gave the other two girls a sideways glance. 'I can't tell you what to do, but I've always taken it as a challenge when people told me I couldn't do something. If you want to be a trainer, go for it.'

33

ANDY

The team sat in a loose U-shape facing the front of the room where an ancient whiteboard stood next to a more modern screen. Alf Badolato strode to the front of the room and scowled as the rest of his team settled.

'Let's take the cases in order. Last week's hit-and-run: Camille Ghani.' He pointed at Andy. 'Thompson? Go.'

'Think we can close that one down. Seems it was made to look like one of the boy racers clipped her and kept going, but Nic got a tip from an "anonymous caller". Seems that Camille and her boyfriend had a blazing row. He was overheard threatening her if she left him. We went to have a word with him, and Williams took a look at his car. Looked like it'd hit something a bit bigger than a squirrel. We've got him in custody and he's waiting on his brief to show up. Forensics are going over the car, but my money's on him for killing her.'

'Good. Last Sunday's murder. Eddie Morley. Got good news for me there?'

'Not yet. Williams and I ruled out Mrs Carstairs. Then we went back to the park to talk to the kids that hang out around there. Same thing as before: Eddie hasn't had much to do with the gangs since getting out of Feltham. No one had a bad word to say about him. Claimed that he tried to look out for them. Protect them.'

'From who?'

'Other gangs, mostly. But some who were new on the streets – runaways – needed some help. Although they said he rarely used them, he knew where the squats were. Knew how to survive.'

'Until he didn't.'

'Yeah, sir. Until he didn't. As far as anyone knew, he had a troubled background, but tried to keep his nose clean. No one could give us anything about who might've had a problem with him. We'll continue looking, but as much as I hate to say this, it might just have been a crime of opportunity.'

Badolato scowled. 'Fine. What about the man found this morning?'

'Mike James, aka Pete the Pusher. Found just after seven a.m. by Mrs Carstairs, outside The Bells pub, near Partridge Park. James had a stab wound in his side and seems to have been killed between two and four hours earlier.'

'Mrs Carstairs? The same woman who found Morley?' The tip of Badolato's nose twitched. 'You're telling me that the same woman found two bodies in a handful of days? I don't believe in coincidences.'

'Not sure if it's a coincidence as much as bad luck, but I get your point. We spoke with her again this morning, and have cleared her,' Andy repeated. 'We did ask her to remain local, in case other questions arise.'

'Hopefully she won't find any more bodies,' Badolato said, his voice heavy with irony. 'If she didn't kill him, any idea who did?'

'Unlike Morley, there's a wide range of options here, guv,' Williams answered. 'Mike James was a local pusher, trying to make a name for himself for being a "go-to" person. And not just drugs. He worked with a couple of local pimps, so if someone wanted some blow and a hook-up, he was more or less the one-stop shop.'

'We know who those pimps are? Or who the other dealers are?'

'Getting a list now. And Forensics are checking to see if anyone left any trace evidence on the body,' Williams added.

'CCTV have anything? Harry?'

'Not yet. And the uniforms have checked along the canal path in both directions. Found lots of crap, but no murder weapon. Yet.'

Andy and Williams exchanged a glance. 'The journalist from *The Chronicle*, Claire Dougherty, showed up.' Andy ignored Badolato's eye-roll and continued, 'She was asking if we were connecting Morley to James.'

'She have any intel that we don't? She's one of your dog people, right?'

'She's part of the Pack, but didn't have anything concrete. That said, I'm not so sure she's wrong.'

'You think they're connected?' Badolato looked sceptical. 'Different type of target, different MO. The kid was garrotted. The pusher was stabbed.'

'I know. That stoned kid probably didn't see it coming, and there were no defensive wounds. But the pusher would know that someone trying to take him out was an occupational risk, especially if he was trying to branch out. He'd have been more alert. Yeah, they were different MOs, but maybe *because* the vics were different.'

'Sounds like you're convinced.'

'No, I'm not. I'm trying to keep all options open.' Andy knew how it sounded and he tried to shrug off his self-consciousness.

'What's your thinking?' Badolato pressed.

Andy met his eye. 'That both men are dead because they pissed off the same killer. For one reason or another.'

Badolato shook his head. 'Highly unlikely. Especially when you take into account the short amount of time between the men being found dead. No. Treat each case separately, at least for now. If—' He held up a single finger. 'And it's a big "if". *If* you can find concrete evidence to suggest these two cases are connected, then we'll connect them. Not until then. Clear?'

Andy fought down a niggling doubt, but nodded his head.

'Clear.'

34

LOUISE

Claire (Tank's Mum)

> I'm going to detour to Mrs Carstair's place. I'll let you know if she can tell us anything new.

👍 Good luck!

I wasn't close to Mrs Carstairs. She had dogs, and took them to the same dog parks we went to, but like many others, she didn't really engage with the rest of the Pack. At least, not socially. Though that didn't mean I didn't know where she lived.

It wasn't far from my home, and I glanced at the sky,

hoping the weather would hold off just a little bit longer. I stopped at News-N-Booze for a bottle of wine and headed towards the park, Klaus marching ahead. When I stopped in front of the red-brick terraced house, he gave me a strange look. *You sure you know what you're doing, Mum?*

I opened the hip-high metal gate between the green and purple rubbish bins, and allowed Klaus to lead the way along the pathway. Mrs Carstairs had made an effort with her tiny garden: Christmas lights hung on the trees and a Yorkie Santa sat on a bench in front of the house beside a half-full mug of cigarette butts.

A light was on upstairs; she was home. Bella and Meeky began to bark as we approached and Klaus joined in, tail wagging.

'Jesus Farkin' Christ,' Mrs Carstairs muttered from the other side of the door before yanking it open. 'What do you want?' she demanded, a lit fag in her hand and a scowl on her face. She wore a pair of cheetah-print leggings and a black top that glittered with rhinestones and sequins. The Yorkies scrambled around her and launched themselves at Klaus, tails frantically beating the air.

'Hey, I heard what happened this morning. Just thought we'd check in and see how you're doing?' I handed her the bottle. 'It's been a rough week.'

'Bloody brilliant,' she growled, but didn't slam the door. 'You wanna come in?'

I took a deep breath of cold, crisp air and followed her into the front room, trying to breathe through my mouth. If Mrs Carstairs was aware of how thick the cigarette smoke was inside, she didn't let on.

I looked around: there were several framed pictures of her children and grandchildren on display, but they were far outnumbered by portraits of her dogs. Every wall – every surface – had something Yorkie-related on it.

Mrs Carstairs put the bottle on the sideboard and poured herself a generous G&T. She glanced over her shoulder and raised her grizzled brows. 'You want one?'

I wasn't sure my liver would be able to handle that strong a drink after the wine I'd had with Annabel. I pulled a bottle of water from my bag. 'No, thank you.'

'Suit yourself.' She sat down in a zebra-print armchair with a sound like a deflating balloon, and I perched on the sofa across from her. 'The Met told me not to leave the country. You believe that?'

'Yeah. They said the same to me when I found Phil Creasy last summer.'

Her eyes narrowed at me. 'That's right. You did find one.'

'Actually, two. Sort of. When my friend Yaz found Jonny Tang last October, she called me. I didn't know what I was walking into there. But it was different with Phil. He was a friend.'

Mrs Carstairs nodded. 'Can't say that the men I found were my friends, but I knew Michael. Knew his family.' She heaved herself out of the chair. The Yorkies followed her back to the sideboard while she fixed a second gin and gin and pressed it into my hand. Her eyes said what her mouth couldn't. *Thank you for your empathy. You understand what it's like, 'cos you've been there.*

I pretended to sip the drink and put it on the coffee

table, hoping one of the dogs cavorting between us would knock it over. 'How awful for you: two, so close together,' I said. 'Do you think whoever killed them meant for *you* to find the bodies, or was it just bad luck?'

She snorted. 'Bad luck, I reckon. No one'd know I'd be where I was either day. Wouldn't've stopped this morning, only I know Michael. I mean, he could piss people off, you know? Didn't lead a good Christian life, but that don't mean he should be killed.'

'No,' I agreed. 'Same, I guess, with the first man – Eddie Morley.'

'Yeah.' She gave me a narrow look. 'You think it was the same person?'

'I don't know. I just think two is a lot when both murders were a stone's throw from each other.'

'Wot you thinkin'? A serial killer?' She seemed to chew on the idea. 'Mebbe. I dunno. Hope not.' She pulled one of the Yorkies onto her lap. 'But if it is, at least we can be thankful that they're not targeting good God-fearing people.'

I wondered how much consolation that would be to Eddie or Mike James's families.

35

LOUISE

Partridge Bark

Indira (Banjo's Mum)

Hi all, just a heads-up. We just got back from the vet. Banjo has kennel cough.

Meg (Tyrion's Mum)

Oh no – sorry to hear that! It can be nasty. T had it once. Fortunately we caught it quickly. I think he hated not seeing his friends while quarantining more than he hated taking the meds. Did Banjo have the jab for it?

Indira (Banjo's Mum)

Yeah. I know it won't prevent them from getting it, but it's supposed to make it milder if they do. Banjo's on the meds (which he also hates) but I'll keep him away from the park for the next few days. I'd feel awful if anyone else's pup caught it from us.

Thanks for that, **@Indy**. Where will you take him?

Indira (Banjo's Mum)

Little square behind my flat. The Housing Authority there popped a swing in the middle of it, declared it a kids' play area and popped up 'No Dogs Allowed' signs everywhere, but dogs go there anyway. Anyone want to guess how I know that?

Irina (Hamish's Mum)

Cos their stupid humans don't pick up after them?

Indira (Banjo's Mum)

Exactly. ☹ Still, I need to keep Banjo away from anyone and that's the only option I can think of. He refuses to use any of the indoor or balcony grass patches.

Irina (Hamish's Mum)

At least you pick up after him …

I lay flat on my bed, staring at the ceiling and trying to make sense of the thoughts chasing each other through my mind.

Mrs Carstairs hadn't told me anything I hadn't already figured out, but one thing was certain: she might be grumpy, she was definitely strange, but she was no killer.

And I hoped she was right: that it wasn't a serial killer, and if it was, that they weren't interested in the Pack – not the way the last two killers were.

I gulped coffee from the mug on my night table, and glanced at Klaus, lounging by the bedroom door. 'When was the last time you played with Banjo?' I asked him, suddenly afraid that I had to worry about him getting kennel cough on top of everything else.

It was a rhetorical question though: he didn't play with Banjo. Or rather, Banjo didn't play with him. A rescue from the streets of Romania, Banjo tolerated the other dogs, but had never learned how to play, which broke my heart. Klaus never pushed him, waiting for Banjo to approach him for a couple of sniffs before he moved on to the next thing. No judgement, no pressure. We honestly don't deserve dogs.

Indy and Banjo hadn't joined us at sniffer dog training, and it had probably been more than a week since we'd even seen him. Klaus couldn't have caught it from Banjo, but what if Banjo had passed it on to another dog? Or the dog who had given it to him had?

Klaus trotted up the ramp to join me on the bed. He moved close and licked my nose. 'Please, just don't get kennel cough, Klaus. Please.' He rolled over and allowed me to scratch his tummy, which I took as his assent.

With one last rub, I finished my coffee and moved to the spare room, which doubled as my home office, and the wall where I'd hung the laminated map of the area. Blue stars indicated where Eddie Morley and Pete the Pusher, had been found.

Two dead bodies in four days. That we knew of. Were there others? Men who had fallen between the cracks of society. Homeless, or with possible drug or gang connections.

There was no proof they were connected. In all likelihood, Pete could well have killed Eddie for some drug connection, and then someone had bumped him off, because, well, pushers weren't usually well loved.

Was that it?

Had Eddie stiffed Pete in some way that had got Pete in trouble with whoever his boss was? Badly enough that he ended up dead next? It would explain why the kiddie park where Eddie was found had no blood, but Pete had clearly bled out. Different MOs because there were different killers?

There had to be some way to check.

Irina (Hamish's Mum)

Evening walk?

I'm meeting Meg to go up to the shelter at 6, but can do a quick one before

> then if you're working from home.

> Fine. Bundle up. I saw snowflakes earlier. You might get your white Christmas yet.

> Three flakes doesn't make it a white Christmas, Irina.

> Be grateful we don't get the sort of snow here that you and I grew up with. Three flakes is all it needs for public transport to halt.

'As if by magic,' I said to Klaus. 'You want to go for a quick walkie with Hammy?'

He didn't.

'Too bad you don't have a choice. I could use some fresh air and I want to talk to Irina.'

Both of us were bundled up to the eyebrows when we stepped out of the building, meeting Irina and Hamish by the gate. Irina wore a beanie and a black coat, open at the neck, and had a large canvas carrier bag slung over her shoulder. Hamish wore a tartan coat and a bandana that said *Suck this, Schnauzer*.

'Didn't you say your American winters were worse than the ones here?' Irina raised her eyebrows at my heavy coat.

'In Connecticut they are. Winters are colder, summers are hotter. But I've lived here for more than a decade. I can't cope with either anymore.'

'Lightweight.'

We passed through the heavy iron gates, hearing the distinctive clang behind us. We turned right, walking away from the canal, away from the High Street. That way was better lit, but came with a higher chance of finding trouble.

'So, I've been thinking...'

She rolled her eyes. 'Here we go.'

'I have a theory I wanted to get your take on.'

'Of course you do.' Her cheeks were already pink. It could have been from the cold, but knowing Irina, it could have been from a glass or two of whatever her poison was at the moment.

'Eddie Morley was homeless. Smoked a bit of weed.'

'Always stoned when I saw him,' she agreed, yanking Hammy's lead to pull him away from a discarded box of chicken bones.

'Right. What if his dealer was Pete the Pusher; the guy who was killed this morning?'

'Lou, almost every night some guy asks me if I want to buy weed, coke, or whatever.'

'Sure, and I'm not saying Pete was the only dealer in the area. I just wonder how big a player he might have been, or maybe thought he was. So, what if Eddie stiffed him, this pusher who may or may not have been a big deal? Do you think Pete would kill him? Have him killed?'

'No idea. Oh shit!' Irina interrupted herself to lunge. 'Drop that!'

Hammy was already frantically chewing before she could pry his mouth open. She fished around, but with no luck. Scowling, she stood up and glared at him. 'What is *wrong* with you?'

Scottish Terrier: 1. Russian Lunatic: 0. She had to be a heck of a lot faster to get anything out of his mouth.

'My dog is half Hoover,' Irina groused, still glaring. Then she turned to me. 'Look, if you're right and that is the case, then who'd be out to kill Pete? If you want to connect them, you need a better theory. Two people don't make a pattern.'

'I was hoping you'd say that. What if there are more?'

She gave me an arch look. 'Are there?'

'I don't know. I did a few searches. The only other person who partly fits the bill is the woman found in Vicky Park last week.'

'Dead woman, not a dead man,' she drawled. Hamish raised his leg against a delivery motorcycle. Klaus, not to be outdone, weed on top of Hammy's deposit.

'Dead person.' I ripped a poo bag from the holder hanging from Klaus's lead as he began to circle. 'But I don't have anything else. A keyboard savant like you can unearth things we mere mortals can't.'

Her wry smile told me she knew she was being played. 'It's more Claire's beat than mine, but I'll have a look and see what I can find. No promises though.'

'Thanks, Irina.'

She thrust the canvas bag into my hands. 'If you're still going to hike up to the shelter tonight . . .'

'Thanks.' It always surprised me how uncomfortable she was when doing something selfless, but I wasn't about to pull her up on it. 'At least I'll be in good company. Jake is coming along too.'

'The ever-elusive Jake Hathaway.' Irina smirked. 'Well, good luck to you then.'

36

CLAIRE

Fiona (Nala's Mum)

> Good luuuuuuuuck tonight with hot Portuguese Jezza!

>> Jeremy is English. Well, half at least.

> Whatevs. Good luck anyway. You gonna tell him that you catfished him with Nala? Fess up and admit that you've got a randy Frenchy who stress voms?

> It's not just stress, but yeah, I'll come clean. Tank's the chonky love of my life.

> Just a bit of unsolicited advice: don't call Tank your spirit animal after telling him about the barfing. Not a good look.

Claire glanced at Tank and her smile faded. He was perfectly fine being by himself for a few hours, but Claire hated leaving him. Lots of people's dogs had separation anxiety, but Claire knew that her anxiety was far worse than Tank's.

She turned away. Leaned towards the mirror and brushed on another layer of mascara, excited despite herself.

When was her last date? The last real one, not just the ones where she wanted something more than the guy was ready, or maybe willing, to offer.

Four years.

Don't look at it as a date, she warned herself. *Think of it as an interview. Find out what you can about Jeremy and his cousin Eddie. And while you're at it, try to figure out if Jeremy is the sort of man you want to date.*

Whether that would make things easier or not was

questionable. Claire turned on the telly for Tank, gave him a chew and topped up his water bowl. She made sure the doggiecam was on and grabbed her coat.

Jeremy was waiting for her at the bar at the Boisdale, wearing a sharp City suit. He smiled and stood up when he saw her.

Butterflies. Not just in Claire's stomach. They'd escaped and were running amok in her bloodstream. Even her skin tingled. 'Hi,' she said.

He kissed her cheeks, the European way. The bar was dark and she hoped he didn't notice her blush.

'I hope you like it.' He gestured around the opulent restaurant. 'It's Scottish.'

Claire blinked. 'Okay.'

'And you're Scottish, right?'

'I'm Irish,' she said. His face fell. When she realised he was trying to impress her, the butterflies took on greater territory, stopping just short of her brain. 'But I've lived here long enough that my accent probably changed a little. Just don't expect me to eat haggis.'

'That's fine, they do a good steak here.' Jeremy gestured to the maître d'. With his hand at the small of Claire's back, they followed the woman to a table by the massive windows overlooking Cabot Square. She left them with a wine list, menus and a friendly smile. Claire tried not to stare; it was like stepping back in time to what she imagined a nineteenth-century gentleman's smoking room looked like, all crimson paint, gold edgework and deep green ceiling, and photographs of famous jazz musicians along the walls. Only on a massive scale – the Boisdale was huge.

'My nan loves jazz. I take her here when I can,' he grinned, revealing white but slightly wonky teeth. Like he had braces as a kid, but his teeth had shifted a little as he'd grown.

'Your nan? You're close with your family?'

'Close with my nan and my mum, yep. You?'

'Close as I can be living in London. We talk on the phone a lot, and I see my parents and my sisters when I can. What about you? Brothers? Sisters? Cousins?'

'Only child.' He flashed her the slightly wonky grin again. 'And not really close with my cousins. Saw them a lot when I was a kid. Didn't have much of a choice, to be honest.' He raised a shoulder in an awkward half-shrug. 'By the time Frank left Auntie Caroline and Ed went off the skids, I was already in sixth form.'

'When we met, you'd said Ed was holding it together until his mum found a new partner? What was it? Jealousy?'

'Jealousy?' Jeremy's tone and expression remained polite, but Claire sensed that he was on his guard. 'About what?'

'I don't know. Another man in the house? Maybe taking his mum's attention?'

'Yeah, I don't know. Kev was always decent when I was around. Auntie Caro and Tracey, Ed's sister, adore him. All this is hitting the family pretty hard. Look, it's not that

I want to change the subject or anything – although I kind of do – but the band is about to start.'

Claire watched an older man in a retro pinstripe suit stride to the mic. 'Is that . . .'

'Yeah. He's a Sinatra impersonator. Nan thinks he's good.' He tilted his head to the side. 'You okay with this?'

'Yeah, sure,' Claire said, trying not to gape. 'It's cool, but I guess it wasn't quite what I was expecting.'

'What? The Scottish-not-Irish venue, or the Rat Pack?' He laughed. 'I'm a man of many talents, me.'

You're out with a hot guy who clearly likes you, Claire could hear Fi's voice hiss in her ear. *You don't have to question him all night. For heaven's sake, just enjoy the bloody date!*

'Yes.' She allowed herself to relax into the seat and smiled back. 'You certainly are.'

37

MEG

Louise (Klaus's Mum)

Running a couple of mins late – we had a quick walk with Irina and Hammy. She'll have a look online to see what she can find to connect our two dead men.

Jake and I will meet you at News-N-Booze and we'll walk up together. Luther's

> staying at home with the Discovery Channel but I'll have Klaus with me.

> Great – T is with me.

Meg exhaled, hating herself for her jitters. She'd quaffed a large G&T when she got home last night, which hadn't helped. Part of her wanted to blame the shakes on the gin, but she knew it was something else.

It was a close call.

Well, tonight would be different. Two sausage dogs would ensure no one snuck up on them. And even though Meg prided herself on her ability to take care of herself, Jake was a lot more intimidating than either Ella or Louise were.

Tyrion sighed, his little legs moving quickly along the pavement.

'No, I'm not being disloyal. I'm sure Lou can throw a punch if she has to. Especially if Klaus or any of us are in danger.' Meg blew on her hands, feeling her fingertips going numb. 'Not that I'm advocating violence, mind. I just think that if you're being attacked, you don't want to make it easy on the other person.'

She saw them before Tyrion did, huddled outside the newsagents on the corner, Jake laughing at something Louise had said. There was something, well, *easy* about them. An easy camaraderie. Meg knew Louise wanted more, but there were worse things than friendship, when that friend truly had your back. And carrying a massive bag of kibble for a half hour walk in the freezing cold went a long way in Meg's book.

Klaus barked and Tyrion responded. Jake grinned and picked up two shopping bags from the ground. One was big and blue, the serviceable sort that IKEA sold. The other was green with koala bears. She stifled a smile as Louise tried to take it out of his hands.

'One of these days, one of them is going to get drunk enough to lunge at the other one,' Meg murmured to Tyrion. She raised her voice and greeted them, 'Hey, strangers. You ready?'

Klaus and Tyrion were happily sniffing each other's bottoms, before Klaus reared up and gave Tyrion a playful push.

'They'll be knackered by the time we get there, let alone get home,' Louise smiled. She had a bulging rucksack on her back, which was probably stuffed with more things for the rescued pups. Meg blinked back tears, grateful for her friends.

They passed The Bells on the left, and the string of shops on the other side. Meg waved to Benny in the hair salon, where he was rinsing a woman's dye out in one of the sinks. She glanced up. 'No lights on in Claire's flat. Guess she's chasing a story somewhere?'

'Not a story,' Louise grinned.

'Ooooh, a date?' Meg felt her anxiety begin to dissipate. 'Do we know who?'

'Can't say.'

'Intriguing!'

'Almost as intriguing as what's in the bag from Irina?' Jake gestured to the canvas bag slung over Louise's shoulder. 'Think it's alcoholic?'

'For a dog? Never. She'll drink until her liver divorces her, but she's always careful about the dogs,' Louise said. 'And with Hamish's Olympic-level skills at foraging, that's just about a full-time job.'

Meg nodded. Hammy was a legend.

'The bag's just old toys that he doesn't play with. She sent apologies that she can't come with us.' Louise looked away, not meeting Jake's glance. Generosity wasn't something Irina was comfortable with, Meg knew. She was always willing to donate, but safely behind her Grinchy exterior. 'She's got a lot of work on at the moment.'

'For her job or for us?' Meg asked.

'Work. But she promised to see what she can find to connect our two bodies when she gets a chance.'

'She's checking out the woman in Vicky Park too?'

'I mentioned it to her.'

'Good. I think the council is trying to convince homeless people to go to a shelter in this weather. Maybe it'll save a few lives.' Meg readjusted the bags in her hands. 'Though it's too late for the Vicky Park woman and Eddie Morley.'

'Victoria Park is a good half hour, forty-minute walk away,' Jake pointed out. His Scottish burr, usually so soft as to be unnoticeable, becoming stronger. Meg tilted her head, wondering whether to call him out on it. 'The other two were within a stone's throw of each other. And the sad truth is that a lot of homeless people are victims of random crimes, even without the dangers of extreme temperatures.'

'You don't think it's connected?'

'I think it's unlikely,' he said. 'And I think it's foolish for you, for both of you, to get involved. Again.'

'We're not involved,' Louise protested. 'We're just speculating. If we find anything concrete, we'll take it to the police.' Her green eyes were wide with an innocence that Meg knew Jake didn't buy into. 'I promise.'

'Marple . . .' His burr made it sound like there were half a dozen r's in there.

They turned off the High Street, winding their way through the dark backstreets. Meg watched Tyrion, trotting alongside Klaus. She was waiting for him to sound an alert, but so far, he hadn't.

It was possible that he was just distracted, but both sausages being distracted was unlikely. Maybe she *had* imagined it yesterday?

Klaus stopped, moving closer to the side of the road, under a tree. He squatted and relieved himself. 'Oh bugger,' Lou said, putting her bag down and ripping a poo bag out of its holder. 'Bloody hell,' she muttered.

'What?'

'Someone dropped a piece of wire.' She scooped it up in the same bag as Klaus's poo and lobbed it into a nearby bin. 'Really fine, with a handle on one side. I don't want a dog – or, you know, a person – to get tangled in it. What's wrong with people that they can't walk two feet and throw their crap out in the bin?'

Meg shook her head. 'I can't tell you how often I pick up used vapes with T's poo. Sometimes chicken bones.'

But Jake was frowning. 'I don't like how dark it is here.'

Meg nodded. 'It's not so bad during the day, but at night? Yeah. The shelter moved here when an old woman left her townhouse to them in her will. It's got a nice garden, and plenty of room inside. And friendly neighbours who understand that sometimes dogs bark. A lot of them volunteer or donate.'

'Admirable,' Jake said. 'Can't tell you what to do or not do, but you want my opinion, I'd say do your volunteering at the weekends, or when it's light out.' He shifted his shoulders in a way that had little to do with the weight of the bags he carried. 'This stretch at night? It's a prime spot for an ambush.'

38

LOUISE

Partridge Bark

Paul (Jimmy Chew and Bark Vader's Dad)

More fireworks ... Jim and Vader are going mental ...

Fiona (Nala's Mum)

@Paul, I hate to break the news to you, but Jim and Vader *are* mental ... 😉 Still, half my kingdom for the silent fireworks.

Ella (Jimmy Chew and Bark Vader's Mum)

> I hear there are towns in Italy that ban the ones that go bang. They only allow silent fireworks to cause less distress to the animals. And people with epilepsy or PTSD. Wish they would do that here. I fear it will only get worse until after New Years.

Meg took the bags inside the shelter, promising she wouldn't be long, while Jake and I sat on the steps outside with the dogs bundled up in our arms. I would have preferred to wait inside, but Klaus was making it clear that wasn't an option, digging in his paws and refusing to move. Whether he sensed the other dogs' trauma or not, I wasn't about to force him to go somewhere he was so uncomfortable.

'You didn't have to scare her,' I said to Jake. 'She's already jumpy enough.'

'*She* wasn't the one I was trying to scare, Marple,' he replied. 'I love what the shelter does, but I don't like the area. Too dark, too remote.'

'I get your point, Jake. I'm not stupid.'

He didn't say: *Then don't act it* aloud, but his look was clear enough, the message undiluted despite the antics of the small dappled dachshund burrowed under his jacket. There was something really sweet about the way a big guy like Jake was so gentle with Tyrion.

'Marple. Louise. That wire thing you found is probably innocent. Maybe someone broke something and threw it away. Maybe it fell out of a bag. Maybe a fox pulled it out of a bin. I don't know. But you know this neighbourhood isn't safe. And that discarded piece of wire? Someone could grab it, sneak up on you from behind and you're gone before you know it.'

'Eddie Morley was strangled,' I whispered, trying not to sound as shaken as I felt.

Jake rolled his eyes. 'Yes, well. There are plenty of ways to strangle a man that don't involve a wire. And plenty of reasons, most of which are crap. All I'm saying is don't jump to conclusions, Marple. And to be careful. Especially in the dark.'

He was right. I knew he was; he knew he was. And it wasn't like we were disagreeing. But for some reason, I couldn't let it go. 'But this one wire was broken. One side of it was frayed.'

'Which is why it was binned.' He shrugged. 'Or discarded. All I'm saying is don't let your guard down. There's a killer out there, and I don't want him to set his sights on you.'

Feeling sick, I pulled Klaus against my chest and hoped we would escape the notice of the killer.

Thursday

39

CLAIRE

Partridge Bark

> Hey, just a reminder, the memorial for Eddie Morley, the man found in the park on Sunday, is at 7 pm tonight. Anyone want to come with me?

Meg (Tyrion's Mum)

> Can't — it's kickboxing night. But I hope the turnout is good and that the poor man rests in peace.

Kate (Percy and Andy's Mum)

I'll go with you. Might leave the dogs at home though. No one needs to hear their commentary during the service.

Louise (Klaus's Mum)

I can do it, but it feels a bit weird to go to a memorial service for someone I don't know.

> Someone whose murder we're trying to solve, so that his family can have closure.

Louise (Klaus's Mum)

That's true.

Irina (Hamish's Mum)

No thanks.

Fiona (Nala's Mum)

> Can't. I'm out for Xmas drinks with old friends. Bundle up – it'll be cold.

Claire sighed. That was fine. At least Kate and Louise would be there. And it would be good to see who else showed up. She'd read that murderers often showed up to their victims' memorials. She was willing to bet the police would have someone there too.

In the back of Claire's mind was someone else she hoped would be there. She hadn't asked last night, and he hadn't brought it up. If he was there, and he saw her, then she could always say she was local – she'd already told him that – and that she'd wanted to show her support somehow.

And if he wasn't? Then she was there as a journalist, observing the family's reactions. Checking out their friends. And maybe, just maybe, spotting a murderer.

40

ANDY

'So, on that point, we've got some good news, and some bad news,' Williams was saying.

'Go ahead,' Andy directed from the front of the room. He cast a discreet glance at Alf Badolato, who sat in Andy's usual seat. *You run with this one,* Badolato had told him. Andy understood: DCS Grieves, who made every effort to be hands-on with any homicide or murder that took place along the canals, was still on holiday. If Badolato delegated the running of these cases to Andy under the guise of training for 'someone with potential' and it went tits-up, then he could blame Andy. If it went well, then jolly good – he could take credit for the win.

'So, a member of the public found the cheese cutter.'

'One of Andy's dog people?' Harriman asked.

'Not this time.' Williams grinned. 'It was one of the swan sanctuary people. One of the birds had taken it onto one of the nests along the canal. Sanctuary woman saw it, figured it shouldn't be there. Was going to bin it, but ran into one of the uniforms doing the door-to-doors. Uniform must have said something and she gave it to him.'

'So, that's the good news. What's the bad news?'

'No prints.'

'Wiped?'

Williams thrust out his lower lip and tilted his head from side to side. 'Maybe. Probably. Don't forget, it's bloody cold out, and with all the crime scene shows on the telly, any idiot knows enough to wear gloves.'

'So, no epithelials?'

Williams pointed at Andy, winked and waggled his finger back and forth. 'Now, I didn't say that, did I?'

'Whose?'

'Morley's. And the swan lady's. Pity it was her and not one of your dog people. They knew enough to gather evidence in their little poop bags. Anyway, Forensics are still testing it, but between Morley's skin cells and the wire matching the marks on his neck, it looks like we now have the murder weapon. The bad news is that they haven't found any transfer from anyone else. Any human, at least. And my money is on the birds, swan lady included, being in the clear.'

'Can you open your mouth without sounding like a tit?' Nic muttered.

'Yeah? What do you have?' Williams shot back.

Nic waited for Andy's nod before speaking. 'I spent the day split between Morley and James's families, and I feel like I need a shower just thinking about it.'

'Why?'

'Morley's stepdad gives me the creeps. He hasn't said or done anything wrong, and I'll hold my hand up here—' She did just that. 'I don't think he had anything to do with Ed's death.'

'But? Come on, Nic. Get it out.'

'He's slick and I don't like how close he is to the daughter. He fawns on her. She fawns on him. They seem closer than he does with the mum.'

'You think he's a paedo?'

'Haven't seen any evidence of it, and everyone in the family thinks he's bloody Superman. Earth revolves around him and all.'

'So?'

'So, it's been bothering me. He's that type of stand-up fella, then why would young Eddie rather have a life on the streets? Why'd he keep going back and checking on his sister? I mean, I know that's not our remit, strictly speaking. Just . . . you know.'

Andy nodded. 'Okay. Keep an eye on the situation and check in with Social Services. I don't want to cause problems if there aren't any, but see if they have anything on him.'

'Will do. I'll be at the vigil for him in Partridge Park tonight. Let's see who shows up.' Her eyes narrowed. 'And who's crying crocodile tears.'

He met Badolato's eyes, beginning to feel the additional stress that came from standing at the front of the room, running the meeting, rather than just presenting your own information.

No, that wasn't it. It wasn't just stress. It was responsibility. For the living, as well as the dead.

'Okay,' he continued. 'Harry? CCTV show up anything?'

'We're just about finished with the footage from Sunday. The killer operated in a known blind spot. Seems the local parents didn't want anyone's camera capturing their children, so they applied a bit of pressure on the council to allow the shrubs to build up where the park borders the street to block out dodgy passers-by and random doorcams. Add to that the fact there's nothing along the towpath and we got the perfect storm. Best we have is the odd glimpse of movement in the park, which could have been Morley or one of his mates. We checked the CCTV from the park exits, and then any exits off the towpath a half mile in either direction. There are more blind spots exiting the park but we would have caught them on one of the doorcams. We didn't see anyone leave within a few hours after the murder. My money is that the killer came and left by the path. Weren't even the usual kids hanging out under the bridges. Too cold for them. And then you get the usual runners, dog walkers, and people heading off to work. We're extending the radius to a mile though. Just in case we just missed him.'

'Good idea. Could the killer have hung about long enough to blend in with the usual crowds?'

'Where, mate? Next to the dead body and chance someone catching him there? Feeling I get, he's not that dumb.'

Andy agreed. 'So what do you think?'

'I dunno. Yeah, maybe he found a place to stay out of

sight for a bit. Could've dressed as a runner or someone going to an office. I can't see him taking a mutt with him while he strangled a man. Too much chance that it would make a noise and draw attention to them.'

'Plenty of foxes in the park to distract a dog,' Williams said. 'It could have been chasing one of them while its master was offing Morley.'

Andy was shaking his head. 'I agree with Harry: highly unlikely he took a dog just to blend in afterwards. So he was wearing something he could move about in. Maybe took clean clothes with him and changed afterwards.'

'In this weather? If he was gonna change outside, he'd freeze his nuts off. And if he goes far, we'd have caught him on one of the cameras.'

It was a good point. 'Anyone stand out for you, Harry?'

'Not really. Plenty of the usual runners or commuters, and nobody overly suspicious. We didn't get one hundred per cent matches to people we saw on a day-to-day basis, but I wouldn't have expected us to.'

'Okay, keep looking, Harry. There's something out there, we just gotta find it.'

41

LOUISE

Claire (Tank's Mum)

> How was the hot date?

Yeah, good. Nice guy. Interesting place. Seems the family's close – or the mothers are. Jeremy hasn't had much to do with Eddie in years. Said the stepdad was decent and that everyone loved him.

> Why are you so fixated on the family? Seems just as likely that some random person decided to kill a homeless kid. I read somewhere that homeless people are, like, 17% more likely to be attacked, and in this neighbourhood, that's a pretty high probability. Especially if he'd been in and out of trouble.

> Yeah, maybe.

> Other than that, then, it went well? You'll see him again?

> 🤞

'That's good news,' I said to Klaus as we left our building and crossed the street on our way to the towpath. 'Not much from a lead perspective, mind. But great if Jeremy turns out to be a decent guy for Claire.'

At the gates to the east side of the complex, Jake was standing on the street with a familiar dark-haired woman.

I slowed down, trying to watch them without being obvious about it.

Kate Marcovici had joined the Pack with her two beagles last October. We'd all been in the pub when they 'met', and at the time it felt like they'd known each other. Both (separately) told me that it was the first time they'd been introduced, but I wasn't so sure.

And now they were standing too close together.

Only, Jake's posture was stiff, his jaw clenched. I didn't think that whatever was between them was romantic, but it didn't look innocent either. If it had been anyone else standing with him, I'd have stopped and waved, but his expression kept me moving forward.

What was going on between them?

I'd asked Jake once, and he'd laughed.

I'd asked Kate once, and she said he wasn't her type.

Whatever it was, it wasn't something they were willing to share with me.

Klaus and I headed along the towpath to the park. At least we made it that far before the green-eyed monster got the better of me.

Jake (Luther's Dad)

> Saw you with Kate. You looked pretty irked. Everything OK?

> Yeah, she was telling me about some idiot with a big dog that went for her beagles.

> Oh no! Are they OK? Is she?

> Yeah. She's fine. They're fine.

> Should I text her? See if there's anything I can do?

> Up to you.

I felt like a heel. Jake wasn't my boyfriend and I had no reason to be jealous over him. He could hang out with, or date, anyone he wanted. And yet, it felt better to know that the encounter wasn't romantic.

Of course it wasn't romantic. It didn't look romantic. But it did look suspicious.

Only I couldn't put my finger on how. Or why.

Mindful of Yaz's warning about the state of the dog park, and Banjo's kennel cough, I kept Klaus on the lead as we reached Partridge Park, my eyes scanning the benches for a familiar face.

Gav MacAdams and his Affenpinscher, Violet, were

sitting on a bench in a far corner, faces turned towards the sun. Violet was again bundled up into her purple fleece, but Gav displayed the same imperviousness to the cold as Irina with his gilet-and-wool-blazer combo. 'Morning, Lou,' he said as I approached.

'Morning! Mind if we join you?' I was grateful for the distraction.

He indicated the bench beside him. Violet looked down at Klaus and then at her master. I could almost hear her wonder if chasing Klaus was worth the effort of jumping down. She must have decided it was, landing neatly in front of him. Both stared at me until I unclipped his lead. He bounced off his front paws a couple of times, flirting with her. She adored him, but that didn't mean she wouldn't roll him if she caught him, something he didn't tolerate from a lot of dogs.

'Good thing he's not a human, or I'd have to have a conversation with him about toxic relationships,' I said.

Gav grunted. 'Guessing you're here to ask me for "my insights". What with those two men being killed?'

No messing around; Gav was direct if nothing else. I felt guilty for not making the effort to seek him out when I didn't need anything from him other than good company.

'If you have insights to share, that's great. If you don't, Violet will tire Klaus out and I'll be able to focus while he sleeps all afternoon.'

He grunted a second time, this time amused. Gav valued a straight-shooter too.

'Right. So, I've been asking around. Your first body, the boy. He wasn't a little arsehole like a lot of the other kids; didn't cause problems, though I heard he did some years back. Sure, he was into drugs. Yeah, he lived rough, but he preferred his own company, mostly. One or two of the others like him – you know: teens who ran away to make a statement, like, but then couldn't cope – he tried to look out for 'em.'

I had an image of Eddie as a teen, probably scared, getting in over his head and with no one to help him get out. It was tragic. Society had failed that boy. 'That makes him sound troubled, for sure, but not necessarily a bad sort.'

'Don't get sappy. He was in and out of Young Offenders.'

'How'd he get by? If he was into drugs, I mean.'

'Begging. Sometimes he'd steal something and flog it. That's the thing: you live on the streets, you know where to buy stuff from. You learn where to make your money.'

'Which meant, what?'

Gav shrugged. 'Doing whatever he could. There's always a go-between. Someone who knows someone.'

My pity for Eddie trebled. 'Maybe like the other dead man? Pete the Pusher?'

'That one,' Gav guffawed. 'Made a big point about only selling drugs himself, but he knew who to point someone to if they were after something else. Would make the calls. He wanted to be a big man. A go-to man.'

'But he wasn't?'

'Nah. Did all right on the streets. Had some kids working for him. But he'd never make it outta the neighbourhood.'

'He wanted to?'

'Lou, you dream big. You wanted to own your own company. Corner office and all, right?'

'Once, yeah. Did it, too.' Although as Gav would point out, it was all about scale. At the moment, my 'corner office' was my spare room.

'Right. Pete wanted to work his way up the ranks too, but was too bloody thick.'

'He pissed off the wrong person? A rival? A boss?'

Gav shrugged. 'Dunno. He pissed someone off. Otherwise he wouldn't be dead, would he?'

42

ANDY

Andy shifted from one foot to the other. It was beginning to make sense why Badolato and Grieves leaned against the wall. It wasn't the nonchalance of a senior officer, it was the pins and needles in their feet.

'Mike James,' he said, switching to the next case. 'Low-level pusher operating in the Partridge Park area, maybe a quarter mile in each direction. Had a cadre of young men working for him – on foot, on bikes, in cars – selling drugs. What else do we know?'

'That's all he was hands-on with, but he had connections. Protection, extortion, flesh,' Williams offered, taking a sip of cold tea from a mug that read *Give blood, play rugby*.

'Regular shitbag,' Harriman added. He put down the empty can from his second diet cola and squelched a belch.

'Yeah,' Andy sighed. 'Interviews with known associates?'

Williams held up his hands in mock innocence. *'Don't know nuffin', mate.'* His voice hardened. 'No one would admit to anything. Not knowing him. Not working with him, good upstanding tax-paying citizens that they are. Hell, even the family is disassociating themselves from him. Claim they haven't laid eyes on him, other than from a distance, in years.'

'You believe them?'

Williams flicked his hand toward Nic, allowing her to answer. 'They all live in the same part of town. Hard not to see him. Especially as he gets his step-count in.' She made a face. 'A fair few people, and their homes, smelled of weed. I'm willing to bet he gave them a friends-and-family discount.'

'Anyone know who he was working for?'

'No one's held up their hands and said they'll issue the P45.'

'But?'

'But we're talking people who have a strong dislike of the police. They see me and they clam up. Give me the bare minimum. If they open up to anyone, it'll be one of their own, but I get the feeling they're distancing themselves, rather than trying to keep things "in the family".'

'What else?' Andy glanced at Williams.

'We're talking to people on the street, trying to find out who hated Mikey-boy enough to off him.'

'Anything yet?'

'Nada.' Williams took a last slurp from his mug and put it down. 'But if you want, we can circle round to Partridge Park when we're done and have a chat with the dog people.'

'Why? As far as I know, they're not involved.'

Williams laughed, a sound that started deep in his barrel chest. 'Mate, if we're gonna question anyone, they're a good place to start. Not because I think they'd have anything to do with killing anyone, but if anything happens in that part of town, they know about it. You saw them on Sunday. You saw them again yesterday. You think your friend Marple isn't already asking questions? And that she hasn't already brought in the rest of the Pack?' Williams's grin lingered. 'Including your Russian friend?'

From the back of the room, Badolato cleared his throat. 'Need I remind you that, for more reasons than I should need to list, we cannot have civilians messing around with our investigations or running parallel ones,' he said. 'If you think they have answers, question them. Formally. If anyone's mucking around, I want you to close them down, pronto. Before someone gets hurt.' He stood up, making it clear that Andy's time in the hot seat at the front of the room was over.

He made no indication of hearing when Harriman whispered, sotto voce, 'Only the last time he tried to say no, it was our Andy that got hurt.' When Andy took his seat, he caught his eye and mouthed, 'Has your heart healed yet, Romeo?'

43

LOUISE

Detective Andrew Thompson

> Would it be safe to bet that, despite our many warnings, you and the Pack are still sniffing around the two deaths near the park?

> What makes you think that? 😇

> You do know that poking around a murder might end up backfiring?

> Who's poking?

> Want me to list off the Pack people I've spotted at both crime scenes?

> We walk our dogs by the canals and in the parks, Andy. Stop the crime in the neighbourhood and I promise you'll see far less of us.
> Unless you'd like to see more of us?
> And by 'us' I mean Irina?
>

'Well, that was fun,' I said to Klaus on the walk home. Usually he walked beside me or slightly ahead, but now he lagged behind, every so often bouncing against the back of my calves. He wanted to be carried home.

'What? Violet tired you out?' I teased, scooping him up. I dropped a kiss on the soft fur at the top of his head, smiling as I considered my next text message. 'Rest up, my love. I suspect it's going to be a long day.'

44

IRINA

Louise (Klaus's Mum)

Andy just texted, warning us off the case.

> OK. So stop looking into it.

Seriously?

> No. I hope you told him that if he did his job, we wouldn't have to do it for him.

> Yeah, but with a little more diplomacy. Did you manage to find any other dead bodies that might fit with the ones we have?

> No and I checked. The ones I found were the usual: drugs and weather, some violence, but in most of those cases the perps were arrested.

> Most, but not all?

> Too many other factors that didn't look right. Even if the perps weren't arrested, the circumstances around it aren't consistent with what we have.

> OK, thanks. Are you sure you don't want to go to the memorial tonight? I'd be willing to bet our favourite detectives will

> have a presence there and be asking around to see what we've learned.

> Interesting, but the sum total of that is pretty much zero. I'll still be stuck in the office, but good luck with it.

It wasn't just an office day. It was an office day that began early with a couple of court hearings. Irina had originally told Angela, her doggie daycare, that she'd pick up Hammy at eight, and she'd still have a couple hours of work to do from home after that.

Louise was bound to have more fun tonight, even with freezing her bits off at the memorial, and that was grossly unfair.

Would Irina prefer to see Andy?

It was complicated. They hadn't met under the best of circumstances; standing beside a dead body that Irina and Louise (or, more accurately, Hammy and Klaus) had found. Whatever flared between them hit the skids when Andy took advantage of her trust, poking around her phone behind her back. And for Irina, trust was a big thing. Break it, and it was a red flag the size of the Crimea.

She wasn't big on second chances, but there was something about Andy. His honest approach, his sense of humour, his Botticelli face alongside the disproportionately low rumble in his voice.

They hadn't spoken for months, and then there'd been the crime wave in October, when a killer had moved like a wrecking ball through the neighbourhood. There'd been a couple of conversations then, and Irina had reached out after the case was closed, but he hadn't responded. Or at least, not the way she'd wanted. Every text was perfectly polite, but left little room for her to manoeuvre.

She wasn't keen to have an audience when she saw Andy for the first time in months, but maybe, just maybe she could wrangle something.

45

LOUISE

Partridge Bark

Indira (Banjo's Mum)

Jesus. If anyone thought the dog enclosure in Partridge was bad, they should see the state of some of these small squares. Disgusting.

Yaz (Hercules's Mum)

It's infuriating. Bad enough that Tower Hamlets has a beef

against dogs, trying to restrict where they can safely go, but these selfish, inconsiderate arseholes are making the council's case for them by not cleaning up after their own dogs.

Kate (Percy and Andy's Mum)

Or keeping them on a lead on the street. Just the other day some big off-lead dog came running after us. Both of mine were on the lead. Percy tried to bolt towards home, tail between his legs, while Andy, bless her, was standing her ground. Barked her head off to tell the other dog off. Had to drag her the last few steps.

Meg (Tyrion's Mum)

OMG – are you all OK?

Kate (Percy and Andy's Mum)

> Yeah. Good thing I've been working out – I managed to drag Andy behind the gate just in time. Scared the living crap out of me though. That other dog was HUGE and his owner was nowhere to be seen.

I heard the distinct *Aroooo* of a beagle's bark before they came into sight. 'Hey, Kate. I heard the beagles had a near miss,' I said, grateful for her message so I didn't have to fess up that I'd heard it from Jake. 'You okay?'

'Shaken *and* stirred,' she said with an irritated smile. Klaus liked her two rescue beagles, but today he was playing it coy, allowing them to approach him. 'We got behind the metal gates outside my building, but this big brute of a dog was throwing his body against them, desperate to get to us. I'm scared senseless that the gates won't hold long enough for me to get the key in the door, and then the stupid owner shows up. The guy looks about twelve. Probably bought the monster "for protection".' She used her fingers for the air quotes. 'Which means he's up to no good. Tells me his dog is really friendly and mine must have triggered him. I mean, seriously. My beagles are about the same size as his dinosaur's head.'

Kate was badass. She'd retired from her job as an investigator with the Environment Agency and was living her best life as an artist with her two rescue dogs. Still in her late forties, she kept herself in shape, and what the gym didn't accomplish, a dabble with Botox did.

If Jake was interested in her – and the thought hurt more than it should have – at least it was someone I liked and respected.

'I'm trying to decide if that gate saved the beagles' lives from his dog, or saved his life from you.'

'The latter. Definitely the latter. If his dog had touched a hair on Percy or Andy, I'd have ripped his bloody jugular out.' Kate's eyes narrowed and I had no doubt that she'd defend her dogs with every breath in her body. As would I. 'The pimply little shit shouldn't be allowed to have a dog if he's not going to train it or keep it under control.'

'I think I want to be you when I grow up,' I said.

'You probably don't,' she laughed. 'Where are you headed?'

'Over to the High Street. I have a couple of questions for the guys who hang out outside Cluckin' Good Chicken.'

She gave me an incredulous look. 'You're kidding, right? The yobs who harass every woman who walks past? Are you seriously looking for trouble?'

'Yep. Wanna come along? You'd be doing me a favour. They're afraid of dogs, and I'd need you to hold Klaus while I speak with them.'

Cluckin' Good Chicken was one of many fast-food chicken shops on the High Street. When it opened last autumn, the owners tried to position themselves as the be-all-end-all in fried chicken. Which might have worked better if they hadn't stepped on the toes of the established chicken shops *and* the local residents within weeks of opening. The result of which was that they imported their own 'security' detail; hard men who lingered outside, harassing passers-by but making sure there was no trouble inside.

I'd had more than one run-in with their unofficial security team, until one of them saved my life by literally pulling me from a burning building when the chicken shop had been firebombed last October. It was that man I was looking for today.

He was standing outside, with a half-dozen other CGC regulars. I didn't know his name, but he was hard to miss with a distinctive scar that bisected his heavy, dark brow.

I handed Kate Klaus's lead and stepped forward. 'Got a second?'

He didn't miss a beat, exchanging glances with his mates before swaggering forward. ''Bout what, Queen?'

'I have a question. Maybe you can answer, maybe you can't.'

'Ask.'

'Come for a walk with me.' It was hard to tell if he was more shocked or horrified. I continued, 'Five minutes. My dog will stay here with my friend.'

One of the other men sidled up and whispered in Split-brow's ear. Split-brow nodded at him, then at me. 'Yeah. Go on then.'

Kate braced herself, two beagles and a dachshund in front of her, looking like a parody of the Boudicca statue outside of Parliament, but I wasn't worried about her. Not with three dogs guarding her. At least, not from the humans. If that off-lead dog that went for Kate's beagles appeared, I could only hope that the CGC crew would have a bigger issue with it than Kate had.

'What'cha want?' Split-brow demanded.

'Have you heard about the two dead men found around here over the last couple of days? One was just there.' I pointed to The Bells pub behind him. 'And the other maybe a quarter of a mile along the canal.'

'So? I didn't kill them.'

'Didn't think you did. But you're smart, and you keep an eye on what's going on around here.' I held up a hand to stop any protest. 'Whether officially or not.'

His lips twitched.

'I was wondering if you knew anything about either of them?' I continued.

'What's it to you?'

'To be honest, I don't know. I just don't like dead people turning up in places where I walk my dog.'

'You the razz?' He glanced over my shoulder, giving the beagles a suspicious look.

'The police? Are you kidding me?' I had to laugh. 'I look like a cop to you?'

'No.' He gave me a reluctant grin. 'No, you do not.'

'Good. Cos I'm not. But if you hear anything about who wanted either of those men dead, I'd be interested in knowing who. And why.'

'Uh huh.'

'What did your friend say, by the way?'

'Who?'

'The guy who whispered something to you before you agreed to talk to me.'

Split-brow's lips twitched again and he glanced behind him at his friend. 'He said you were the bird that stopped that crazy broad from threatening the shop.'

'Kinda glad you saved my life now?'

He nodded, stopping just short of a smile. 'Yeah, kinda.'

This was my chance. 'You could have left me to burn to death when those idiots firebombed CGC, but you risked your life for me. I'm grateful. Will you help me now? Again?'

'Got nothing to offer, Queen.' He shrugged and dug his hands into his pockets. 'Heard about both murders, y'know. Hard to miss, innit? But I don' know who killed 'em or why.'

'Okay.' I struggled to pretend I wasn't disappointed. It wasn't as if I expected him to know – or to tell me – but he was one of the few leads I had. 'If you hear anything, would you tell me?'

'Yeah, sure.' He was about to go, then stopped and looked me up and down. 'See you around here regular, like, but guessin' you don't like chicken?' His face took on a stern expression, and I wasn't sure if he was joking or not.

'I like chicken fine, but the hound would go mental in there, and the bones are really bad for dogs. They splinter and ...' I realised I was babbling. Hopefully he wouldn't require me to start eating CGC's wings.

'That's awright. I get it.' This time he did smile. 'Anyway, yeah. I hear something, I'll tell you. I promise. You're easy to find – you're always out with the little dog.'

'Yeah, that's me.' I smiled back. He wasn't a friend, yet, but maybe there were the beginnings of it. 'I'm Louise.'

'Right. I'm Rafiq,' he said, flashing bright teeth before turning back to join his mates.

I followed him, waving at Kate. The dogs' leads were wrapped around her wrist while she texted, looking effortlessly cool, until Klaus saw me return. He cried and pulled her towards me, his bottom wagging hard.

'All okay?' she asked, slipping her phone into her pocket.

I nodded, going to one knee to hug my needy dog. I took his lead from Kate and we doubled back, towards the bridge over the canal. Kate paused at the crossroads. 'You okay?' she repeated.

'Yeah. He couldn't help, but that's fine. He said he'd tell me if he hears anything.'

'You believe him? That thug?'

'Yeah, I know it sounds strange, but I do.' I rolled my shoulders, not realising how tense they were. 'I just hope that trust isn't misplaced.'

46

MEG

Ethan (Cat Boy)

> With everything going on, are you sure you want to go out to your class? I mean, I know I can't tell you what to do or anything, but I'm sure you can miss one class and still be OK?

> There's always something going on in this neighbourhood, Ethan. And I need to blow off

> some steam. Kickboxing helps.

Yeah. And I know you're good at it, but I don't like the idea of you putting yourself in harm's way.

> You're welcome to come take the class with me you know.

Kickboxing? If it's VR, sure. With someone literally trying to kick the 💩 out of me? No thanks.

> LOL! Well, thanks for the sentiment, but I'll be fine. I'll text when I'm home.

I can pick you up after the class. Maybe go somewhere for a late dinner?

> Nah, don't worry – you've got to meet your deadline.

> Besides, after class all I want is a hot bath. I'll be fine. X

Meg put the phone away and zipped her pocket closed. She took a deep breath, wishing she felt as confident as she'd made out to Ethan.

She was a mess and she knew it. Had been since that walk to the shelter with Ella. It wasn't like she wouldn't go back there, but maybe during daylight over the weekend. With Ethan.

Her mind hadn't stopped whirling. If it was the same attacker – the same creep who killed Eddie and Pete the Pusher – then why lurk after her or Ella? It wasn't like they fit the same profile. Hell, Ella was *pregnant*. Who would want to attack, or even scare, a pregnant woman?

And it wasn't like Meg went around pissing people off. She tried to be friendly with everyone. Someone who was happy to help, who had her friends' backs.

No. It had to be someone else. Someone who maybe wanted to scare people, just because he could.

The wire flashed through her mind. Jake's voice saying, 'I'd think it was just junk if anyone else found it. You two, you and your friends, you're magnets for trouble. All of you.'

Was she? She never had been before.

It had to be a different person, if the creep existed at all.

Only, she wasn't sure how much better it made her feel, with a lurker *and* a murderer out there.

Because Jake wasn't the only one who didn't believe in coincidences.

47

LOUISE

Claire (Tank's Mum)

> OK, so it looks like we're dealing with two separate murderers. The MOs are too different. Highly unlikely to be the same person.

> Isn't it possible that the same person could have switched things up?

> Sure, but this different? I have a source that has unofficially confirmed

that Eddie was killed by someone garrotting him.

Unofficial? Like Eddie's cousin?

Can't tell you, Lou. All I can say is that I agree: someone who's more comfortable strangling a stoned kid from behind is probably not the same person who'd be comfortable stabbing a drug dealer.

Maybe two people working together? Like part of a gang?

Anything's possible, but in order to figure out the 'Who', we need to figure out the 'Why' and TBH, I don't have a clue. Do you?

Sadly, no. What does your new date, I mean contact, think?

> I didn't say Jeremy was my informant. If the family knows anything, they're keeping it schtum.

> Guess you need to have another date to get closer? 😉

I frowned at Klaus, curled on his bed. 'It's not that I'm not delighted Claire's getting along with Jeremy,' I said to him. 'I just hope it doesn't blow up in her face when he finds out she's a journalist.'

Klaus tilted his head questioningly at me.

'I know. I'm just glad at least one of us is dating.'

I turned to look at my new map, my eyes drawn upwards, towards the place where a rash of murders maybe started. Victoria Park.

I looked back at Klaus. 'I know, I know. I'm probably making more of this than there needs to be. Tomorrow, when it's light out, we'll walk up there.' I rubbed at my suddenly cold arms, wondering where the breeze had come from. 'I doubt we'll see much there. The dead woman would've been gone for a good ten days, but there's no harm having a look around, is there?'

48

ANDY

Irina Ivanova

> Got time for a quick chat and a cheeky 🍺, Detective?

Andy knew Badolato was right; that the Pack would take any encouragement to heart, and that for their own safety, not to mention any pending trial once they caught the murderer, he had to keep them away from the investigation.

And for his on sanity, he had to keep Irina away from, well, everyone.

She was trouble. A lawyer with the *modus operandi* of a wrecking ball; yet despite her questionable personality, she was close to the centre of the Pack.

Which made him wonder: had Marple put Irina up to texting him, to find out whatever the police knew? Or was the message just Irina being Irina and wanting him only when she didn't have him?

Anything was possible.

Andy knew that he should ignore the message. Or better still: block Irina's number.

And yet, his fingers weren't complying with that order.

Irina Ivanova 🦇💩

> Quick one – I have an early start tomorrow. The Prospect in an hour? 8-ish?

He was tempted to delete the message, but she responded with a simple thumbs-up. Maybe he could kill two birds with one stone: find out what the Pack knew, while following Badolato's orders to warn them off.

Irina wouldn't listen, of course. Neither would Louise or the others. And Andy was self-aware enough to know better than trying to convince himself that was the reason he accepted her proposal.

'You're an idiot, Thompson,' he muttered to himself. 'But at least you had enough sense to suggest a pub away from the Pack's prying eyes.'

49

CLAIRE

Louise (Klaus's Mum)

Give me 5 minutes – I'm on my way! Klaus saw the jacket and bolted. Took a while to coax him out from under the bed.

'Louise is on her way,' Claire said. 'Looks like she'll have Klausi with her.'

'Wouldn't expect anything else,' Kate replied. 'At least he's better behaved than my two. Do you recognise anyone?' The crowd gathering just outside the children's play area wasn't large, but Claire knew she meant the trio paused just outside of it. The woman she'd last seen on

Sunday morning with the two brown mongrels now held an enormous bouquet of flowers. Beside her, slightly off to the side, stood a middle-aged man and a young woman.

'The family,' Claire said. Caroline Carr's face was puffy and tear-stained. She looked ravaged, but it was the people around her who interested Claire. The man would be Caroline's husband, Kev Carr. He had a rolling gait, hooded eyes and stony expression. The pictures that Caroline had posted of him online were flattering. Which meant the young woman was Tracey, Eddie's sister. It might have been her age – sixth formers had perfected the *so bored* look as if it were an artform – but this was her *brother*. Even if she hadn't seen him for years, she had to care, right?

Two other women moved forward and enveloped Caroline in their arms. 'The sisters,' Claire explained. She tried to distinguish which one was Jeremy's mother, but in the weak light, wasn't able to. An older woman stood apart, her back straight, eyes forward, face resolute. *Nan*. The woman who taught Jeremy about music from the Forties and Fifties, although that had to be even before her time.

There was no sign of Jeremy, of course. Claire hadn't really expected him to be there for the cousin he clearly disliked, but she had put on a bit of makeup, just in case.

'What about the others?' Kate asked.

'The vicar,' Claire guessed. 'Based on their ages, maybe a few friends or family. I guess they're friends of Eddie's mum. There's Lou.'

Louise was trotting up from the canal path. Her dark

hair was captured under a bobble hat, and she wore a sling diagonally across her chest. Unlike most dachshunds, who submerged themselves in bags, blankets or pretty much anything else they could burrow into, Klaus sat upright in it, supported by Louise's arm. Like a meerkat clad in a tiny blue jacket. 'Sorry we're late,' Louise puffed.

'Don't worry. It hasn't started yet.'

One of Caroline's sisters moved through the small gathering, handing each person a candle and staying to light it. She had two more boxes under her arm, but Claire didn't think that, including the three of them, there were enough people there to account for even one box. She accepted a candle with a simple 'Thank you.' The sister didn't know her and didn't linger.

On the far side of the loose circle Claire noticed a woman standing close to Caroline, but not directly beside her. She watched the individuals present with the same sharp gaze as Claire, and although she didn't recognise her, Claire knew that she was one of the detectives.

She allowed herself to relax infinitesimally; maybe the police weren't as uninterested in solving the murder of a homeless boy as she'd feared.

Or maybe the Pack's involvement had fired a rocket up their arses.

The vicar began to speak, murmuring generic words for a young man he hadn't known. He talked about the bright young boy that Eddie had been, and the potential that had been lost with his death. Claire found herself becoming almost as angry with him as she was with the killer. The bright flame of Eddie's potential wasn't extinguished by his murder. It had been guttering for years, dimmed by whatever tragedy had set him out onto the streets in the first place. The vicar's speech, she realised, looking at the stony faces of Mr Carr and Tracey, was more to comfort Caroline than any eulogy for her son.

Claire had originally intended to disappear after the service, but instead she found herself moving forward, holding out the store-bought flowers she carried to Eddie's mum. 'I am so sorry for your loss, Mrs Carr.'

Caroline blinked, surprise clear on her face. 'Did you know him? Were you the one . . . ?'

'No.' Claire shook her head. 'I'm sorry, but no. I never met him, but I saw you when you came to the park on Sunday, and I've been following his story. I wanted you to know—' She broke off, unsure what she wanted to say until the words came out. 'I lost a good friend a few months ago. It's not the same as a child, but I wanted you to know that I'll do whatever I can to make sure Eddie gets justice. You have my word.'

50

MEG

Ethan (Cat Boy)

> Heading home. Going to pick up Chinese on the way. Glad I went – I really needed the exercise.

> Cool. You sure you don't want me to come around? I can meet you en route.

> I'm fine. Hot food, hot bath and my 🌭dog.

Meg rolled her shoulders. She'd needed to work off the stress of the last few days. Her kickboxing coach had sensed it in her and assigned a sparring partner who would give her a proper workout. One hour later, and every muscle in her body ached. She knew it would be worse tomorrow, but it was a good sort of pain. The type she relished.

She glanced down realising how close she'd come to stepping in a large pile of poo. She reached into a pocket for a poo bag. Picking up your own dog's poo became business-as-usual pretty quickly, while picking up another dog's for some reason remained gross.

Although not as gross as stepping in it. 'Better I sort it before someone has to clean it off their shoes,' Meg muttered.

She tried not to gag as she rubbed her fingers along the top of the bag to open it. Tyrion was five-and-a-half kilos; his poos were fairly small. Whoever left this pile must have been the size of a small brontosaurus.

As she bent over, she felt something whizz past, hitting something with a soft *thunk*.

She didn't think twice. She threw the bag of poo behind her and, hunched over as far as she could, dove through the nearest open door – an off-license – as something else pinged past her.

'Someone's shooting something out there,' she panted at the young Asian man behind the till.

He gave her a curious look. 'Stay here,' he directed, and came round from the counter, peering out onto the dark street. 'I don't see anyone.'

'Someone was there,' she insisted. 'They were shooting something at me.'

'I didn't hear anything. Did you hear anything?'

She thought about it, heart still racing. She hadn't heard the bang of a gun, but guns could be silenced, right? In crime books, they'd make a soft cough, and she hadn't heard that, had she? A cough? Or any sound, really.

So stupid, she castigated herself. *You knew someone was out there the other night, but you were still in your own head. Would've served you right if they'd got you.*

'Look, lady. Sit down. You ain't looking too good. There someone I can call?'

'There's really no one outside?'

'No one I can see,' the man said. 'But that don't mean no one's there.' He crouched beside Meg on the floor. 'Don't know how far you live, but maybe it's best to take a car home tonight?'

51

IRINA

Partridge Bark

Yaz (Hercules's Mum)

> Congratulations to my downstairs neighbour, Susan. She's not in this group, but her Shih Tzu had puppies last night.

Kate (Percy and Andy's Mum)

> Awww! You got pics?

Yaz (Hercules's Mum)

Haven't seen them yet.

Claire (Tank's Mum)

Wait – the thirty-something-year-old woman? Blonde-ish/brown-ish hair? She wouldn't let Tank anywhere near her dog when she was in season. Guessing she wanted to mate it with another Shih Tzu?

Yaz (Hercules's Mum)

Yeah, you'd think so, but from the cursing coming from her flat, whatever hijinks the little thing got up to, they weren't sanctioned.

Louise (Klaus's Mum)

Well, I can 💯 guarantee that Klaus isn't the baby

> daddy. She wouldn't let him get close either. See if you can get a look, @Yaz — you might get a clue from the pups.

Boring, Irina thought. *You'd think there would be something more interesting to discuss.*

She sat in the corner of the Prospect of Whitby, with a clear view of the entrance and the bar. Behind her was a wall of windows and the Thames beyond. A gallows stood outside, a grim reminder that a couple of hundred years ago, pirates and smugglers were hanged here. Execution Wharf, it used to be called. Or something like that.

The pub had the sort of rich history that Louise loved. Built in the time of King Henry VIII, she'd said. Original floors and all.

It could have been built by Caligula, for all Irina cared. What was more important was that it was Andy's local, and despite her best efforts, it was the closest she'd been to his flat.

'He's playing hard to get,' she mused aloud, ostensibly to Hamish, although the Scottie was deep under the table trying to nibble something hiding in a corner. She pulled him out and propped him on the seat beside her. Snapped a pic of him on her phone and was about to add it to her Insta feed, but then stopped herself. Lou followed her accounts. If she saw a pic of Hammy here, she'd know that Irina was out with Andy.

'Next time,' she said, determined not to make it too easy for Lou. She might be her best friend, but she knew Lou didn't approve of her relationship with Andy.

Such as it was.

But then Lou hadn't approved when Irina was with Tim Aziz either, so she could take a flying—

Irina looked up and smiled. Glad to see Andy's wry grin as he made his way over to her, carrying a beer and a large glass of white wine. Bless him, he'd remembered that she drank sauvignon blanc.

'Right,' she said, as he set down the glasses. 'Let me pre-empt the next few minutes and save us both a bit of time. One: I acknowledge that you can't share anything about the murders the Pack is interested in, or any other case and as such I will not waste time asking.'

Andy blinked and sat down.

'Two: my Pack friends have already proven that, despite whatever warnings you level at them, they do what they want. There is no point in wasting your breath warning us off, or warning them off via me.'

He took a sip of beer and waved at her to continue.

'And three: you and I have had a bit of ... ah ... bumpiness since we met. I won't dwell on it, if you won't.'

It took that last point for Andy to look surprised, but to his credit, he didn't spit his beer across the table. 'You know, you really are something else,' he said.

'Wouldn't it be terribly boring to be just like everyone else?' Irina sipped the crisp white wine. 'So?'

'All right. No talking shop,' he agreed. 'And no past. Just two friends enjoying a drink together on a Thursday evening. All right?'

'All right,' she said, clinking her glass against his. 'Happy to start there.'

Hamish, who hadn't expected the tug on his lead when she raised her hand, tried to bolt. Sauvignon blanc sloshed out of the glass, onto the table and Irina's coral silk top. She muttered something in Russian, and Andy looked away, suppressing a laugh.

Her phone buzzed while she patted down her chest with rumpled tissues. She picked it up, intending to turn it over, but the message caught her eye, and the responses kept moving quickly. She uttered a curse and held her phone up for Andy. 'Sorry, we literally just agreed not to talk about work and crime and shit.'

Partridge Bark

Meg (Tyrion's Mum)

I'm OK now and I'm home, but I think someone tried to attack me tonight.

Louise (Klaus's Mum)

OMG – what happened? You sure you're OK? Do you need anything?

Ella (Jimmy Chew and Bark Vader's Mum)

Non! Where did it happen? Are you certain you're OK?

Meg (Tyrion's Mum)

I'd just left kickboxing and was on my way home. I'd felt like someone was watching me for the last couple of days, but tonight someone tried to shoot me.

Paul (Jimmy Chew and Bark Vader's Mum)

With a gun? Here? I did not think gun crime was that common here.

Meg (Tyrion's Mum)

No. I didn't hear a shot. Shots. Whatever. But something – a couple of somethings – 💯 whipped past me. If I hadn't bent over, they'd have nailed me.

'Just how many times?' Andy asked.

Irina shrugged and started typing.

Partridge Bark

> Plural? How many times were you shot at?

Meg (Tyrion's Mum)

> Twice, I think. I don't know what it was TBH. But there were a couple of thunks when whatever it was landed wherever it did.

Kate (Percy and Andy's Mum)

> Do you want us to come over? Percy and Andy are pretty good guard dogs.

Ethan (Cat Boy)

> I'm on my way.

Irina looked up at Andy from under her lashes, trying not to look as disappointed as she felt. 'I think you need to go see Meg, Andy.' She handed him her phone so that he could message directly instead of dictating the questions to her.

Partridge Bark

> Log a call with the police, Meg. And if you have his number, text Andy the coordinates of where it happened. He'll look into it.

Irina cleared her throat and raised her eyebrows. 'Want to phrase that so the Pack doesn't think I'm out with you tonight?'

He grimaced and nodded.

Partridge Bark

> I'll message him and let him know to expect your message.

Yaz (Hercules's Mum)

> You sure he's not blocking you, Irina?

> Hope springeth eternal.

'You really had to write that?' Irina said, not sure whether to laugh or cry.

Andy grinned. 'Yep. Absolutely.'

Standing, he pulled his own phone out of his pocket. It was already vibrating with new notifications; Meg must be messaging him. He held the phone to his ear. 'Hey, Scott. I'm going to send you some coordinates. Can you have a look around and tell me what you find?' He glanced at Irina. 'Yeah. Looks like we might have an attempted attack. I'm going to speak with the intended victim now.' He picked up his jacket, dropped a brief kiss on the top of her head and, still talking on the phone to Scott Williams, gave her a thumbs-up.

She took a gulp of wine and watched his tall, lean frame disappear through the door into the night.

'Bloody hell,' she muttered, leaning back in her chair. 'Shortest. Date. Ever. Least he could have done was make sure I got home okay.'

52

ANDY

'Please tell me you weren't out with Irina tonight,' Scott Williams said, his breath coming in sharp pants as they sprinted towards their nearest Tube stations.

'Don't be daft. Why?'

'Because I'm still in that bloody chat. And Marple only just told Meg she'd DM her your number.'

'She already had it.'

'Uh huh.'

'Look, I sent you the coordinates. See what you can find there. Meg said she took shelter in the nearest shop – Sammy's. See if they know anything. I would've preferred for her to stay there until the uniforms arrived, but I get why she wanted to get out of there.'

'Yeah.'

'The uniforms are on the way?'

'Yeah. They'll do a perimeter, but my money's on the guy being long gone.'

'Probably. Let me know how you get on.'

A PC was waiting for Andy outside Meg's building. 'What can you tell me, detective?' the officer asked.

'Ms Barnes thinks she might have been the target of someone shooting at her.'

'Might have been? Don't take this the wrong way, but you're the murder squad. Has someone been offed?'

'Too many,' Andy said, entering the number for Meg's flat on the entry panel. 'I don't know the ins and outs of what happened – that's why we're here – but I have met Meg Barnes before and she's not the sort to overreact. If she thinks something happened, it probably has.'

The intercom buzzed, and Andy pulled the door open. Took the lift to Meg's floor and knocked once. 'Detective Andy Thompson with PC Michael Miller.'

A series of loud, deep barks erupted behind the door. Miller gave Andy an apprehensive look.

'I wouldn't worry.'

'Because that thing knows you?'

'"That thing?"' Andy echoed with a smile. 'Wait for it.'

A skinny young man, with crazy hair styled á la manga, opened the door. He had a small dappled sausage dog tucked under an arm. The dog's fangs were bared, and he struggled to escape from the "air jail" to protect his home from the intruders.

'Hey, Ethan,' Andy said. 'Hey, Tyrion. Don't worry, buddy. We're here to help.'

'Jesus, I thought that'd be a much bigger dog from the way it sounded,' Miller whispered.

'Shh, don't tell him. He thinks he's Cerberus.' Ethan held a finger up to his lips. 'Meg says that where other dogs bark, daxies bork. Deeper sounds.' He shook his head. 'Sorry, I'm rambling. It's been a shit night. Come on in.'

He stepped back and Andy followed him into the living room. Meg sat on the couch, dressed in an oversized unicorn onesie, looking childlike. Her hair was pulled back into a plait dyed in shades of red and gold for Christmas.

'Thanks for coming, Andy. I'm so sorry to ask you to come out this late at night.'

Andy couldn't understand why anyone would target Meg. Irina, maybe – that one made a living from irritating people – but not Meg.

'Not a problem. Sit down. Tell us what happened.'

Meg recounted everything she could remember. As she reached the end, her face fell. 'I left the bag of poo on the street.'

'You won't be the first to have done that,' Miller said with a gentle smile.

'I threw it and ran. I wanted to distract him, but I'd picked it up to stop someone else from stepping in it and then left it there, for someone else to step in.'

Andy made a noncommittal sound. 'Not sure you need to worry about that. You distracted whoever it was for long enough to get into that shop for safety. Did you see who it was? Rough size, shape? Anything?'

'Nothing. At first I thought it might be some local kid having fun, but there was definitely more than one thing that was shot at me.'

'Do you think it was a bullet?'

Meg lifted a shoulder, then pulled her legs in, hugging her knees. 'I didn't hear a gun. Or any footsteps.'

'Is there anyone who might want to hurt you, ma'am?' Miller glanced sideways at Ethan. 'Maybe an old boyfriend?'

She didn't have to think about that, shaking her head with certainty. 'No, no one.' Andy believed her: Meg struck him as that rare breed who managed to stay friends with all her exes.

'I'd like to say it was just one of those wrong place, wrong time things, but on Tuesday, when I walked to the dog shelter with Ella, it felt like someone was watching us. And then when I went back the next day, the dogs found an old wire cutter thing. Broken. Jake said that if it was anyone else, he'd have thought it was just junk that someone binned and the foxes pulled from the rubbish, but not when Louise or I are involved.'

A wire cutter? Like a cheese cutter, maybe? Red warning lights flashed behind Andy's eyes, but he managed to keep his voice steady. 'It could have just been that, a broken bit of wire.'

'I know, but I just thought of poor Eddie, strangled . . .' Meg's wide eyes met his, pleading.

'We have the weapon used in Mr Morley's death,' Andy said. 'Can I assume you left the broken wire where you found it?'

'Don't be daft. Louise binned it.'

Of course she had. Andy gritted his teeth to stop his eyes from rolling. It would be gone by now. And Eddie Morley's killer had been smart enough not to leave his prints on the murder weapon. If the broken wire was his, he would have cleaned it before disposing of it.

Andy's gut told him that these crimes were connected, but what stumped him, and what he would struggle to justify to Badolato, was the different MOs. It wasn't unheard of for killers to change their methods, but it wasn't all that common either.

As he thanked Meg and left her flat, he was struck by a more perplexing question: What on earth could Meg Barnes, beloved by almost everyone, possibly have in common with Eddie Morley?

53

ANDY

'Right, you free to talk?' Scott Williams boomed from the other end of the phone line.

'Finished up and heading home. What have you got?'

'Well, for starters, I've got you on hands-free, mate,' Scott Williams said.

''Kay. What else?'

'Forensics will test it, but we found something embedded in a tree close to where Meg said she was earlier.'

'Something?'

'A nine-millimetre ball bearing, to be exact. Forensics extracted it and bagged it up. With a little luck they'll find a finger mark, or even a partial. I did a quick search online. You know how easy it is to get hold of ball bearings?'

'Every online hardware or general goods shop?' Andy sighed.

'Not every one, but an awful lot. And not just online. A bit of cash changes hands and there's no paper trail.'

'Fantastic.'

'So, you get a handful of ball bearings, and maybe a slingshot. You don't even need to buy one, they're easy enough to rig if you don't want to have it in your basket history. Then you've got yourself a primitive but effective weapon.'

'Which could have taken Meg out.'

'If she hadn't stooped to pick up the poo. Yes.'

'Jesus. Who would want to kill Meg?'

'Good question, and I don't have an answer, but here's another one for you: if it is connected to one of our other cases – and I'm not saying it is – which one, and why? Moreover, mate: you're looking at someone who's decompensating quickly enough to be murdering his targets in rapid succession. Are these kills planned, or is he – let's assume it's a man – being opportunistic? Is it one man, or more than one? 'Cos if it's one guy, what's with the different MOs for each case?'

'That's been puzzling me too. Maybe he wants to keep us on our toes? Maybe he's experimenting to find which one he likes best. Or maybe he's trying to choose the right weapon for each victim. Or attack.' Andy rubbed the back of his neck, wishing he had better answers. Or rather, any answers. All he had was a little bit of speculation and more questions. 'Got anything else?'

'Checking to see if we find any other ball bearings. The more we find, the greater the chance that he made a mistake and left something for us to trace back to him.'

'I don't like this.'

'Yeah. Not sure any of us do.'

54

ADRIAN

Adrian peered out of the window. The park was still, frost glittering beneath the lampposts. Christmas was coming and fairy lights lit up The Nest and people's balconies. The season of love and joy, and all that bollocks.

Just because it was pretty, just because the ground sparkled outside, that didn't mean it was safe. And Adrian was scared.

Eddie was dead. Sweet, broken Eddie. Her friend, her protector, the only one who'd *understood*.

She'd wanted to go to his memorial, but couldn't bring herself to. Even if her foster dad would've allowed it. No one she knew was going. The razz would be there, watching, and asking questions. Instead, she'd raise a can or a spliff in Eddie's honour tonight. He'd understand that, too.

She'd stopped by Tesco on her way home from school

and picked out a bouquet of flowers. She'd taken it to the kiddie park, after the last family had extracted their screaming child, and laid it in the basket swing where he'd been killed, along with a note. It wasn't signed or anything, but it didn't need to be. Eddie'd understand.

First Eddie, and then Pete. Pete wasn't a good man, but that didn't mean he should be murdered, left to die alone on a park bench. Although the irony wasn't lost on her: it was the same thing Pete used to say to Eddie. *C'mon, work for me. You don't want to end up dead on a park bench, do you?*

The police were investigating, but would they understand the links? Would they understand *why* Eddie was targeted, from a sea of young homeless men? Or Pete, of all the drug dealers in the neighbourhood?

Or that woman from Hackney. Well, not *from* Hackney. From around here, Adrian had heard. Lived here most of her life, but moved up that way for a man. Same old story though: a troubled youth. Anorexia. A thing for the bad boys. One thing leading to another. What was her name? The cops hadn't released it, but Eddie had called her Laura. He'd pronounced it the Italian way: *L'owwra*. Was she Italian? Adrian didn't know, but she hoped that the woman's family had given her a decent send-off. The poor thing had been so addled at the end, she barely knew her own name.

At first Adrian didn't see it, but there was a pattern. And if she could see it, maybe the police could too. Maybe they'd be clever enough to spot the thread connecting the victims. Realise that Danny was cleaning things up, and that Eddie – foolish, foolish Eddie – had probably set everything in motion.

Her shaking hand closed around the knife that she'd lifted from her foster dad's fishing box and she closed her eyes. If this were a movie, she'd stare at herself in the mirror and tell herself she was ready, but it wasn't a film, and she wasn't naïve enough to fool herself.

Danny knew where she lived; she had nowhere to hide, and nowhere to go.

Not much faith in the police either. They'd never been there when she needed them before. And now it chilled her that she was trapped here, hoping they'd be able to catch him before he came for her.

Adrian opened her eyes, and turned away from The Nest's bright lights, towards the kiddie park. The memorial'd been over for hours, but when she blinked, she could still see *those* lights. They'd had candles.

'Fire in the night,' she murmured aloud, a tear slipping down her cheek.

Eddie would have liked that.

55

GAV

Gav stretched, but every muscle in his body still felt tense.

The George and Dragon pub was his home away from home. It was dark, and according to his Doris, dated. 'Stuck in the Sixties,' she'd declared. That was fine. He didn't need some chichi wine bar. He was comfortable here, with the burgundy flocked wallpaper, the dark wood floor and the wonky chairs. The beer was good, the food was all right and there was always someone to have a laugh with.

Violet pawed at his leg. Gav took a sip of beer, set the glass down further towards the centre of the table and picked her up. He knew people laughed at him: the crusty ex-con with the ridiculous little dog. Knew the joke: that he'd wanted a Doberman pinscher and ended up with an Affenpinscher instead.

He was okay with that; hadn't bothered to confirm or deny the rumour.

Truth was, he'd found her. It were nine years ago, a few days after he'd been let out from prison that last time. After a couple of years Inside, he was still trying to find his way around Outside. It was raining. In London, if it was properly pissing down, it wouldn't last more'n ten minutes, but could drizzle for weeks on end.

He'd left the house to go for a walk. Doris had been ratty about something, and he left, needing fresh air and his own company. Didn't care about the incessant rain. Didn't care about the cold. Just knew that if he stayed at home, he'd say something they'd both regret.

So he walked. Didn't care where he was going, his head full of what he thought he should be doing versus what he really wanted to do. Barely noticed the traffic whizzing by.

It were no small miracle that he heard scratching from a cardboard box beside a rubbish bin. It would've already melted in the rain, but'd been wrapped up tight with packing tape.

'Bloody hell,' he muttered, giving the box a gentle nudge with his toe. It erupted with furious howls. Whatever was in there was *alive*. Too weak to scratch through the tape, but alive.

Heart pounding, Gav ripped the tape from the box. What was wrong with people? He was no stranger to violence, but how could anyone could harm an innocent animal?

Anyone who could do that, was effin' sick in the head.

Maybe he'd find out who they were. Couldn't be that difficult. Grab 'em and stuff 'em in the boot of his Fiat for a coupla hours. See how much they liked it.

Inside the box was a ball of dark fur, enormous black eyes and bright white teeth, all bared at him. It bit his hand when he reached in to take it out, its teeth like tiny daggers.

Puppy teeth, a part of his brain registered.

It were strange looking, with a squished in little face, like them gremlins from that Eighties movie. The ones that became crazy when they got wet. And whatever this was, it was plenty wet.

He took off his muffler and wrapped the little thing in it, unsure if he meant to contain it or to protect it from the weather. Maybe both. He tucked it under his arm and turned around, heading for home. He could always tell Doris that the little thing was an *I'm-sorry-I'm-an-arse* present. Even offer to walk it, if she didn't want to.

He stopped in his tracks, double-checking to make sure that it wasn't a rat. Some people kept rats as pets. Swore they were intelligent an' all. But Doris? If he brought a rat home, she'd tell him the rat was smarter, then she'd kill him.

No, the nose was definitely squished in, not pointy. Not a rat. Not a cat, neither.

Puppy teeth, something in the back of his brain insisted. *Means it's a dog, you dimwit.*

Didn't matter whatever it was – he wasn't about to leave it out there alone.

He stopped by the vets on the way home. The woman behind the desk confirmed that the little dog wasn't microchipped. There was a protocol to follow, she told him, but Gav didn't believe in protocols. The pup was young, alone and had just been discarded like garbage. Taped up, so she couldn't get out – not that a tiny thing like her would last long on her own.

He bought the smallest collar they had – it were designed for a cat, but at least it fit. He'd sort out a chip and order a tag for her when he got home.

'Got you something,' he said, proudly presenting the little beast to Doris with a hopeful smile on his face. Rainwater streamed down his face – at least, he thought it was rain – and he held his breath, aware that the last time he'd smiled like that at Doris was when he asked her to marry him.

'What the devil is that?'

A good question, considering the way the little thing fought to get free from the muffler. And the vet. And, well, him.

'It's a puppy. Her name is . . .' He looked around, trying to think of something. His eyes landed on the little purple collar around her neck. 'Violet.'

'Uh huh.' Doris frowned at him, sceptical.

'I thought you'd like to have a, uh, companion. For when I'm out.' It sounded lame as he said the words aloud. He'd been away at Her Majesty's orders for years. Hell, he'd been away even when he was here. Still, he couldn't leave the little thing out on the street. 'You don't want it, I'll see if Jenny wants to take her.'

'Jenny's in university. She can barely take care of herself, let alone a dog.' Doris stepped closer, holding out a tentative hand. At Violet's warning snap, she drew her hand back sharply.

'I'm not taking care of it, Gav,' she declared.

'Aw'ight.' He felt the little body in his hands relax a fraction, as if she knew. As if Violet had already decided that he was Her Person. 'I'll take care of her.'

'But you gotta train it. I'm not having a feral beast in my home,' Doris declared.

Gav could have pointed out the number of times she called him and his mates feral, but wisely held his tongue. Tucked Violet under one arm and nodded.

In the intervening years, Violet and Doris had reached a polite détente. Violet wouldn't bite or snap at Doris, and in turn, Doris allowed her to sleep in the kitchen. A policy that Gav broke every time Doris was out of town, allowing Violet to sleep on Doris's pillow. Violet was his shadow, his conscience and maybe his soul, following him everywhere.

Gav would never admit to anyone, but on that day, Violet saved him every bit as much as he saved her.

Now she moved from his lap to the table, eyeing up his beer.

'Violent's mean when she drinks, mate,' Mo reminded him from across the table, using his nickname for the dog.

'And mean when she doesn't.' Jono completed the joke, taking a seat between the two.

Gav let it slide. 'Let her.'

'Guess Doris isn't home tonight?' Jono said. 'Guess you didn't go down to that vigil at the kiddie park with your dog friends today?'

'Nah. Figure that crap's gang on gang. They'll go after each other 'til the last one's standing. Keep it like that, keep it away from me and mine, I don't care.' Gav leaned forward, his elbows on the table. 'What I do care about is that some arsewipe took a shot at one of my friends.'

'Stupid of them,' Jono said. 'Which one? The one with the little dog who came with you to ask me and Norma about the guy she found in the park? What was it? Six months ago?'

'No, the other one with the little dog. The one with the crazy hair that saved Violet's life.' *I owe her.*

'Oh shit. She okay?'

'Will be. I spoke to Baz, told him to get his arse back to London. I want him to keep an eye out for her. Subtle-like – I don't want her to know.'

'Good choice. If he don't want to be seen, he *won't* be seen. And he won't let no one near that girl.'

'That what I'm hoping. Putting out the word as well, making sure the locals know that Meg, and the rest of the Pack, are off limits. Or they'll be answering to me.'

He didn't need to explain what that meant.

Gav took a last mouthful of beer and stared out the window for a few moments. If it were just about him, he could deal with it. But the Pack, they were naïve. Probably still believed in effin' fairies. Someone had to look out for them.

He'd tried to keep his old life separate from the new one. His old life – it had been about violence. Anger. The new one, well – it was about dogs.

And dogs, they were worth protecting. Not just Violet, but her friends. His friends. If'n he couldn't protect them, then what good was he? They didn't have to know; they didn't have to see it. Best if they didn't, actually.

If he had to call in favours or get his hands dirty to sort this shit out, well. That's what he'd done for decades. He wasn't afraid of a bit of confrontation, 'specially not when the stakes were this high.

'Mate, I think Violet is violent so you don't need to be,' Mo said, breaking into his thoughts. 'But if anyone thinks you don't have it in you no more, they're in for a nasty surprise.'

Gav put his glass down on the table and glared. 'Count on it.'

Friday

56

LOUISE

Claire (Tank's Mum)

> Hey Claire, quick one: what was the name of the woman found dead in Vicky Park a couple of weeks ago? The original article didn't have a name for her. Were you able to find something?

The police named her as Laura Rossi, but haven't put much out about her. Born in Poplar, with Italian

> parents. She'd been living on the streets for years.

> How did she die?

> First reports were of a suspected overdose, although it sounded like there were enough inconsistencies to raise a big question mark.

> Maybe a murder staged to look like an OD?

> Anything's possible, and I'm getting really tired of using that phrase.

> I get that. Thanks.

> Something's set off your radar, Lou. What is it?

> Right now? Just a feeling that there's more going on than we think. If I turn up anything else, you'll

> be the first to know. I promise!

> You'd better. And you'd better take care of yourself. If anything happens to you, Jake will string me up by my innards.

> What a lovely thing to say.

I itched to ask her why she thought that. Despite the speculation it generated among the Pack, what Jake and I had was firmly grounded in friendship, with a large dose of Unrequited on my part.

Klaus, bundled up to his eyeballs in the blue parka he hated, gave me the nasty dachshund side-eye: *Bad enough you drag me out of a warm bed, but this isn't just the usual morning walk for a pee and a poo. What the actual fluff?*

'Blame Auntie Fi,' I told him.

I'd woken up with her words from last Sunday ringing in my ears. That she'd gone to Victoria Park a week early because the original date of the sniffer dog class had been pushed back at the last moment because Sarah the Trainer had the flu.

The light turned green. We were halfway across the A11 when Klaus decided to dig in his paws, a sausage protest for being dragged on a long walk. The green man was replaced with a digital countdown, telling me I had ten seconds to cross. I had no choice: I scooped him up and sprinted to the other side just before the cars blasted past.

I set him down on the sidewalk. 'Come on, it's not that far,' I insisted, knowing that by the end of the block, I'd be carrying him again. A few kids whizzed past on stolen Lime bicycles chirping "Hackney birdsong".

By the time we turned onto Grove Road, I still wasn't sure what I hoped to accomplish with this trip. Laura Rossi's body was long gone. The police tape would be long gone. And the probability of anyone telling me anything useful was pretty low.

Maybe all I wanted was to allow my brain to catch up to whatever my gut feel was insisting on. Keeping an open mind, I went over what I knew:

1. Laura was found in a park that was a local favourite with the dog community.
2. Eddie Morley had been killed in a kiddie park, separated from the rest of the park by a waist-high fence.
3. Pete the Pusher was found on the canal path, not that far from where Eddie was killed.

From the perspective of someone who walked her dog past all three sites on a regular basis, they were all not only accessible, but had quite a lot of foot traffic. Whoever was killing them had to commit murder and get away without being seen. How likely was *that*?

Eddie and Pete were killed in our neighbourhood. Was it a coincidence that we had planned on being in Vicky Park that day? Maybe not early enough to find Laura, but not long after.

Add on the attack on Meg last night, and there were too many coincidences lining up.

And I didn't really believe in them.

The Meg thing felt like the outlier. The first three were vulnerable. Meg, for all her diminutive size and little-girl looks, could kick someone's butt into next week if she had to.

Unless, of course, she'd been targeted because of the questions we were asking?

It was still all circumstantial, and far too soon for me to bring any theories to Andy, but standing by the pub in Victoria Park, I felt a chill that had nothing to do with the cold December sun. What if, somehow, the killer already knew about the Pack? And what if he thought we were a threat?

57

ANDY

Most of the team wore out the loyalty cards from the coffee shop outside the station on a weekly basis. The coffee was overpriced but the location was convenient. Moreover, cliché as it sounded, the station's coffee tasted like it'd been brewed with Thames water and filtered through old socks.

Scott Williams preferred to walk a bit further, to the smaller independent café a few streets away. The coffee was better, reasonably priced and they stocked the sort of gluten-free banana bread that Williams ate because it would have appealed to his late wife. Andy picked up his pace, intent on meeting his partner there.

He pushed through the door of Que C'est Belle's. Scott was easy to spot – his bashed-in face and powerful body gave *rugby prop/don't mess with me* vibes, but his smile was easy and his eyes intelligent. He'd been leaning back, joking with the proprietress behind the counter. His smile faded when he spotted Andy. 'Andy, you know Sybelle, right?'

Andy nodded, fine with maintaining pleasantries. 'The beautiful Sybelle, who was once the bane of the courts before she had enough and got out of Dodge.'

'Not that far, Andy. I hear that you're acting DS at the moment. Congratulations.' Sybelle smiled, showing a small gap between her front teeth. She had to be in her late fifties to have been appointed as a QC before appointments were paused in 2003, but she looked younger. Andy guessed that was due to good genes and knowing when it was time to leave the law in favour of an easier life.

He shrugged uncomfortably. 'I have a feeling it might be a poisoned chalice.'

Sybelle unhooked the container of used grinds from the coffee machine and banged it a few times to dislodge the brown sludge. 'If it helps open the doors that'll enable you to better do your job, then you take it.'

'A natural, he is.' Williams raised his coffee, saluting his friend.

'Don't be an arse. Badolato just wants someone to do his job while he politics his way up to DCS.'

'And none better than you.' Williams's grin widened. 'Or rather, better you than me.'

Sybelle pressed fresh grounds into the container and shoved it into the machine with a sharp twist. 'You'll have your usual, Andy?' She didn't wait for his nod, but gestured to the men. 'You two look like you need to talk. We're not busy right now. Just move to the corner, will you? For my peace of mind.'

Scott placed his empty plate on the counter and picked up his coffee, carrying it two tables over. He settled himself into the chair in the corner, with a good view out onto the pavement, and the entrance door. It was the spot that Andy'd been eyeing up, but he held his tongue, sitting beside Williams rather than opposite him. 'What'd you find last night?'

'Three nine-millimetre ball bearings. One in the tree, and two more on the ground. No prints.'

'So, clear enough that Meg was an actual target, and not just a random person passing by.'

'Looks that way.' Williams gazed out at the street, frowning. 'But that bothers me. I mean, *Meg*. I know I said it before, but Marple or your lunatic Russian friend would make more sense.'

Andy was happy to let that slide. 'It's the big picture that bothers me.'

Williams nodded thoughtfully. 'You've got a homeless man who might've dabbled in prostitution when he needed the dosh. A pusher with connections in the flesh trade, trying to be a one-stop shop. If we just take those two men, there's a connection, I'll give you that, but it's tenuous. Maybe we can connect them, maybe not. But I don't see the sort of person who'd kill them going after a female IT programmer who loves everyone.'

Andy didn't disagree, in theory, but when he tested that theory, his gut protested.

Sybelle approached, placing a tiny cup of espresso in front of Andy. He waved his phone in the universal sign to pay. She waved it off, knowing as he did that he'd only leave cash instead.

'Right. Sooo?' Williams said, once Sybelle's attention was on a new customer.

'So, you're right. Everyone loves Meg. Because everyone *knows* Meg. You ever see her walk down the street? She stops every few feet. Not just because her dog needs to stop, but because people stop to chat.' Andy shook his head, bemused. 'She's like a Goth crossed with some utopian suburbanite from the Fifties. She knows *everyone*.'

Williams leaned back and nodded. 'You think she knows more than she realises?'

'It makes sense, right? Whoever it is has been careful not to leave any evidence. Not to utilise the same MO in any of these cases. And let's face it, some yob with a slingshot taking a potshot at a some random woman isn't going to be clever enough to make sure their prints aren't on anything. That there's no trace passed on.'

'Let's go with it. You think there's a clever killer, who might have a list of people he wants to bump off.'

Andy nodded and waved at Scott to continue.

'OK. So, there's this woman. She and her friends have been involved in two cases so far. Some might say they were *instrumental* in taking down the killers. So, if you want to bump someone off, you might not want Meg and her friends sniffing around your work.'

A thought popped into Andy's head. 'Unless you do.'

'What?'

'Unless you do want them involved. Don't forget, the men's bodies were posed in places any local dog walker would pass. Maybe he wants to prove how smart he is. That he's smarter than the Pack. He might not think they were interested enough initially. So, he finds a target that will get them involved. One that has the added bonus of potentially knowing who he is. Take her out before she takes him out. Then he can play a proper game of cat-and-mouse with the Pack.'

An ominous silence swelled between them.

'A perp who doesn't want to outwit the police, he wants to outwit *the Pack?*'

Andy nodded.

'Kind of messed up, right?' Williams pushed his coffee away. 'Why the Pack?'

'As you said, they've been in the news a couple of times over the past year.' Andy scowled at his coffee.

'If he wanted the Pack's attention, you'd think he'd have toyed with them before now.'

'Given where the bodies were found, maybe he has.' Andy leaned back in his chair, unable to get comfortable. Something that had little to do with the café's seating. 'Let's say – for argument's sake – that the murders are all the work of the same guy. Just to rule out the theory.'

Williams nodded.

'Okay. So, he does have one eye on the Pack and did attack Meg. What then?'

'Lots of reaches in there, Andy, but what it would give us would be a bigger problem: not only do we need to protect a vulnerable community, the homeless, the drug users and the dealers, but we now need to protect the Pack, who should know better, but can't seem to stay away from trouble.'

'And don't listen when we tell them to.'

Williams's heavy brow lowered, consternation etched on his face. The Pack might be a nuisance, interfering in their cases, but it came from a good place. And over the last six or seven months, they had gotten to know them. The Pack weren't just busybodies. They were *friends*, who happened to be busybodies.

'Shit. Right.' Williams stood up and shrugged into his jacket. 'So, what's the plan to find our killer before he finds someone else?'

'Uniforms spent the night rounding up the other known dealers operating around Partridge Park. Most'll keep quiet, but I'm hoping someone might give up a name. Or a direction we can look into.'

'Which means, we still have nothing solid to go on?'

Andy shook his head, feeling like they were running out of time. '*Nada*.'

58

CLAIRE

Jeremy Silva

> Running a little late – soz! Meet you outside the Notes in 10.

> Right, so, just a reminder. I'll have Tank with me, not Nala ...

> Not a problem. Sushi is Mum's dog. I don't take him to work with me.

> Fab. See you soon!

Tank sprawled on the floor beside the table at the Crossrail Place Notes, his legs splayed out behind him as if two turkey drums were attached to a massive, pale kiwi fruit. Claire knew it was because the floor was cold, but didn't want to think too hard on it.

'Right. So, I like this guy,' she said to him. 'Please don't embarrass me. No humping. No farting. No stress voms. Nothing creepy, right?'

Tank blinked his green eyes. *Mum, seriously?*

Claire ordered another cup of coffee from the server. It was her third, and she hoped she wouldn't be shaking from a caffeine overdose by the time Jeremy arrived. Although maybe that was better than shaking from nerves. She knew she needed to tell him she was a journalist before he found out some other way, and while she was at it, confess that she had gone to Eddie's vigil last night.

It was a double whammy of nerves. She liked him, *really* liked him, and didn't want to lose him. Not yet.

'It'll be fine,' she told Tank. 'Just two friends meeting for a pre-work coffee.'

He seemed to roll his eyes – something she'd never considered possible in a dog. The side-eye, sure. But this sort of censure? Seriously?

'Who are you talking to?' Jeremy said, looking better than any man had any right to look this early on a Friday morning. He took off his black wool coat, sat beside her and waved over the server. Instead of a suit, today he wore a pair of well-made dark grey chinos, a black rollneck jumper and a black blazer; a panther incognito.

'Tank,' she said, her mouth dry.

The Frenchie, having successfully ignored the intruder sitting beside his mother, raised his head at his name. He blinked at Jeremy and got to his feet, suddenly interested.

'Here, give him this,' Claire pressed a small dead fish into Jeremy's palm, hoping he wouldn't retch. Or throw it away, because Tank would be interested in either option.

'Fish, huh? Just don't tell Sushi.' He held the sprat out, palm flat. Maybe he didn't like seeing the little eyes, or wasn't taking a chance in case Tank was half shark. Sensible.

Tank, open to bribery, gobbled up the fish and rested his head on Jeremy's lap. 'Want another piece, do you?' Jeremy laughed.

Claire relented, handing him another sprat, which Tank promptly inhaled. She would have relaxed a bit, if not for what Jeremy was saying.

'Sorry I'm late, Mum was in a state. Seems the police aren't able to release Eddie's body for burial yet and Aunt Caro isn't coping that well.'

'Of course she isn't,' Claire said, one hand on Tank's head to keep him from demanding another sprat. 'It's her son.'

'Yeah, well. Not like he's been much of a son.' Jeremy didn't seem to register Claire's noncommittal sound, and continued, 'You know what the irony is?'

She tilted her head. Several theories popped to the tip of her tongue, but thankfully remained there. 'Tell me.'

'The last message he sent her, he said he had someone in his life. Someone who'd recently come into money who he thought could take care of him. She was so bloody happy for him. That he'd finally found a woman who made him happy. Who cared enough about him to take care of him.'

'Wow.' Claire took a slow sip of her coffee, trying to find a way to phrase her question so that it didn't sound like an inquisition. 'Did she know who it was?'

'No, of course not.' Jeremy shook his head. 'You think Eddie would bother telling his mum anything that might calm her mind?' His voice was laced with the sort of bitterness that had developed over a lifetime.

'You didn't like him much, did you?' Claire spoke before her filter could engage. She held her breath as he contemplated the question.

'It's not a question of like or dislike,' he answered slowly. 'It's more complicated than that. He was ... all right ... when we were little. But then, things changed. He kept things to himself. He was always angry. Like he blamed us for something we didn't know we did. And he wouldn't tell us what it was. He held his mother to ransom like some sort of terrorist. She'd've jumped through flaming hoops for him, but did he care? Did he not.'

Jeremy leaned back in his seat, his anger spent. 'Sorry. You didn't come here to hear me vent about my dead cousin.'

'No,' Claire said. 'It's all right. I'm just glad that he had someone who made him happy before he died.'

'Are you?' He snorted. 'She must have been masochistic AF. Ed was hard work.'

Jeremy's black brows furrowed into something fierce. Claire watched the emotions play across his handsome face, fascinated. 'Maybe he was hard work to his family – a lot of us are – but it was different with a partner?'

Jeremy looked like he wanted to shoot down the theory, but instead turned his gaze towards Tank, bemused. 'I've got to say, while Nala was pretty, for some reason, Tank seems to suit you more.'

Claire put her mug down, trying to process that. Was he saying she wasn't pretty? Or that she better resembled a muscular, farting, vomiting, well, Tank?

'It's a compliment,' Jeremy said, and as if he understood, Tank grinned at him. 'He's got character.'

'That he does.'

Tell him, Claire's inner voice urged. *Tell him you're a journo.*

She quashed the voice and smiled, hoping it looked better than Tank's. 'I wanted to thank you for the other night, I had a great time.'

'Me too. Didn't realise you'd be up there high-kicking to "New York, New York" though. You're full of surprises too, you know.'

'Good. Well, ten points for planning a super night. You set the bar pretty high. I'm going to have to think of something equally cool for the next time.'

'Next time?' he asked, with a fake (she hoped it was fake) coyness.

'Yes,' Claire said before she could change her mind. 'You choose the day, I'll plan the evening.' She would tell him then. It didn't really have to be today.

59

LOUISE

Claire (Tank's Mum)

> So, before he died, Eddie Morley was in a relationship. Someone who'd 'just come into money' who he thought was going to take care of him.

> God, that's sad. Do you have a name? Is she someone we want to talk to?

> Nope. My source didn't give me a name. Yet. And yeah, I want to talk to her 💯.

> So, Eddie's cousin doesn't know who it is? 😉

> Didn't say my source was Jeremy.

> No, huh. Did you tell him you're a journalist trying to help find his cousin's killer?

> Jeez, Lou. I wanted to. I really did. I planned to meet him for coffee this morning to tell him. I just couldn't manage to get the words out. But I will. I don't have a choice.

> Eek. 😬 Good luck.

I couldn't fault her assessment. I just didn't know which direction to point any of us in.

The sun had burnt off the frost from the grass, but Klaus wasn't interested in lingering around Victoria Park, even with the lure of the ball, and we were walking home among the early morning commuters. A pair of teenage girls wearing school uniforms saw him and jumped. He glared, planted his feet and barked. *You're scared of me? I'll give you something to be scared of!*

'Sorry,' I apologised to the girls, now trotting away at pace. 'He is friendly,' I insisted, knowing they wouldn't believe me that it was just him asking for attention.

We entered Mile End station, ready to head home. I had a lot to think about, not least of which my speech at the company Christmas party this evening. Something I wasn't sure how much I was ready for.

60

CLAIRE

Partridge Bark

Yaz (Hercules's Mum)

> So ... guess who I saw arguing with Shih Tzu Sue early this morning? I have a feeling I might have a clue as to which dog knocked her girl up.

Ella (Jimmy Chew and Bark Vader's Mum)

> Oooh, tell! And I have news too – I think we may have finally found tenants!

Kate (Percy and Andy's Mum)

That's great news! Do they have a dog?

Ella (Jimmy Chew and Bark Vader's Mum)

No, but they like dogs. Two young women who have just graduated from university. Fingers crossed that they come back and sign the lease!

Louise (Klaus's Mum)

🤞🤞🤞

Yaz (Hercules's Mum)

Maybe they'll want one of Shih Tzu Sue's new pups, once they're old enough? 😊

Claire tossed her phone onto the desk. It was too much of a distraction when she had work to do. How could she find this elusive woman who had unexpectedly come into money and wanted to take care of Eddie Morley? A woman who was open to a relationship with a homeless young man with drug issues and a history that included time in Young Offenders?

Had they been involved together before the newfound wealth? Because if it was afterwards, it might raise more questions about motives on both sides.

She opened her laptop's browser, fingers hovering over the keyboard, checking for people who might have won a lottery. Something significant enough to enable them to care for someone else.

She narrowed it down to the local area, simply because Eddie Morley was homeless. He wouldn't have the resources to swan around the country and meet someone from afar.

'Although, that said ...' Claire frowned at the screen. 'It doesn't mean he didn't meet them online.' She made a note to find out if Eddie had a phone.

'Of course he'd have a phone,' she answered her own question. 'He might not have had a lot of credit on it, but it'd be easy enough to get onto The Nest's WiFi. And as for the device itself, the Baby Gang stole mobiles on a regular basis, and they're not the only act in town. If he didn't still have the old phone he used before leaving home.'

Did the police have it, or was it missing? How hard would they search for it?

'Bloody everlastin' hell,' Claire muttered. 'How hard would they even search for *his killer?*'

Tank, lounging under her desk, stopped chewing and tilted his head at her. 'Don't worry, Tank. We're not giving up.' She frowned. 'We just need to bring out the bigger guns.'

61

IRINA

Claire (Tank's Mum)

> Hey, Irina. Are you busy?

> On the last Friday before Christmas? Are you serious?

> OK. Never mind then. Wouldn't want to bother you.

Irina was bothered, all right. Just when she was making some sort of progress with Andy, something had to go and scupper it. And Meg, of all people. Little Gothy Swot, so keen on her self-defence class, almost had her clocks cleaned.

It wasn't as if Irina wished harm on Meg. She didn't; she actually *liked* Meg. Didn't understand her, but liked her anyway. She looked at her caseload and winced. Two other associates had dropped the ball on their cases, and the senior partner asked Irina to pick up the pieces. Like, why was their ineptitude her problem?

And it was ineptitude. Their cases, both of them, were straightforward. She'd agreed to help, hoping that whatever the problem was, it would distract her; but now all she could see was Andy's long, lanky frame heading out of The Prospect, without so much as a backwards glance, damn him.

She got up and went to the kitchen to refill her wineglass and forage about for a bag of crisps.

Against her better judgement, she shot off a message.

Detective Andy Thompson

> Hey. Not sure what your plans are for Xmas. Festive drinks 🥂? Preferably on a day you're not working?

> Can't guarantee that something won't come up, but I'd like that.

Irina felt her mood lift. Scrolling back to Claire's chat, she began to type. If they could close the case before next week, he might not need to run out on her. Again.

Claire (Tank's Mum)

> Can't guarantee I can help, but I'll see what I can do. What do you need?

> I'm looking at the Eddie Morley case. I heard that he had hooked up with someone who'd recently come into money and wanted to take care of him.

> I'm assuming by 'take care of him' you mean in a long-term romantic way, and not as in getting rid of a problem. Cos if it's the latter, they seem to have done a good job.

> Good point. Let's assume the former. Not sure if he'd brag to his mum

> that someone wanted to hurt him. Is there any way you'd be able to find someone who might have been romantically attached to Eddie, and who was still willing to be there for him?

> As I said, no guarantees. But I'll do a couple of searches. I'll let you know what I find.

Irina leaned back in her chair and opened up a new browser window. In the spirit of getting the case closed before the date ... because she'd be really irked if Andy had to run out on her again.

62

ANDY

Irina Ivanova 🦇💩

By the way, you know that Eddie Morley, the dead guy from Sunday, had a girlfriend? Someone who 'wanted to take care of him'.

Heard that. Found no evidence to support it. Have you?

Not yet, but according to my sources, this woman

> had recently come into some money. But I'll bet you knew that too?

'Shit,' Andy muttered, turning the phone so Williams could see.

'Who would want to take care of a homeless drug addict? Some Dorothy Do-right?'

'Maybe they knew each other before. Maybe she wanted to save him. Some women are like that.'

'Would have been a hell of a lot easier if we'd found his phone,' Williams said.

'Still no luck?'

'Nada. Either the killer kept it or did a damn good job getting rid of it, and I'm talking not just turning the phone off, but taking the battery out and smashing it. No luck tracking it.' Williams shrugged. 'I'll see if Nic can get anything else out of the family.'

'Okay. And I'll have one of the analysts look for anyone local who might have come into money. Jesus.' Andy sighed and leaned back in his chair, staring at the ceiling. 'You ever get the feeling the Pack are getting good at this?'

'Every bloody case, Andy. Every bloody case.'

Andy cracked an eye open and asked, 'Anonymous caller?'

'You think I'm brave enough to tell Badolato that we got the tip from the dog people? Are you mad?' Williams laughed, then sobered. 'Although if you're still hanging out with that Russian nutjob, maybe you are.'

63

INDIRA

Partridge Bark

Ella (Jimmy Chew and Bark Vader's Mum)

> WE HAVE TENANTS! The two women came back with an offer. We've accepted it. The agency is doing background checks, but assuming all goes well, they'll be moving in at the end of February.

Fiona (Nala's Mum)

Is that enough time for you to do everything you need to do and relocate?

Ella (Jimmy Chew and Bark Vader's Mum)

Yes, we hope so! They'll rent the flat as furnished. So, we just need to move our clothes and personal stuff. Anything we can't take with us will go into storage. And we're lucky – we'll be staying with Paul's family. They have a little cottage on their property that we'll take over, so they'll be close enough to help with the baby.

Louise (Klaus's Mum)

Moving house and getting ready for the little one at the same time sounds like a lot. Let us know if you need any help.

Claire (Tank's Mum)

> We'll miss you. How long are you planning on going for?

Ella (Jimmy Chew and Bark Vader's Mum)

> Paul got approval to work from France for one year, travelling to the UK as needed.

Paul (Jimmy Chew and Bark Vader's Dad)

> Don't worry – we'll be back!

Indira was heading to work when she saw Mrs Carstairs, with her two Yorkies in tow, all three matching in cow-print coats.

She'd known Mrs C for years. As one of the local paediatricians, she'd had care of the woman's grandkids, and sometimes the old woman had brought them in for appointments when their parents couldn't. 'Morning, Mrs Carstairs,' Indy said.

The old woman paused and inclined her head politely. 'Dr Balasubramanian. Y'aw'ihgt?'

'Yes, thanks. How are *you* doing? I heard you found both dead men this week. Can't have been easy.'

'Easier for me 'n them,' she replied.

'I believe the council offers—'

'Yeah, yeah. Counselling. The detectives said when they came to question me t'other day. Truth is, I'd rather just get outta here for a bit. See my sister in Spain. Bit of sun an' liquid therapy. Know what I mean?' Her voice was raspy and her eyes were intense.

Indy nodded. 'A change of scene isn't a bad idea, but I wouldn't dismiss the idea of talking to a professional too.'

Mrs C snorted. 'What? Six five-second sessions when they spend the whole first one coverin' the basics of who I am and why I need a shrink? Better to sit wi' my sister on a beach.'

'Okay.'

'But the razz told me to stay put until the killer's caught.' She leaned close and Indy was overwhelmed by the smell of cigarette smoke.

'Okay?' she repeated, not sure how else to reply.

'I mean, seriously? Like I have anythin' to do wi'it.'

'Maybe it's just procedure?'

'Procedure, this.' Hazel Carstairs made a rude gesture and Indy had to smother a grin. 'Tell you somefin', Dr B. I got an appointment at the vet's in an hour.'

'Are the pups okay?'

'They're fine.' She knelt down and rubbed each one behind the ears. 'It's cos I'm getting 'em the health certificate wot lets 'em travel. Got ten days to use it after it's issued. Either the razz solves this before then and Bob's your uncle. Or we're goin' anyway.'

Indy was about to remind her that however polite the

detectives' request had been, it wasn't a good idea to ignore it.

'This place, Dr B. It ain't safe.' Still on one knee, Mrs C looked up at Indy. 'I found two bodies in a coupla days. Police want me to stick around, and maybe the killer does too. Why? Well, not because I farkin' did anyfin' other'n have bad luck.'

'Do you know who it is, Mrs Carstairs? Who might want to harm you?'

The older woman scowled, hard enough to hurt. 'If I did, I'd farkin' sort 'em out, razz or no. People like that, they ain't normal.' She paused. 'Look, I got two dogs. They mean more to me 'n just about anyfin'. I'd take a bullet for 'em. Either of 'em. But what d'you think'd happen to 'em if anyfin' happened to me? No one loves 'em the way I do. My kids? You think they'd take care of 'em? Hell, they'd put 'em in a shelter as soon as I was in the ground. Me, I can't risk that.

'You got dogs too, Dr B,' she said, her eyes sharp, and a little desperate. 'Would you take that risk? Or would you do what you could to keep you an' your family safe?'

64

MEG

Partridge Bark

> Who do you think the puppy daddy is then, @Yaz? Not saying there aren't a lot of unspayed dogs around here (T was done at 18 months, before you ask), but Shih Tzu Sue seemed pretty on the ball. Who could have gotten there before she could stop them?

Yaz (Hercules's Mum)

The million-pound (or 3-pup) question!

Fiona (Nala's Mum)

Do you have an answer?

Yaz (Hercules's Mum)

An answer? No. A theory? Maybe. But let me check one or two things. Don't want to rat out someone who, well, isn't a rat. This time.

Meg sat at home in her onesie, Tyrion on her lap. Her boss insisted she take the day off, but she needed a distraction. They compromised on her working from home, although her concentration wasn't what it should be.

'Tea?' Ethan sat at her kitchen table, his laptop open in front of him. His hair was standing on end and he looked tired. No – worried. Both of them had been up late last night, unable to sleep. He'd gone home early this morning to feed his cat Marlowe, returning an hour later with two coffees and a bag of pastries from The Nest.

'I'm okay,' Meg said, her voice listless, even to her own ears.

His eyes made it clear he didn't believe her, but how could she explain it? She started taking the kickboxing classes because as a youngish woman, barely over five feet, she didn't want to be easy prey for some opportunistic thug.

She'd worked hard. Learned what that first instructor had to teach and continued on with her training. But what would it take to be good enough to not only sense when she was being watched, but to deflect, or at least evade, a bullet screaming at you? This wasn't a game, and she wasn't a ninja.

Ethan cleared his throat. 'Detective Thompson asked if you had any ideas about who might want to hurt you. Did anything come to mind?'

'No,' she snapped. 'Same as I told Andy last night.' Knowing how bitchy she sounded, she softened her tone. 'Ethan, you know me. I try to be friends with everyone. If I have any faults, it's trusting people too much.' She raised one shoulder in a haphazard shrug. 'It's what's landed poor Lou in trouble more than once.'

'Pretty sure Louise isn't holding that grudge against you.'

'Yeah, I know. I won't say she'd take a bullet for me, but she *would* take a metal rail and swing it like a baseball bat at the back of my attacker's head.'

He smiled. 'She's pretty fierce.'

Meg returned his grin. 'She can be.'

'There are a lot of people who have your back, Meg.' Ethan looked down and then up again, his blue eyes clear.

'The police. Your Pack. Louise.' *Me*. He didn't say the word, but it hung in the air nonetheless.

'I know,' she said, reaching out for his hand. 'And, if I don't say it enough, I really am grateful.'

He nodded, looking like he wanted to say something else but was holding back.

'What is it, Ethan?'

'I can't help thinking that detective was right, Megs. I don't think it'd be an ex out to get you, but maybe ... someone you know?' He deliberately echoed her words: 'Because you know everyone. Because you're friends with everyone. Maybe someone thinks you know something?' He tilted his head from side to side. 'And maybe you do, even if you haven't realised it yet.'

65

LOUISE

Partridge Bark

Meg (Tyrion's Mum)

Hi @Indira, how's Banjo's kennel cough doing?

Indira (Banjo's Mum)

He's taking the meds – which he hates. He's figured out the pill-in-cream-cheese trick. He even looks suspiciously at peanut butter. I think he's doing a little better each day but I'm still trying to keep him away from the other pups. It's bad enough that he's going through it – I wouldn't want to pass it on to any of the others! So, another few days of lurking around the grim squares.

Indira (Banjo's Mum)

How are you doing, @**Meg**? Pretty 💩 experience you've had. Have the police got any leads?

Meg (Tyrion's Mum)

Yeah, I'm fine. It could have been worse. @**Ethan** and Tyrion are taking good care of me. Keeping busy trying to figure out who it might be.

The Sipping Room was alight with festive cheer, from the fairytale snow globes out in front, to the decorated boughs and Christmas tree inside. We'd taken over the left half of the pub for the night. I'd offered the team three choices for our annual party: a swish cocktail bar with magnificent views, an escape room type of event or a more laid-back thing at one of our favourite haunts. Same budget, but whatever wasn't used on the venue would go behind the bar.

Babs caught my eye and winked. She was elegantly dressed in a cobalt sheath dress, her dark hair loose around her shoulders. Her trademark blazer had been left at home for a change; tonight she was going for the 'professional but approachable' look. I, on the other hand, had taken advantage of the opportunity to go out without the risk of being decorated with pawprints and black fur and wore a wide-leg cream wool trouser suit with a pair of high heels. The elegant Bardot-cut jacket was now slightly obfuscated by a strand of red tinsel that a tipsy intern had draped around my neck.

'You okay with this? I was worried you'd have preferred the more cerebral escape room thing,' Babs said, trying to read my mind.

'Not this time,' I admitted. 'I want to just relax tonight.'

'How about that.' She said the words deadpan, and set her glass of wine on the table between us. 'Want to talk about it?'

I smiled. 'After. I've got a speech to do first.'

I clinked a fork from one of the nibbles platters against my glass. When the noise had settled down, I took a deep breath and began.

'You didn't come here to hear me witter on, so I'll keep this short. First, I wanted to thank you all. This hasn't been an easy year. There've been difficult projects, difficult clients, and a challenging economic climate to boot. And yet, working together, we've succeeded, and I couldn't be prouder.'

'Hear, hear!' someone shouted, and applause followed.

When it died down, I continued. 'I started this company in 2018 with two friends. One left within six months—' There were a lot of boos and I held up my hands. 'No, no disrespect to Ryan. He was expecting a kid. He needed more stability than a startup could provide. But then there was the pandemic, and Stubby left.'

'Bought out!' someone said.

I laughed. 'You bet. He thought the pandemic would beat us.'

'Sucka!' was the response.

I gestured to the maître d', and a pair of servers came out with trays of champagne.

'So, you've been stuck with me since then. Thing is, when you start a company, you need a different skillset from when you're running it. I had an idea, a methodology, a vision – but over the last year, it was Barbara Lane who executed it. So, please join me in raising a glass to Babs.'

I took a sip and waited for the cheers to subside. When the room was quiet again, I took a beat and swept my gaze around the room, trying to meet everyone's eyes. 'The next step isn't the end of an era, it's building on one that's already in motion. While I'll remain chairman and chief exec, I am delighted to let you know that Babs will be stepping up as Managing Director, the new boss hoss.'

Babs's face sagged with surprise, and then lit up as the room erupted around her. She closed the gap between us and wrapped me in a tight embrace. 'Thank you, Lou. I – I don't know what to say. But thank you.'

It was a good thing she didn't expect a response; I wasn't sure I'd be able to speak around the lump in my throat. I hugged her back, certain this had been the right decision.

66

ADRIAN

The Nest's lights blazed and their Christmas music carried on the cold night. Adrian stepped back from the window and rubbed her hands along her thin arms. It was safest to stay here. Not least because it's what her foster father ordered. But she felt a sense of inevitability. Maybe futility.

And claustrophobia. She was trapped. If Danny got in – and he could, she had no doubt – she'd have nowhere to hide. No way to escape. No one who would protect her. Outside, maybe she could outrun him.

Maybe there were people out there who could help. There were the Others. The people who knew Eddie, owed him in some way. Maybe they'd help, but these things were sometimes transactional.

Inside, she was like a rat in a trap. Not the kind that snapped closed on its victim's neck, killing them, but the kind that people called 'humane', even though it took away that most basic of rights: freedom.

Tonight everyone would be at The Nest. Maybe Danny would be there too. It was cold outside. At five degrees below zero, if people were going out, it would be straight from one warm place to another.

Adrian didn't *need* to go outside. Didn't *need* to go anywhere. But she craved fresh air; itched for the chance to stretch her legs.

One lap around the park, that's all she needed. She reached for her sweatshirt and parka. Her foster parents were in the front room watching some crappy Christmas game show. They wouldn't hear her, wouldn't notice she'd gone.

She'd be back in fifteen minutes. Tops. No harm, no foul, right?

67

LOUISE

Partridge Bark

Fiona (Nala's Mum)

Any update on Shih Tzu Gate, @Yaz?

Yaz (Hercules's Mum)

Well, the puppies are super cute!

Claire (Tank's Mum)

She invited you in? She wouldn't even talk to me!

Yaz (Hercules's Mum)

Don't be daft. I went and knocked on the door. Told her I'd heard about the puppies and wanted to drop off some stuff for them.

Meg (Tyrion's Mum)

I thought you gave Herc's old stuff to the shelter?

Yaz (Hercules's Mum)

Yeah, so? I didn't say that it was Herc's stuff. Even when he was a pup, his stuff would've been too big. I stopped off at the pet shop this afternoon.

Babs sat beside me, toed off her high heels and clinked her glass against mine. 'Thank you again, Lou. I genuinely didn't see this coming tonight.'

'It's well deserved, and maybe a little overdue. You've done a brilliant job.'

Her head tilted, but her sharp eyes remained on me. 'You sure you're okay with this?'

'If I wasn't, I wouldn't have done it.'

'Then something else is on your mind. Want to talk about it?'

I waved her concern away. 'Neighbourhood stuff.'

'Want some advice?' she offered.

'From you? Always.'

She pursed her lips and nodded. 'Good. Then, Lou: you overthink things. The simplest explanation is usually the right one.' Her expression softened. 'I'm kind of surprised not to see Klaus tonight. The Sipping Room is super dog-friendly. That's why we chose it.'

I shook my head. 'The Christmas party should be about the team, and about you. Not about my dachshund.'

She grinned back. 'Fair. But let's take him out on an evening soon. Who's he with tonight?'

'Jake.'

'Ooooh. Give Klaus a kiss from Auntie Babs. And give Jake a— ' She made a raunchy sound and I laughed.

'Well, not sure about that. He's a good friend, and I'm okay with that.'

'Sure you are.' She winked.

'But on that happy note . . .' I stood up and placed my empty glass on a table. 'I'm going to head out.' I cracked a smile. 'Lest I show up pissed. It's never a good look.'

And, quite honestly, I didn't trust myself around Jake after I drank too much. The last time, I'd lunged at him, only to be gently knocked back. Proverbially, that is.

As I walked away, Babs called me back. 'Lou?'

'Yeah?'

'If he invites you in for a drink, take him up on it. You deserve a little joy in your life.' She gave me an empathetic look. 'And if you want one last piece of advice, there's nothing wrong with showing a little vulnerability once in a while. You don't need to be superwoman *all* the time, you know.'

68

LOUISE

Jake (Luther's Dad)

> Just about to get off the DLR. Should be at yours in about 10.

You didn't need to rush – we're fine. Good time?

> Yeah, it was good. K's behaved?

As always. C U soon.

By the time I got off the DLR, I regretted not wearing more comfortable shoes. For heaven's sake, I had Klaus's ball in one pocket along with his treats and a spare poo bag.

'Bloody hell, I pack better for Klaus, even when he's staying at home,' I said aloud. 'The least I could have packed was a pair of flats.'

'Not sure what's more bonkers, you talking to yourself, or wearing cream trousers.'

The voice, unexpected, surprised me and I whirled around, one hand clenching Klaus's ball. It took a moment to register the slim Asian woman standing in front of me, her long hair swept back with a faux-fur headband. She smiled, but the black-and-white mixed-breed at her feet watched me with serious eyes. 'Jesus, Indy,' I gasped. 'Gotta say, I've gotten used to Klaus not letting anyone get close.'

'I was wondering about that. I didn't think you'd wear pale colours with him about.'

'Absolutely not. They'd be covered in pawprints in seconds.' I reached into my pocket and offered one of Klaus's treats to Banjo. When he wouldn't take it, I put it on the ground in front of him. Banjo had been rescued from a Romanian shelter and he was still learning to trust. His progress was slow, but steady.

He inhaled the treat and sat down, tail wagging. He licked his lips, politely asking for a second one, which I duly provided. 'I can't resist.'

'He knows that.' Indira smiled. 'He totally knows how to play us.'

'Let him.'

We watched Banjo eat the second treat and sniff around for more. He was about to sit down again to repeat his beg, when Indy gave a gentle tug on his lead. 'Stop trying to fleece Auntie Lou out of Klaus's goodies.' She was still in her scrubs, with a heavy parka zipped over them. 'Where are you heading?'

'Home, by way of Jake's, to pick up Klaus.'

She eyed my feet dubiously. 'If your shoe situation will permit it, I'd be happy for the company. I'm used to talking to someone else on the late-night Pack walk, but with Banjo's kennel cough . . .'

I nodded and fell into step with her. 'He's sounding okay right now.'

'Definitely better. Chances are that he's no longer infectious, but the vet said another day or two in isolation as a precaution. Lou, it's doing my head in.'

'I get that.'

'Anyway, catch me up. Have we figured out who killed those two men?'

'Nope. Not yet.'

We walked along the High Street, Banjo occasionally trying to pull us down one of the side streets. 'Do we think it's the same person who attacked Meg?'

I shrugged, digging my hands deeper into my pockets, wishing I'd grabbed my defence spray instead of Klaus's treat bag. 'No idea.'

'Damn.' Indy turned her attention to Banjo. 'What's with you? You *never* like going down the alleys!'

'Cluckin' Good Chicken's up ahead. He probably smells the fried food.'

'Well, he's not going to get it.'

Debatable. Banjo was straining against his harness. I'd never walked him myself, but had the impression he was usually quite mellow with the lead.

'I ran into Mrs Carstairs this morning,' she said, trying to maintain a conversation when her dog had other ideas.

I pretended not to notice. 'Poor woman. Seeing one dead body in a week is bad enough, but two? Did you get any sense that she was talking to a professional?'

'Yeah, I've suggested that to her. She thinks sun therapy would work better. Doesn't want to find another body, and doesn't want to become the next one. I've got to say: I don't blame her.'

'Nor do I. She's taking the Yorkies with her?'

'Like she'd leave them behind? Seems she's taken them with her to Spain before, so their rabies jabs are up to date. She just had to get the Health Cert.' She moved Banjo's lead to the other hand. 'What's your body count at the moment?'

'Two, spaced about six months apart. And before you ask, that's two too many.'

Banjo started whining, a high-pitched keening sound. His nails scraped on the pavement. 'Do you mind?' Indy asked me.

I would have loved to continue home, but I didn't want to walk alone, any more than I wanted her to.

As I hesitated, a scream cut through the night.

We looked at each other, and without a word, let Banjo show us where we needed to go.

69

CLAIRE

Jeremy Silva

> Hey Jeremy. Good to catch up with you this morning and looking forward to seeing you again soon. Just so there are no secrets between us, I went to the vigil in Partridge Park last night. Partly out of respect, and partly because I wanted to see what Eddie's family is like. What your family is like. I know that sounds stalkery,

> but I'm not like that. It's just that I'm working with my friends to try to get justice for him. Not because I'm a journalist and out for the story, because that's not the way I work, but because I believe no one deserves to be murdered like that. Just wanted you to know.

Claire stared at the message, knowing she should send it, but couldn't bring herself to. Not yet. Maybe once the case was closed and the killer was behind bars she could tell him. Maybe he wouldn't hate her so much after she found justice for his cousin. The cousin that he didn't much care for.

She deleted the message without sending it. Went to the window and stared out across the High Street, over The Bells, to the other side of the canal.

Her phone pinged, jerking her from her reverie.

Fiona (Nala's Mum)

> Hey darl, sorry I didn't check in earlier. How'd the

coffee date go? You tell him?

> It was good, but no. Not yet.

Your call. You bringing him to The Hound for the Pack do tomorrow?

> No. Not sure we're at a point where I'm ready to introduce him to you lot. Or that it'd be the best place to take him when everyone'll be talking about his cousin.

Fair point. You can tell me all the details when I see you then. Without blushing every time he looks your way.

> I don't!

No, Claire. You blush every time you TALK about him . . . 😊

Claire sank onto the floor beside the dog bed. Tank looked at her curiously and gave her a sloppy kiss. 'I love you too,' she said and pulled him into her arms.

Holding his warm body tight, she stared out the window at The Bells. The Christmas lights were on, but the pub remained closed while the police continued their investigation into Pete's death.

'There's got to be something else we can do to chivvy this along,' she said.

70

LOUISE

Jake (Luther's Dad)

> askfdjjd

I jammed my phone into my coat pocket and slung the strap of my evening bag over my head and across my chest as I ran, struggling to keep up with Indy and Banjo. The little rescue mutt, who usually tried to make himself invisible, raced forward, barking his head off.

The lighting was poor, the street lamps long since broken and never replaced. What little light there was came from the moon, Christmas decorations and other people's windows.

We approached a small patch of green. On our left was

the back of Claire's building, and on the far side was its small car park.

Suddenly I could see them – two people struggling with each other. A big man and a smaller figure, maybe a woman.

'Hey!' Indy shouted to be heard over her dog's howling. 'You there!'

The bigger figure froze, then began to run, heading towards the far side of the square. The smaller one took a few steps, only to sink to the ground.

'I've got the girl,' Indy said. 'Go after the guy!'

I sprinted, even knowing there was no way I could outrun him. I caught a glimpse of a tight ponytail over a shaved undercut but he was moving too fast to see anything more.

I wasn't an athlete. Never had been. As a kid I played sports, because in Connecticut that was more or less expected. I'd been assigned a role based on what I wasn't rather than what I was. For soccer, I was fast, but not fast enough to be a striker. Had a decent kick but not big enough to be a defender. So midfield it was.

For softball, I had a good throwing arm, but no concentration, so was relegated to the outfield, with instructions to stop daydreaming. There was never any point in confessing that it was a lack of interest more than any lack of skill.

My right hand closed around Klaus's little orange ball. It was the hard one, not the soft squeaky one. I hadn't thrown a ball with any seriousness in years – tossing it for Klaus didn't count – but the muscle memory remained.

Aim for his torso, I told myself. *It's the biggest target.*

I threw the ball, hoping for the best, and stopped, wheezing. The ball moved straight and true, as if launched from an RPG. Only, it didn't hit the man's torso, it hit the back of his head.

Better, I thought. *If it hit his back, it'd only bounce off his puffer jacket.*

He stumbled, righted himself, and powered forward, arms and legs pumping.

Shit. I began to run after him. He'd exited the little square, and by the time I got there, he was gone. What I was looking for was the orange ball.

It took a few minutes, but it was there, half hidden by a denuded bush. I scooped it up in the poo bag, stuffed it into my pocket and retraced my footsteps.

'Here,' Indy called. 'She's bleeding. I've packed the wound and called an Uber. I don't want to wait for an ambulance to take her to A&E. Really sorry to ask this, but can you take Banjo home? I think he's past being contagious?'

Banjo's ears twitched at his name, but he remained on the ground, pressed against the girl, her fingers tangled in his fur.

'Don't worry. Do what you need to do.' I got to my knees, to help Indy get the girl to her feet. Her head hung limp, her hair falling across her face, one arm clutched across her waist.

'Are you sure you don't want me to go with you?'

'No.' Her face caught a rare bit of light, looking strained in a way it hadn't ten minutes ago. 'It's all right, Addie.

Walk with me,' she told the girl. 'We're safe. We're getting you help.' It was spoken like a litany, as if Indy was trying to convince herself as well as the girl. She caught my eye. 'I'd tell you to take Banjo back to mine...'

'No,' the girl whispered.

'He can't come with us to the hospital,' Indy explained gently. 'He'd be okay at home, he doesn't mind being by himself, but I'd rather Louise not walk around outside any more than she needs to. Not with that man out on the streets.'

'He can stay at mine,' I said. 'Klaus and Luther have both been vaccinated against kennel cough.' I slipped the loop of Banjo's lead over my wrist, noting how close he stayed to the injured girl. As if he knew that she needed his presence.

'Dogs always know who's a good person,' the girl murmured.

'That's right,' I said. 'And you can trust Indira. Banjo does.'

She nodded and, careful of her wound, we half carried, half dragged to the girl back to the High Street, where the Uber was waiting.

Indira (Banjo's Mum)

> I'll let the police know what happened. Maybe they can find something on CCTV.

> Poor girl. How is she?

She was stabbed. The jacket took most of the brunt of it, I think. Maybe. I've packed the wound with a sanitary napkin and my scarf but I can't see how bad it is and don't want to do anything in the back of an Uber.

> How far away from A&E are you?

Couple of min. You home yet?

> Almost at Jake's.

K. Text me when you're home.

> 👍 Let me know how you get on. How the girl is.

👍 Thx.

I tapped out Jake's apartment code and he buzzed me into the complex, then again, a minute later, into his building.

Unlike mine, his block didn't have a lift, so Banjo and I trudged up several flights of stairs. I felt drained, but on the plus side, Banjo wasn't a dachshund and could do the stairs on his own.

Before I could knock on Jake's door, I heard the barkpocalypse that was Klaus's joy at my return. The door opened and he shot out as if from a cannon, pausing only when Banjo barked in his face, stepping between us to protect me. Then Banjo shook himself, maybe registering that Klaus was my boy, and was allowed to jump on me. He stood back, still cautious but at least silent.

Jake's expression was thunderous. 'Are you okay?' I asked.

'You tell me you're ten minutes out, then you butt message me, then you show up looking like you were dragged backwards through a hedge.'

My cream suit had survived the company Christmas party, only to be massacred on the walk home. My shoes were caked with mud. My trousers were ripped and looked like they'd been painted in layers of brown and red. I tried not to think too hard about what the red meant, but knew the trousers would end the night in the bin.

Jake stared at the remnants of my once-smart attire. 'You do know that's not your dog, right?'

I blinked. 'Banjo? I know.'

'Want to come in and tell me what happened?' It was phrased like a question, but Jake's intonation, and his dark blue eyes, were steely. He pushed the door wider, to allow us to enter.

'Sure.' I could hear Babs's words, reminding me that it was okay to show a bit of vulnerability once in a while. I sighed. 'I don't suppose you've got a spare glass of wine going? It's been a hell of a night.'

71

LOUISE

Indira (Banjo's Mum)

> She was triaged as soon as we got her admitted. Stab wounds to her side and right forearm. She lost a lot of blood but thankfully it looks like the knife missed her vitals. The ER doc says we got her here in time.

> Well done, Indy. Thank you for doing that for her.

> Thanks for your help. How's Banjo?

Sleeping by the door.

> Yeah, he likes that. Mind keeping him a little longer, maybe overnight? I'd like to stay here a bit longer.

Not a problem. But once you speak to the cops, let them know I may have a possible sample of the assailant's DNA. Can you let Andy know the case number once you have it? I'll message him now and let him know what happened.

> Why? It wasn't murder. Assault maybe?

Close enough in my book. Be safe, and let me know when you're home.

There was no point in telling Indy that I hadn't made it back home yet; that I was still at Jake's flat. My nerves had begun to dissipate with my third sip of Malbec. My trousers, on the other hand, had given up the ghost and had been replaced by a pair of Jake's sweatpants.

A point I was trying hard not to fixate on.

Klaus had returned to Luther's bed by the balcony, his usual spot when we were here. Banjo, as I'd told his mum, was curled by the door, protecting the flat from any intruders. If Jake thought it was odd, he didn't say anything.

At least, about that.

'So, you don't know who the attacker was, or who the girl was, but you and Indira decided to put yourselves in the middle of it?'

'Yep,' I said, huddled on his couch, my glass of red cupped in my hands.

He scowled at me. 'And with everything going on, you thought that was a good idea?'

'The girl was attacked, Jake. Stabbed. You can't really have expected us to leave her there to bleed out?'

'No. I would have expected you to call the cops though.'

The cops. Oh hell, I'd almost forgotten. I reached for my phone.

Detective Andrew Thompson

> Hi Andy, sorry to text so late on a Friday night. Indy and I interrupted an attack

> this evening, in the green area behind the CGC building. A man stabbed a young woman.

R u OK?

> Yeah, I'm fine. Indy took the girl to A&E. Got her checked in.

You made a police report?

> Indy will. But I might have a sample of his DNA.

Explain.

> He was running away and I couldn't keep up. I had one of Klaus's balls in my pocket, and threw it at him.

And?

> Well, it hit him. So, I'm guessing epithelials. It

> didn't stop him, but I'm guessing that if you find whoever it was, he'll have a bump the size of a goose egg on the back of his head.

'You know what?' Jake said, reading the messages from over my shoulder. 'You're a right piece of work, Marple.'

'Thank you.'

'You do know that every dog in the park has stolen Klaus's ball at one time or another?'

'Technically, he allows them to steal it so he can chase them and then ninja them to get it back. But between that and the usual park sludge, I wash it every time I get home. But good to point that out. Thanks.'

Detective Andrew Thompson

> Indy will send you the case number. When your guys test the ball for trace they should know that I wash it every time we come home, so there'll be my prints and my DNA there too, maybe a bit of

> pocket lint, but anything else should be his.

It's a bit more complicated than that.

> Is it? Well, I picked it up in a clean poo bag, just to be on the safe side.

Of course you did.

> Let me know when you, or one of your guys, can pick it up. It doesn't need to be tonight, tomorrow morning is fine. I know there's a lot on your plate, and this isn't a murder — or rather, it wasn't because we got there. You can thank me later. 😊

You know, you're beginning to sound like your Russian friend.

> Am I? I'll take that as a compliment. 🤣

'I don't think he meant that as a compliment,' Jake drawled, pausing with the red wine bottle hovering over my glass. '*She* can drink like a sailor. You . . . ?'

I took the bottle out of his hand and refilled my glass. 'I get squiffy and make bad choices. I know, I know. And right now? I don't care.'

'Not all the choices are that bad,' he said, replacing the bottle on the counter and dropping onto the sofa beside me. 'Just most of them.'

The kiss? Is he really talking about the time I drank too much and tried to snog him?

I stared at him. At his mouth. *Oh my God.*

'Your phone's buzzing,' he pointed out.

Did he want me to lunge at him again?

Could I cope if he knocked me back again?

'Marple?'

'What?'

'Your phone.' He held it out to me.

Oh.

Indira (Banjo's Mum)

> I'm taking a car home. They've done what they can and are keeping her in overnight. The police told me they'll interview her tomorrow morning.

> Any protection in case the guy decides to come back and finish the job?

> You watch too many crime shows, Lou.

> Yeah, probably. Anyway, you did a good thing tonight. I'll text you tomorrow when we get up. We'll head towards Partridge.

> Great – breakfast on me at The Nest. I'll bring Banjo's with me.

Jake and I finished our drinks in an awkward silence. When I drained my glass and stood to leave, he reached for his leather bomber jacket. 'It's late, and you've had a long day,' he declared. 'I'll walk you home.'

'You don't have to. I live just across the canal.'

'And tonight you were just going to your company's Christmas party. Marple, you could get into trouble on your way from your couch to your loo, and I'd rather nothing else happened tonight.'

I nodded, grateful for his company, although less

grateful for what could have been a missed opportunity to make another pass at him. Even though it would have probably ended just as badly as the last time.

As we entered the hall I caught sight of myself in a mirror and shook my head. My cream-coloured coat looked ridiculous over black tracksuit bottoms and high heels and my makeup, immaculate when I'd left home, now seemed like it had been applied by Harley Quinn.

I shrugged into my coat, picked Klaus up and followed Jake's broad shoulders down the stairs. If I had any chance of getting anywhere with him, I'd really have to up my game. This Damsel in Distress thing was getting old. Fast.

72

ADRIAN

Adrian looked around. The hospital lights were bright, the beeping from the machines unnaturally loud. As grateful as she was that the women had found her, she knew that Danny wasn't done. That he'd only try another day.

The doctors had patched her up. Stitched her arm and her side while telling her that she was lucky, that his blade had caught on her jacket and missed her vitals.

They'd hooked her up, given her blood 'to replace what she'd lost'. How could she tell them that they could *never* replace everything she'd lost?

A female police officer came in to talk to her, but she turned away and pretended to sleep. No point in telling them about Danny; they wouldn't believe her.

No one did.

73

LOUISE

Partridge Bark

Paul (Jimmy Chew and Bark Vader's Dad)

> The party at The Nest was shut down an hour ago but there are still drunk people shouting in the park.

Yaz (Hercules's Mum)

> @Paul – there are *always* drunk people shouting in the park. And shooting off fireworks.

Ella (Jimmy Chew and Bark Vader's Mum)

Non-stop. And I think someone vomited on the street under our balcony.

Paul (Jimmy Chew and Bark Vader's Dad)

By the front door. More for the foxes and rodents to eat.

Meg (Tyrion's Mum)

And dogs, **@Paul**. Some dogs go for that as well. 🤢

It was only a stone's throw from Jake's gate to mine. Technically we were part of the same complex, but it was bisected by the canal, so you had to go out to come back in. As soon as we got outside, Banjo lifted his leg on the side of the building. Klaus, not one to miss an opportunity, circled behind his friend to wee in the same spot.

'Nice try, but not much vertical lift, mate,' Jake told him.

'Smaller radial,' I agreed. 'Doesn't stop him from trying though.'

Once the immediate needs were taken care of, both

dogs began holding back, clear they didn't want to move towards the gate.

'I know Klaus can be stubborn, but Banjo too?' Jake said.

'Klaus doesn't like the cold. And he didn't want to leave Luther, I think,' I said, not blaming him. 'As for Banjo? I don't know. Maybe he's doing the simpatico thing with Klaus.'

My hound had put the full brakes on now, refusing to go any further. 'Although usually Klaus is keen to go home.'

I scooped him up, and he burrowed closer in my arms. He rested his head on my shoulder, but his eyes were alert, as they always were when we left the flat.

We waited while Jake searched for something in his pocket. Banjo wasn't huge, maybe a little more than ten kilos. Jake could have picked him up as well but instead dangled a chew in front of him. Whatever it was, it was interesting enough to get him to start moving. 'Bribery works,' Jake said, flashing a grin at me over his shoulder as he pushed open the gate. Bribery, and understanding that Banjo had trust issues and that picking him up would have made things worse.

We were far enough from Partridge Park that we couldn't hear any shouting, but a firework went up further along the canal and Banjo dropped close to the ground, whimpering.

'Poor thing, he's afraid of fireworks.'

'Let's move quickly. I don't think he'll relax until he's back indoors.'

We were crossing the bridge, when I heard the faintest

whistle. Banjo reacted, jerking Jake sideways. Something passed over my head and struck a ground-floor window, cracking the glass. 'Jesus,' I whispered, staring at it when Jake's body slammed into mine. I fell, throwing one arm out to break my fall, the other holding Klaus tight to my chest to protect him.

'Keep down,' Jake hissed in my ear. The slight burr in his voice broadened with each word, an audible barometer of his stress. His right arm was over my back, the left was wound around Banjo, keeping the small dog close to his side. 'Someone's shooting at us.'

I froze, unable to process what he was saying.

Jake's head moved, scanning the area. 'I can't see whoever it is, so listen to me carefully: we're going to stay close to the ground, all four of us. While we're on the bridge we've got little protection. Once we're on the other side, we can stay close to the bushes.'

'It passed over my head. I guess we have to keep hoping he's a bad shot,' I tried to joke.

'He wasn't aiming at you,' Jake said, inching us forward. 'He was trying to take me out. Would have hit me if Banjo hadn't jerked me to the side. I owe him.'

We crossed the canal, every inch hard won. A second missile pinged in front of us, bouncing off the pavement into the brush.

'Slingshot,' Jake whispered, his voice grim. '*Keep your head down.*'

Another projectile shot past, brushing past my back. I whimpered, hating the sound, and Jake cursed. 'Give me your fob,' he said, steering us closer to the gate.

I reached into my pocket and passed it over. He rose just enough to tap it on the reader, pushing at the heavy iron gate before it clicked open. We scrambled inside, letting it close with a satisfying clunk behind us.

Jake handed me the fob and Banjo's lead. 'Get inside.'

'Not without you.'

'I'll be up in a sec. Just want to see if I can find him.'

'Don't be stupid, Jake. You're not friggin' Superman. That man is *shooting* at us. At you!'

'I know. That's why I want to know who it is.' He gave me a gentle shove. 'I'll be right behind you.'

I opened the main door, moving the dogs far enough inside that they were out of view, but close enough that I could see Jake when he approached. Did a quick triage to make sure both of them were okay. No blood, no bumps, thank God.

I mentally scanned myself next. Scraped knees from where I'd fallen – I'd managed to mangle Jake's sweatpants as well as my own trousers – and my right elbow hurt, but didn't seem broken.

It could have been worse; much, much worse.

Jake arrived a few moments later, out of breath. 'Come on, let's get upstairs.'

I nodded, allowing Klaus to lead the way to the lift. Once at my flat, I turned off my intruder alert and opened the door. Took off my shoes and did a second check of each dog. Still sitting on the floor, I watched Jake shrug off his jacket.

'Did you find him?'

'No.' His left hand was idly rubbing his right arm.

'Are you okay?'

He looked at me, his dark blue eyes confused.

'Your arm.' I pulled him further into the flat and reached for his arm. There were no holes in the sleeve that I could see, and no blood underneath. But when I touched a spot on his bicep, he flinched. 'I think he hit you.'

'Must've bounced off.'

'Jesus, Jake. Maybe you really are the Man of Steel.' I shooed man and dogs into the kitchen. Filled the water bowl for the hounds and gestured for Jake to roll up his sleeve so I could get a better look. He held up a finger and pulled out his phone, dialled 999 and asked to be put through to the police.

While I waited for him, I took out my phone for my own police report.

Detective Andrew Thompson

> Hi Andy, me again. Sorry to keep bothering you.

> You know what time it is?

> Late. But someone with a slingshot came after Jake and me tonight. We're OK, but TBH I'm pretty shaken. Jake's phoning the police now. Can't help

> but wonder if it's the same guy who went for Meg.

> Glad you're OK. Make sure you give the police a statement and let them know I'll interview you tomorrow, so you can get to sleep tonight. I'll make sure they have the area cordoned off and check for any evidence. I can swing by The Nest first thing tomorrow. Pick up the ball and take your statement. Will that work?

> That's perfect. Thank you.

> See if you can get some rest tonight.

That done, I poured water into the kettle and waited for Jake to finish his call. Then I grabbed his arm. Tried to fight down the chills when I pushed up his sleeve to see the dark swelling as a bruise began to form. 'Do you think it's broken?'

'No.' He stepped away and yanked his sleeve back into place.

'Okay, you didn't answer my question. What are the chances it's the same guy who shot at Meg?' I asked, ignoring the boiling kettle.

Jake took a deep breath. 'Look, I don't like saying this, but with everything that's going on, I think you two have got someone seriously spooked. Bad enough that they want to take you out of commission.'

Permanently. He omitted the word, but my nerves didn't.

'Make that pot of coffee, Lou. I think we'll be up for a while.'

I nodded, and took the grinds out of the cupboard.

'And once you do that, I need you to walk me through what you and the Pack have worked out so far. Because whoever's doing this thinks you've got something, and if we know what it is, we might be able to figure out who they are.'

74

LOUISE

Claire (Tank's Mum)

Lots going on that I need to catch you up on. Give a shout when you're up tomorrow.

Jake and I stood in my home office, in front of the large map of the area. I'd added two yellow stars, one for where Meg was attacked and one for where we were. Banjo was still curled up in the entranceway, but Klaus lay in his dog bed by the window, watching us with tired eyes. It was his version of solidarity: if I was awake and stressed, he should be too.

Or maybe it was FOMO.

'What bothers me is that whoever it is knows you. Knows your schedules. He knew to wait for Meg after her class.'

'Everyone knows about Meg's Thursday kickboxing.'

'But he knew where it was. He knew about the trips to the shelter when you were all going, and that you'd be out tonight.' Jake leaned back against the exposed brick of the opposite wall, looking edgy and far too attractive. His usual five o'clock shadow had deepened to eight o'clock, and I was discovering that when he was tired his eyes had a *come-to-bed* sort of look about them.

I held the mug between my hands, trying to rein in my thoughts. I cleared my throat and answered, 'What are you saying? That whoever's shooting at us is part of the Pack?' Alarm spiked through me.

'No. At least, probably not. But if he isn't, maybe he knows someone who is. Someone who's sharing information with him.'

I wasn't sure how much better that was. Who would . . . ?

Jake. Jake was asking questions. He couldn't have been the shooter tonight, but maybe he was working with them?

No chance, my gut guffawed. *You've got to be really knackered to clutch at that straw. He wouldn't have saved you if he wanted you dead.*

He continued, 'He knew where to find you tonight. Under normal circumstances would you have been dragging in this late?'

'No. I didn't even know where I was going to be, so I don't know how he could have. I mean, I didn't know what time I'd leave the Christmas party. Or that I'd end up with Indira and Banjo in that little square.'

'He knew you'd be out,' Jake continued. 'Maybe even knew you'd be coming to mine to pick up Klaus, or at least, that you'd be coming from the DLR. He might have been watching your route.'

'It's minus five degrees outside tonight. Do you really think he'd have been sitting out in the cold for hours, waiting for me to come past? And let's not forget, it was you he was shooting at.'

He shook his head again. 'He wanted me out of the way because I was the bigger threat. Without me, you'd have been an easy . . .' He cleared this throat. 'Eas*ier* target.'

That made a sick sort of sense, but my stomach clenched at the thought that I'd put him in danger. Not just him, but him, Banjo and *Klaus*. I glanced at Klaus again, just to convince myself that he was all right. My throat clenched, and I had to force the words out. 'Okay. Let's assume Meg and I are the targets. Maybe Claire too.' My voice rose with each word, and I could feel panic begin to take hold.

'Step by step, Lou.' Jake's low voice, that soft burr, was like a salve. It didn't fix the problem, but his steadfast common sense made it less frightening. 'Let's clarify: whose killer?'

'We've been looking into Eddie Morley and Pete the Pusher.' I pointed first to the two blue stars on the map, and then to a green one a little further away. 'But there might be a third murder. Laura Rossi.'

'I don't remember hearing about her. What happened?'

'Exactly? I don't know. But we saw an article in the news about her body being found in Victoria Park. Usually, I'd say it was far enough from Partridge not to be linked, but Fi reminded me that we were originally going to do the sniffer dog training there a week earlier, which would have been when and where her body was found.'

'Okay,' Jake said, watching me carefully. 'How is she connected to Eddie and Pete?'

'Well, two of them were homeless with a troubled past and a history of drug abuse. The other was a dealer.'

'Okay, maybe we can connect the two homeless people, although during winter, in inner city London, that's a reach. We can connect the men by their proximity to each other, but that's a stretch even if we exclude the differences in the MOs. Which we can't.' He yawned, but his eyes were still sharp. 'We have three deaths and potentially as many MOs. Maybe more if you want to include the wanker with the slingshot who came after us.' He rubbed his arm; I could see it ached. I wanted to help him, but didn't know how. He'd already rejected the painkillers I'd offered. *It's my fault he's hurt.*

'The only link that seems clear is the coward who tried to pick Meg and us off. I get that you're keen to find justice for the first guy, but I'll be honest with you, Marple, I'd love to shove that slingshot down the shooter's throat.'

I didn't blame him; it had gotten personal. 'So, even if we start there, we're looking at someone who knew where Meg was; where we were.'

He grunted, which I took as encouragement. 'Let's circle back to whoever's after you and Meg. Someone who may or may not be involved in the murders. I don't like the idea, but yeah, they might have an in with the Pack.'

'We share a lot in that chat.' I felt physically ill, but he was right – I couldn't rule anything out. 'There are a lot of people in the chat that I don't know. People who moved away, or joined because they walk their dog in our neighbourhood every Tuesday. Whatever.'

'Can you check them out?'

'I'll ask Irina to do it. She's one of the administrators and has been regularly removing anyone who doesn't look legit.'

He raised his dark brows. 'Seriously?'

'She's been doing it since finding out that Andy added himself in last June.' I offered a weak smile. 'Don't get me started on the Irina-and-Andy thing. Best as I can figure, it's complicated.'

'Okay. What else have you got?'

He was tired, and his accent had gone all Braveheart. My sleep-deprived, over-stimulated mind conjured an image of him in a kilt. Just for kicks.

My mouth went dry as I desperately tried to think of something else. 'Claire found out that Eddie had a lover who recently came into money. Who wanted to take care of him.'

'But he was still on the streets, instead of living with her. Which means, either he *was* with her and was caught outside and posed to look like he was still living rough . . .' His tone made it clear that he didn't believe this theory. 'Or he wasn't living with her, which means that she, or someone connected to her, might have thought he was a ... uhm ... problem that needed to be resolved.'

'And killed him.'

'The pusher might have known about their connection.'

'Pete was trying to be all things to all people. What if ... *what if* Eddie, to fund his drugs habit, was trying to, uhm ... find other income. And Pete put him in contact with this mystery woman.' Maybe it was the urgency of the evening, of being a target, but the theory was beginning to make sense.

'Who, now that she has money, doesn't want him weighing her down?'

I leaned forward. 'But he doesn't want to be cut loose?'

'So, he's, what, blackmailing her?'

'So, she finds someone to get rid of that problem. And while she's at it, she goes after the person who introduced them. Because he could point the finger at her.'

Jake lifted his chin, scratching at his budding beard. 'But to eliminate one, no, two threats, she hires someone else to remove them? And then whoever's trying to piece together the details?'

'Okay. It made sense up until that point.'

'I don't think it's necessarily wrong, mind you,' he conceded. 'It feels like we might be on the right track.' He got up and stretched. 'I need to sleep.'

'I don't want you walking home alone. What if he's still out there?'

'I'll take the couch. Luther has plenty of water and he'll be good until morning.'

'Okay, let me open up the sofa bed.'

'Don't worry, the couch in the other room is fine.'

'Okay.' I turned away, busying myself with the task of getting a pillow and clean blanket for him.

'And Marple?'

'Yeah?'

He gave me a tired smile, and took the bedding from me. 'If I didn't compliment you earlier, you really did look good when you dropped Klaus off.'

I looked down. I was still wearing the smart jacket with the Bardot collar and Jake's ripped sweatpants. My muddy shoes were by the door and would probably be binned in the morning. 'And now I look like a hobo.'

He kissed the top of my head. 'I'd say "a crusader" who's already been in enough battles for one day,' he said. I hadn't expected those words, unexpectedly poetic, and I felt a little tug in the area of my heart. 'Thing is, you've got to be careful. Because crusaders aren't invincible.'

'Would you miss me?' The words were out before I could stop them.

'Haven' I just said so?'

Saturday

75

LOUISE

Indira (Banjo's Mum)

> Morning! I'm getting Klaus and Banjo ready now. We'll leave here in 5 and head towards Partridge Park. See you at The Nest.

> 👍 I'll have your coffee and cinnamon bun waiting.

The icy wind assaulted my face as soon as the dogs and I stepped outside. People talk about "the bracing cold" but today it only made me want to slither back inside and crawl into bed.

Andy had been on the case. The area where Jake and I had been attacked was cordoned off, with a small pedestrian corridor open on the other side. A few PCs were hovering around. It still felt surreal.

'I hope they found whatever evidence was left,' I said to Klaus. Bundled up to the eyeballs in his hated blue puffer jacket, he gave me an unimpressed side-eye. Banjo ignored me and marched us towards the entrance to the canal towpath.

Indy had staked out a table by the window at The Nest, underneath the overhead heaters. Banjo gave a little yip when he saw her, his tail wagging. I let go of the lead, letting him run across the café to greet her. She dropped to one knee and burrowed her face into his soft, thick fur. 'I missed you too,' she told him. Then she drew back and told him, 'You did well last night.'

'He didn't just save the girl last night,' I added, sitting down across from her and lifting Klaus onto my lap. 'He saved Jake too.'

Indy blinked. Her long dark hair was as immaculate as ever, but she had shadowy circles beneath her eyes that her makeup wasn't able to cover. 'Jake? What else happened? I'm assuming Banjo didn't need to save Jake from you.'

'No. Not this time.' I took a sip of coffee and closed my eyes in bliss. 'He walked me home yesterday – I guess he didn't trust me to cross the canal on my own – and good thing too. Someone took a couple of shots at us.'

Indy's mouth sagged open. 'With a gun?'
'Slingshot.'
'Same as Meg. You think it's the same guy?'

'Dunno.' The cinnamon bun suddenly tasted like dust and I pushed the plate away. 'He – I'm assuming it's a he – shot at Jake first. Jake thought it was because he was the bigger risk to the attacker.'

Indy made a face. 'Could be. He's okay? You're okay?'

'Tired. We were up kind of late trying to figure this thing out.'

'You and Jake?' Her face fell into an expression of polite interest, which didn't quite mask her curiosity.

'Yeah.'

'... And?'

'And he stayed on the couch. Left before I got up.'

'Without a word?'

'He left a note on my table. "Stay out of trouble, Marple." Klaus heard him leave and woke me up. Banjo hadn't moved from the front door, but he let Jake go without a sound.'

'Hmmm.' Indy let that go without further comment. 'What's next?' she asked.

'What? With Jake and me? Nothing.'

'I meant, what else do you have planned for the day?'

'Oh.' Of course. Not everything was about my non-relationship. 'Andy said he'd meet me here in a half hour. I need to give him the ball I threw at the guy last night and give him my statement about getting shot at.' Saying the words aloud to Indy didn't make it feel any less surreal. 'I got the impression that neither of them are his case, but he's helping out.'

Indy's posture began to relax. She kept one hand on Banjo's head but gave me an impish smile. 'Out of the kindness of his heart, or to get back into the Tsarina's good graces?'

I smiled, appreciating her attempt to raise the mood. 'Anything's possible.'

Detective Andrew Thompson

> There in 5.

*

Indy and Banjo had already left, citing last-minute Christmas shopping, although I wouldn't be surprised if that shopping was by way of the Royal London Hospital.

What were the chances of getting caught up in the stabbing and then getting shot at an hour or two later? Was it just random bad luck or something worse?

'You okay, Louise?' Andy looked as tired as I felt.

'Sure,' I lied, handing him the poo-bag-wrapped ball. In a puckish moment, I'd added a red bow to it. 'Merry Christmas, Andy.'

He patted Klaus's head and ruffled his ears. 'Thanks for this. I'll give it to Forensics with a note about you and your pocket fluff. And I asked Harriman to have a look to see if we can get any CCTV footage. There's a Nisa shop around there that might have something.'

I pushed the cinnabun crumbs around on my plate. 'Yeah? Well, if you don't mind, see if he can find anything on the stretch between Jake's entrance to the complex and mine. I saw the area's still cordoned off, but it'd be nice to know that someone might get arrested for trying to shoot us. Strikes me as being similar to the attack on Meg.'

'Can't make any assumptions yet, Louise. You know that.'

I did. It was police procedure, but I wasn't Police, so that procedure didn't apply to me. 'Right. Of course. But can I at least ask to be kept in the loop on this?'

He nodded.

'And can I share with you what we've been thinking so far?'

Andy sighed and rubbed his eyes. 'Louise. If I had a quid for every time I've asked you not to get involved and you've ignored me . . .'

'Then you'd be rich, but maybe your caseload would be a case or two higher.'

'And you wouldn't have people breaking into your home, or trying to shoot you with ball bearings.'

Ball bearings. *Jesus*. What next?

76

INDIRA

Steve Starzyk

> Sorry I missed your late-night visit, Indira.

> NP. How's Addie doing?

> Got her stabilised and moved onto the wards. She gave us her first name, but nothing more.

> Have the police been to see her? Do they have someone guarding her?

> Not as far as I know. And, sorry, but not as far as I know.

> FFS, someone tried to kill her last night!

> Would have succeeded if you hadn't run them off and brought her in, from what I hear. Look, the girl isn't talking. And if she won't talk to us, you really think she'll talk to the police?

> Do you think it would help if I came in and had a word with her?

> Can't hurt, can it?

> OK, I'm on my way. Text me her room number.

Indira stood in the bright, white-tiled hallway outside the ward. After the big hello at The Nest, Banjo had been happy to go home, retreating to his safe space at the corner of her couch. She'd returned to the café, bought a bag of pastries and walked towards the Tube station, grateful that she didn't have to go to the DLR and pass the square where the attack had happened.

She hovered outside the half-open door for a few moments, gathering her thoughts before knocking. 'Morning, Addie,' she said, stepping inside.

The bed closest to the door had the curtains pulled around it. Indira passed by it and peered into the second bed.

The girl lay flat, one arm hooked up to an IV and several monitors. Her face was turned towards the window, but even so, Indira was struck by how young she looked. Fifteen, maybe sixteen, but no older than that.

She didn't turn as Indira approached.

'I'm Dr Indira Balasubramanian,' she said out of habit. Then softened her voice. 'But I think you might remember my dog Banjo more.'

The girl turned towards Indira. Her voice was little more than a whisper. 'You're the one who saved me, yesterday.'

'Yes.'

'Why?'

That wasn't the question she was expecting. 'What do you mean?'

'Why did you save me? You didn't have to.'

'That's debatable.' Indira perched on the window ledge. 'Want to tell me what happened?'

'Tosser came at me. Cut me. Then you showed up.' She tried to shrug, but the effort seemed too much. 'Not much more to tell.'

Indira put the bag of pastries on the table. 'In case the hospital food is as bad as I remember.' There was a wary look in the girl's eye that felt like a punch to her chest. 'No strings attached, but if you don't want them, I'll take them home with me.' She reached in and broke off a crust of the first pastry, popping it into her mouth, as if to prove it wasn't poisoned.

'Your dog . . . ?'

'Dogs can't eat raisins,' Indira said.

'I know.'

'But that wasn't what you were asking.' Indira gave her a gentle smile. 'He's fine. Happy to be home. Interestingly, he seems to have a knack for finding people who need him.'

It was a throwaway comment to make Addie feel more comfortable, but Indira noticed a spark in her eyes. 'My mates think I'm delulu, but I want to be a dog trainer when I'm older,' she whispered.

'Nothing crazy about that. Good trainers are hard to come by.' Indira tore off another piece of pastry. 'My friends took their pups to sniffer dog training last week. We didn't go – I didn't think Banjo would be interested, but now I wonder if maybe he'd be better off training as an emotional support dog.'

It wasn't something she'd ever considered, but being a paediatrician, having an ESD around to calm anxious children (and their parents) might not be a bad idea. She made a mental note to discuss it with the practice manager.

Addie also seemed to consider it. 'I think he can do it.'

'Banjo can do *anything* he puts his mind to.' Indira leaned forward. 'So can you.'

The girl offered her a fake smile. 'Sure.'

What had happened to this girl to make her believe so little in herself?

'Look.' Indira kept her voice firm but reassuring. 'What happened last night was horrible. My friend hit him and might have a sample of his DNA. She's giving it to the police this morning. They'll need to ask you some questions to help them find the man who did this to you.'

The girl ducked her head, her hair falling over her face. 'He'll just come back for me.'

It wasn't random. She knows who he is. Indira wanted to ask for a name, an address. Some way to help the police find him, but knew the girl wouldn't give her a straight answer. She let it slide. 'Not if he's arrested.'

'He'll find a way.'

'Not if we can get him first.' Indira stood and stared out of the window for a few seconds. 'I don't expect you to trust me enough to tell me, but there's a detective I know, who I trust. Who I would want to find my attacker, if it were me in that bed instead of you.'

The girl made a noncommittal sound.

Indira pulled a small notebook out of her handbag and wrote down Andy's number on a piece of paper. Ripped it off, folded it in half and placed it on the side table, weighed down by a plastic jug of ice chips.

'If you believe only one thing I say, believe this: you can trust him.'

77

ANDY

Doug Harriman

> Found something. Can you swing by here?

> Can't you just tell me?

> I think it's something you should see.

Andy entered the CCTV Monitoring Centre. One wall was a mosaic of monitors, maybe a dozen across by three deep. The man closest to the wall was older, balding and intent, squinting at the screens, chin propped up by a fist.

Harriman sat hunched next to him, looking the sort

of tired you can only get from watching multiple screens over the course of several hours. There was no sign of the Velcro back brace in sight.

'What do you have?' Andy asked. 'And why so bloody cryptic?'

Harriman pointed to a screen with a grainy image frozen on it. Andy moved around to stand behind Harriman. 'Right. You were spot-on: the Nisa had CCTV. Not the best quality, but better than sweet FA.'

'Okay.'

Harriman rewound the video for a few seconds, then hit the arrow to play. There was nothing, then more nothing, until a blurry figure appeared, sprinting across the screen. From the size and the body language, Andy could tell it was a man, but his face was averted, as if he knew the CCTV was watching him.

'Look familiar?' Harriman asked, pausing the reel.

'Should it?'

'Okay. Maybe not yet.' He hit Play again. 'Keep watching.' A small object moved quickly, bouncing off the back of the man's head. For a moment, he stopped, one hand on the spot where the ball had hit him.

'And now?'

Andy squinted at the screen. The man was tall, with hair pulled back into a short ponytail, revealing a buzzed undercut.

Harriman pointed at another screen. A different image filled it: a short stocky woman wearing a fedora, walking beside a taller man. Same pony. Same buzzcut.

'That woman is Caren Hansen, who's serving at His

Majesty's pleasure for the murder of Jonny Tang and the attempted murder of Annabel Lindford-Swayne,' Harriman clarified. 'We'd been unsure whether that man had helped her or not. Looks like whoever he is, he hasn't stayed underground for long.'

Andy sank into the nearest chair, his thoughts bashing each other, unable to deny what was on the screens in front of him, but struggling to believe what he was seeing. As bad as the video quality was, the man who attacked the girl last night bore a striking resemblance to the man with Hansen.

If the man on the screen was as tight with Hansen as he looked, he'd know she was behind bars. And he might also see Louise and her friends as the reason why, given their role in her arrest.

Which meant that the attack on her and Jake Hathaway might not be unconnected to the attack on the girl, or to the attack on Meg Barnes.

The girl was key.

And that made her an even bigger target.

Scott Williams

> Harry made an interesting connection. Meet me at the Royal London in Whitechapel. There's a vic there we need to talk to.

> K. I can be there in 20.

78

LOUISE

Claire (Tank's Mum)

> Are you up? Got another entry for your crime beat. Klaus and I are heading towards yours. You're welcome to join us for a little detour and I can catch you up.

> An offer like that? Not gonna say no.

Claire and Tank were waiting for us outside News-N-Booze, Claire was bundled up, but Tank was still happily naked.

'You're just showing off now,' I told him on Klaus's behalf, stroking his ears.

'I swear, he doesn't feel the cold.'

We started walking. With the exception of Tesco, which was doing its usual brisk Saturday-morning business, the other shops along that stretch of the High Street were closed. 'I would have expected the salon at least to be open. Benny's been doing some long hours since Caren was put away, trying to keep it going.'

'He can't hire anyone?'

'Too much business for one person, I guess, but maybe not enough for two full-time staff?' Claire said. 'I'm getting the impression that they've lost some clients though.'

'I feel bad for Benny. He's doing his best but fighting a losing battle. Any luck on your list of who might have come into money? Cause maybe we can fix him up?'

'I don't think he's into women. And no luck yet. I've drafted Irina in as well. Figure if she's can't unearth something, there's not much to find.' Claire shot me a glance. 'So, cheer me up. What've you got? The sneaky goss on Shih Tzu Gate? Yaz is being uncharacteristically discreet.'

'My money is on her wanting to announce whatever she's found out at The Hound tonight. You're going, right?'

'Course.'

'With Jeremy?'

'Haven't asked him.'

I raised an eyebrow. 'Why not?'

'Too soon. It's only been a couple of dates.' She shrugged. 'And I don't want us speculating as to who killed his cousin, while he's standing right there. Help a girl out, Lou. You know when my last relationship was? Any idea who the killer is?'

'Why me? Y'all usually tell me to leave it to the cops.'

'Hell, Tank does a better "leave it" than you do. No one *expects* you to listen anymore.'

We'd come round to the back of Claire's building, entering the square from the same street Indy and I had last night. For a few moments I narrowed my eyes, trying to juxtapose what I remembered with how it looked in daylight.

'Last night I was coming back from my Christmas party and ran into Indy and Banjo. Banjo pulled us here, then we heard a scream. A man stabbed a young woman, just there.' I pointed to the far corner. 'It wasn't that well lit, but we yelled, and got his attention. He ran, and Indy went to see that the girl was okay.'

'What did you do?'

'I threw Klaus's ball at the back of the attacker's head.'

Claire stifled a giggle. 'I know it's not funny, but *really?*'

'I've got one in every coat. I don't wear my dress coat that often, and the ball in there isn't Klaus's favourite. It was the hard orange one, instead of the soft blue squeaky one.'

'So, it must have hurt.'

'Hope so. I retrieved the ball and gave it to Andy this morning.'

'How could I have missed it?'

'Your flat faces in the other direction.'

'I didn't see anything in the building's chat. Did anyone else come out to help?'

'No,' I said. 'Although it's cold so the windows are closed. Maybe they didn't hear anything?'

'You mean, if they did hear something, they didn't want to get involved.' It was a fair assessment. 'I'll bet at least one person tried to video it.'

'With the crap lighting, they wouldn't get much.'

'True,' Claire sighed, poking at her phone. 'Shit. There's nothing in the news about this yet.'

'Maybe stabbings aren't that uncommon, Claire. Not unless someone ends up dead.'

She raised her eyebrows meaningfully. 'Like the someone in the kiddie park, and the other someone across the street?'

'Yeah. I think I recognised the girl from last night. I saw her with her friends on the DLR a few days ago. They sounded a bit rough, but this one, she just wanted to pet Klaus and tell me that she wanted to be a dog trainer.'

'That's really sad. I hope she'll be okay.'

'Me too.'

'Rough night though.'

She didn't know the half of it. 'It didn't end there. I went to pick up Klaus from Jake's and on the way home someone attacked us.'

'What?' Claire's voice lowered to a horrified whisper. 'Was it the same guy? Did he try to stab you?'

'I couldn't see who it was, but he tried to bean us with a handful of ball bearings.'

'He missed, of course?' Claire stopped walking and eyed me up. 'You're okay? The handsome Jake is okay?'

'Yeah.' I tried to make light of it. 'Good thing my throwing arm is better than the guy's slingshot, or the night could have ended far worse.'

'Shit,' she repeated. 'I'm so sorry.'

'On the plus side, Jake and I were mulling this over until crazy o'clock last night. We do think whoever Slingshot Man is, he's coming after Meg and me because he thinks we're getting close to figuring out who he is.'

'Are you?' Claire asked. 'Cos if you are, you wanna share?'

'That's the tricky bit. The only real theory we have is that the woman Eddie was with, who came into money and wanted to take care of him, might have gotten cold feet. Or he might have been pushing her for more.'

'More?'

'More money, I guess. I don't know. Either way, he'd become a threat. Maybe to her, maybe to her family. Then we've got Pete the Pusher. Small-time drug dealer and casual pimp. It's possible that he provided the ... ah ... introductions. And then this woman ended up hiring someone to get rid of the inconvenient lover as well as the man who knew her secret.'

'How does a normal person even go about finding a hitman? You think there's a website? Crims-R-Us?'

My skin began to tingle. *Hitman?* The *woman* Eddie met. 'Claire, when Jeremy told you that Eddie had someone, are you sure he said it was a woman?'

'I think so, but I might be wrong there. Why?'

'Not all prostitutes are women, and I'm suddenly feeling that we might have jumped to the wrong conclusion.

We've been looking for a *woman* who came into money. What if it was a man?'

'Okay.' Claire shrugged. 'Gender aside, how many people do you know, who might know us, who have just inherited a lot of money?'

'None,' I said, deflating.

'Me neither, but let's keep an open mind. And Lou?'

I looked at her, feeling my stomach clench.

'I don't know anyone who's come into *a lot* of money, but "a lot" is relative. And to someone who doesn't have much, even something modest might seem like a windfall worth killing over.'

79

ANDY

'Hi,' Andy said, approaching the young woman in the bed. 'I'm Detective Andy Thompson. This is Detective Scott Williams. I hear you ran into some trouble last night?'

'You think?' the young woman said, holding up her arm, which was attached to an IV and a monitor.

Beside her, Louise's friend Indira Balasubramanian blinked at him. Andy was as surprised to see her there as she clearly was to see Williams and him, but she gave the young woman a gentle nod. 'It's okay to talk to them, Addie. This is the detective I told you about.' She stood up and picked up her handbag.

'Stay,' the young woman whispered. 'Please?'

Indira glanced at Andy questioningly.

'Sure you wouldn't rather have your mum or dad here instead?'

The girl shook her head. 'I'm over sixteen. Don't need 'em here.'

'Okay,' he said, taking out his notepad. 'We'd like to ask you a few questions about what happened last night.'

'Can't help you. I didn't get a good look. Don't know who he is.'

'That's all right, one step at a time. Can you please confirm your full name and where you live?'

Silence.

'We can take your picture, show it to people and ask around to find out, but really, it'd be easier if you just told us,' Williams pointed out.

The girl looked like she wanted to bolt. Then her shoulders sagged and she shrugged with a studied nonchalance that spoke of deeper trauma than the average sulky teenager. 'Adrian Barlow. I live ... my foster family lives on Nobert, right next to Partridge Park.'

'All right.' Andy exchanged a glance with Williams. 'Can you tell me what happened last night?'

She shrugged. 'There was a party at The Nest. It was getting loud and I needed air. I just ... needed to get out for a bit.'

'Because your friend had just died?' Williams said, not unkindly.

She looked up, alarmed. 'Who told you that?'

You, just now, Andy thought. Up until that point, it had only been a guess based on her age and proximity to the park.

'Do you think last night was a coincidence, Miss

Barlow?' he asked. 'Or do you think that whoever hurt Eddie was also targeting you?'

'I don't know.' Her voice vacillated between glum and aggressive.

'Do you know who killed Eddie Morley?'

'No!'

'Do you know who attacked you last night?'

'Sod off! No!'

Andy didn't believe her, but decided to change tack. 'Right. Rumour had it that Eddie had a new lover, someone who wanted to take care of him. You know anything about that?'

Her face dropped, dumbfounded. 'What're you talking about?'

'A woman who'd come into some money. Who could give him a better life.'

'You on drugs or somfin'? Who'd you even hear that from?'

'Our understanding is that he was involved with someone . . .'

'Sure. Someone. But it weren't no woman. It were the blokes that wanted Eddie. Always the blokes.'

'All right,' Andy said, slowly, the puzzle pieces beginning to come together in a way that was surprising but felt right. 'Was there any one bloke in particular?'

She shook her head, trying to hide the tears that streamed down her face.

'Miss Barlow?'

She hung her head, allowing her hair to hide her face, and another piece clicked into place. 'You were the one to let his mother know he was dead, weren't you, Miss Barlow?' Andy said gently.

Her shoulders slumped and she nodded. 'He hated his stepdad. But his mum? He'd've wanted her to know.'

'I think that's enough for now, detectives,' Indira said. 'You can ask her more questions later.'

Andy was about to protest but Indira handed him her phone. Her messaging app was open.

Louise (Klaus's Mum)

> If you're still at the hospital and see Andy, tell him to get in touch. I tried messaging but he's not responding. I think I know who the murderer is, or at least who organised everything. And why.

> He's here. I'll tell him. Whatever you do, *stay away from this*.

> Ofc. On my way home now.

Andy muttered a curse under his breath, not believing Louise for a second. She'd be out putting herself in danger somewhere. He had an idea who they might be after, but would he be able to make the arrest before Louise or one of her friends got into trouble?

That was the question. And the clock was running down.

80

LOUISE

Indira (Banjo's Mum)

> He knows – he's on his way to make the arrest. I think he figured it out too when we were interviewing Adrian. Seems that Eddie's clients were male, not female.

> Yeah, we just figured that out.

> Before he left, he told me to remind you to go home,

> lock the door and 'not do anything stupid'. His words, although I don't disagree.

'Right,' Claire said. 'I don't disagree either. Look, the cops are on the case. Come back to mine. I'll make a pot of coffee, lock the door and if we're lucky, we can watch whatever goes down from the window.'

We began walking across the green. We were almost at the car park when Klaus began to bark. Tank, not one to be left out, joined in.

'What're they barking at? I don't see anyone,' Claire said.

I shrugged. 'Could be a bird, or a paper bag dancing its way down the street. If it were a squirrel, Klaus would have yanked my arm out of its socket trying to get to it.'

'Same, same.'

What we heard next wasn't a paper bag. It was a delicate *ping*, followed by the sound of splintering glass. For a moment my body froze as I watched cracks radiate out from a small point in the windscreen of a red Toyota. Then my brain registered what was happening.

'Shooter!' I scooped Klaus up and dove behind a tree. 'Move! Get down!' I screamed at Claire.

'I didn't hear a gun,' she said, confused.

'So what? He could have a silencer or a slingshot. Move your arse!' The words came out before I could think them through, but they made sense. The idiot with the slingshot hadn't got me last night, so he was trying again today? It wasn't a crime of opportunity – he was trying to kill me. But that didn't mean he wouldn't shoot at Claire too, if she wasn't already on his list...

'Oh my god!' She ran at a crouch, dragging the still-barking Tank behind her.

My fingers shook. Hell, my whole body shook. Klaus nuzzled my jaw and licked my face. I gently pressed his head against my chest, trying to make us as small a target as I could. 'We'll get through this,' I said to him. 'I promise. I don't know how, but somehow we'll get through this.'

I closed my eyes to stop the tears. I'd been in danger before, but never had I felt so helpless.

I'd seen films where someone lobbed something further away to distract a shooter, and had always thought that was ridiculous. The shooter would see them move, see them throw something. Now it didn't seem so crazy – I'd try anything to get us out of there.

The road on the other side of the green wasn't far, but there wasn't enough foliage to hide us if we made a run for it. He knew where we were, he was just waiting for us to make that sort of move.

I glanced at Claire. She was huddled to my right, her forehead resting on Tank's.

Something Gav said the other day bubbled to the surface. *You're not on your own. You've got the rest of the Pack.*

He was right. It wasn't just Klaus I needed to protect.

I needed to protect my Pack. And I wasn't afraid to ask for help.

I eased my phone out of my pocket, trying to make as little movement as I could. With fingers trembling from more than the cold, I opened WhatsApp and messaged Andy, hoping he wasn't that far away.

81

ANDY

Marple

> Claire and I are in the green area behind her building. Someone's shooting at us. We're sheltering behind a couple of trees. We're safe, I think, maybe. But we're trapped here. Can you send help?

> On it. Keep your head down, we're almost there. Are you both OK? Can you

> tell where he's shooting from?

> Somewhere in the building. I can't check what floor, but I'm guessing the flats rather than the shops. He wouldn't have as good an angle if he was on the ground level.
> Scared, but not wounded. Every time we move, something pings by. Pls hurry!

>

'Shit,' Andy said, updating Williams as they sprinted towards the newbuild on the High Street. The Bells was behind them, and ahead he could see a squad car parked outside Cluckin' Fried Chicken. The uniforms had already blocked vehicle and foot traffic and were herding pedestrians into the nearby shops. A third PC waited in the doorway of the charity shop with a worried looking woman. Sirens heralded the arrival of backup.

'I'm Deborah Bay,' she said. 'The building manager. Can you tell me what's going on?'

'Suspect is inside, shooting ball bearings at two women trapped around the back,' Andy said. 'Make whatever announcement you need to. Let people know to stay in their flats, or out of the building. Away from the building. Down the street or behind The Bells, by the canal.'

'Email or text messages,' Williams added. 'Nothing through the intercom.'

She nodded. 'Of course. I can do that.'

'Good. You have fobs so we can get in without breaking down the door?'

She held out two plastic discs. 'There are two entrances, each corresponding to a stairwell. The lift is midway between them.'

'Thanks. And ma'am? Stay where you are in here. The shooter's focused on the back of the building for now, but it'd be easy enough for him to start firing out the front as well.'

She hunched and retreated further into the charity shop.

'You got the whole area cordoned off? Back as well?' Williams barked at one of the PCs.

'Of course,' the PC replied. 'You want us to go get the women out back out of there?'

'You got riot gear? Helmets and shields?'

'Helmets, yes. Shields, no.'

'See if you can get some. Until then, you get close, you'll make yourselves a target. Clear the area as best you can, but stay out of sight. We don't know for certain what sort of weapon he might have. If it's a slingshot, they can go some fifteen, sixteen metres, but we can't rule out him having a gun. The women will have to hang tight for now. Has anyone engaged with them?'

'Yeah. They know we're here. We told them to stay in place.'

'Good.' Andy pointed at him and a second PC. 'You two. I want you to stand at each exit. Don't let anyone in or out.'

The third one said, 'And me?'

'I want you to get a helmet on and get into the lift. Disable it. Then get your arse outside. More help is on the way to take care of crowd control.'

'What are you going to do?' the third PC asked.

'Williams will take one stairwell, and I'll take the other. Unless the suspect has access to one of the flats, he'll be shooting out of the windows in one of the stairwells.'

Williams was already moving towards the far side of the building. He waited until Andy was level with him and gave the thumbs-up.

Andy took a deep breath, pulled out his Taser and pushed the door open.

82

DANNY

The stairwell had windows on both sides; he'd known the moment the filth arrived. Had hoped he'd have more time, but he had a job to do, and he'd do it.

Danny looked down. The rozzers were taking the stairs. There was one cop on this side, one on the other. He knew the drill. He'd grown up on a council estate rough enough that the police didn't go there. Not unless they were armed and out in numbers. When they'd clear a building, they'd take the stairs, stopping at each floor to check for whoever they were after.

It was *supposed* to be that they'd work in tandem, stopping at each floor at the same time, to make it harder for their suspect to go unnoticed, but there was usually a fit one and a fat one, so that never lined up.

Even if it did, there were ways of getting around that.

He glanced down, seeing the stairs turn onto each

other, like a Dali painting. The only movement a left hand on the banister, two floors down.

Stupid.

He'd been playing this game from the time he was a boy. Cos either you were with the troublemakers, or they were out to get you. And Danny wasn't a victim.

Adrenaline surged, drowning out the bass thumping of his headache. He wanted to laugh, but couldn't afford to make a sound.

Maybe a flat door would be open. He could force his way in, have a bit more fun from their windows, maybe. Harder to make his way out though, if he took a hostage.

The hand on the rails disappeared while the cop checked out the floor below.

Every cell in his body screamed at Danny to run.

He ignored them. *You run, you're done* was the motto he lived by. You had to be brave, or you'd be dead.

There were refuse rooms on each floor. He edged out of the stairwell, careful not to make any big moves. Not because of the headache – it was bad, but he could cope – but because big moves attracted attention. He slipped into the refuse room, holding his breath to keep from gagging. There weren't any bins to hide in; the room only had chutes – one for recycling, one for trash, but someone had thoughtfully left an old cabinet in there. Danny took off his jacket, making it easier to move, and stuffed it on top of the cabinet. Wedged himself between it and the wall, pulled a small steel ball bearing from his pocket and tucked it into the elastic sling. Drew it back as far as he could, in case the cop thought to check the room.

He'd have loved to rub the cold steel between his bare fingers for luck, but knew better than to give the cops his prints. Make them work for it: they find him, good on 'em. But not bloody likely.

If the copper did check, he'd take him out and continue the job.

When he finished, he'd leave. Walk out of the building, with no one even thinking to stop him.

He had the perfect disguise.

83

ANDY

'Third floor, clear,' Andy whispered into the Airwaves radio. A door opened and a harried-looking older woman took three steps into the hallway. Andy glared at her, held up a finger to his lips and gestured her back into her flat. He heard the door lock behind her and moved forward, his heart beating a rapid tattoo in his chest.

Hopefully she'd stay there, safe, until this mess was over.

84

DANNY

It was Benny's fault, of course. Danny was sick of bailing him out of trouble. He'd been cleaning up after him since they were kids, and it was getting old. That idiot didn't know when to keep his mouth shut and his flies zipped. Never had. Probably never would.

Far be it for Benny to date like normal people. Find someone in real life. Maybe at a bar or on an app. Have a normal relationship. But Benny was *strange*. People sensed it and stayed away. If he managed to swing getting a date, he ended up scaring them off.

He bloody *stunk* of desperation.

So, he paid for it. And he couldn't even do that right. No, he had to get an intro from a pusher. And it wasn't as if Benny did drugs. A single drink made him pissed.

Danny had a good idea what had happened: Benny'd been nervous and poured himself a glass of wine. Probably had another with the rent boy. Then when it was done, a bit of oversharing with the pillow talk.

Which would have been fine, but the rent boy got greedy. Thought that Benny was flush, what with Caren signing everything over to him when she was found guilty. Not like she wasn't planning on having it back when she got out, but maybe ol' Ben didn't share *that* part.

The rent boy wanted money. Far more than his fee. Something to keep him going, 'cos Benny, a pillar of the community, wouldn't want his dirty secret to come out, eh?

He couldn't cope with running the business.

Couldn't cope with telling the rent boy to sling his hook.

Couldn't cope with the pusher lurking around. Of course Pete knew what the boy was doing. Probably wanted part of the action.

They were gone, now. No thanks to Benny. But there were people who wouldn't let it go. Who were asking questions. Making Benny sweat.

Hell, *everything* made Benny sweat.

So, once again, Danny had to bail him out. All because Benny couldn't keep his bloody kit in his pants and his gob shut.

This was the last time. Quite frankly, he'd had enough.

85

LOUISE

Partridge Bark

Fiona (Nala's Mum)

> @Claire, there are police cars parked outside your building again. No one allowed in or out. You OK?

Claire (Tank's Mum)

> Some idiot is trying to shoot us. @Louise and I are hiding behind a tree behind the building. I hope the cops get him

> soon, it's bloody freezing out here!

'He hasn't shot anything at us for the last few minutes,' I whispered to Klaus. There were no other people in sight, which I guess meant the cops were keeping people away. 'Maybe they got him?'

In the far corner, a police officer in a helmet edged towards us. He held a massive clear shield in front of him. Each move was deliberate, as if he didn't know whether he'd be hit.

The shooter hadn't been apprehended yet.

I wanted to run to the man, duck behind his shield and have him get me out of there, but my body wasn't complying. I was shaking, hard, and trying not to cry. I was even more terrified for Klaus. If he got hurt, it'd kill me. And if something happened to me, what would become of him?

'I'm so sorry, Klaus. I never meant to put you in danger.' My breath misted on the air and I held him closer, despite his struggles to get out of my arms and kiss my face.

The police officer hissed, trying to get my attention. I wasn't sure whether my legs would work and jerked my head towards Claire, indicating that she should be rescued first. Pressed my back against the tree and whispered to Klaus. 'I don't know what I did to make him hate me bad enough that he wants to kill me.' I knew it was self-pity, and knew that it wasn't personal. The hitman, or maybe his boss, saw me as a threat, and they were out to cover their tracks.

But knowing the reason why didn't make me feel any better.

The police officer had reached Claire. Held up the shield while she picked up Tank. Crouching, they moved towards the safety of the car park. I held my breath, waiting for another shot, but the only thing I heard was Klaus's breath and Tank (maybe Claire) vomiting.

As the officer made his way back for us, I could hear Claire muttering all sorts of things that she'd do to the shooter if she ever got her hands on him. And I really hoped she had the opportunity to put those words into action.

86

ANDY

Andy crouched, easing open the refuse room door with his foot. He led with the Taser, careful to keep his body shielded as best he could until the room was cleared. Something pinged past at head height. 'He's here!' he breathed into the Airwave, and then did what was possibly the stupidest thing of his career.

Hoping that the target didn't have enough time to load up another ball bearing, he sprang forward, keeping low, one finger squeezing the Taser's trigger.

There's only one shot with a Taser. Let it be good!

Two thin copper wires shot forward as Andy crashed into the far wall, between the refuse chutes.

The barbed darts at the ends of the wires landed a couple of inches from each other in the mark's chest.

The circuit completed, and the target dropped to the floor, spasming.

Andy swatted the slingshot out of the way and got to his feet. He watched the man convulse and felt no pity. 'Benjamin Daniel Bryce, I'm arresting you for the murders of Edward Morley and Michael James, and the attempted murders of Meg Barnes, Louise Mallory, Jake Hathaway and Claire Dougherty.'

'I'm coming in,' Williams panted through the Airwave. 'Clear.'

Williams yanked the door open, flooding the room with the hall's bright lights.

'Glad you could make it,' Andy said. He took out his handcuffs and turned back to Benny. 'You do not have to say anything, but it may harm your defence if you do not mention when questioned something which you later rely on in court. Anything you do say may be given in evidence.'

87

LOUISE

Detective Scott Williams

> All clear. Got him.

> Safe to move?

> Yeah. Bringing him out now. You and your mates are safe.

> Thank you – you got Benny too?

> Everyone in connection with the murders and the

> attempts on your and Meg's lives has been apprehended.

> Thank you. I owe you and Andy a drink. We'll be at The Hound tonight. Please join us.

'They got the shooter!' I breathed, putting down my phone and turning to Claire. The PC who had escorted us to safety had moved a few steps away and was talking into his radio.

'Did Andy say who it was?'

'It was Williams, but no. Not who. I don't think he'd be able to . . .'

Despite how close we'd just been to being shot, or maybe because of it, mischief lit Claire's eyes. 'No, but if they're bringing him out, we'll be able to see for ourselves.'

Two exits, on opposite sides of the building. There was a fifty per cent chance they'd pick the door nearest us and we'd be able to see who'd been trying to kill us.

'Split up?' Claire suggested.

We were about to do just that when we heard the door on the far side open. With the dogs leading away, we raced over to it in time to see Andy and Williams emerge, holding the arms of a man wearing black jeans and a black long-sleeved top. A black jacket was draped over him, hiding his face. Williams put his hand on the man's head, helping him into the back of a squad car, and just for a moment, the jacket slipped.

'Jaysus,' Claire breathed, turning to me in shock. 'Benny? The shooter is Benny? I can't believe it.'

I struggled to process it as well. Benny was so mild. Scared of his shadow ... 'I thought maybe he paid someone to kill his lover, and then his blackmailer. I didn't think he'd be the one to do it himself. Or to go after us.' I frowned at the departing squad car. 'Meg's gonna have a really hard time with this. She thought Benny was her friend.'

'I can't imagine what she's gonna be going through.' Claire pulled out her phone. 'But one thing that today's taught me is that life is short. You find something that makes you smile, you've got to hang on to it.'

'You're texting Jeremy?' I guessed.

'Yep. I'm breaking the story. But I don't want him to see my byline and think I was only after him because of his family.' She gave me a self-conscious smile. 'It might have started that way, but I'm not gonna let it end there.'

'Change your mind and invite him to The Hound later? I mean, we can now give him some closure.'

Claire's mouth sagged in horror. 'Yeah, but it's still far too early to introduce him to you lot!' She cleared her throat and continued, 'It wouldn't be appropriate anyway. It's closure, but his family's been through a lot. They'll need to mourn, not celebrate.'

I nodded. 'Well, I wish you luck.'

Tank got to his feet and shook himself hard enough to lose his balance. He looked at Claire, at me, then choked out a small puddle of clear vomit.

'A lot of luck,' I added.

88

LOUISE

Detective Scott Williams

Ain't over until the fat lady sings, and I gotta tell you, this one sang soprano.

??
He talked? Admitted everything?

Can't give you details ofc, but I can tell you that you and your friends are safe. And we'll join you for a jar or two. Andy was called in

> to meet with the boss. As soon as he's done, we'll head over.

'You know, this is the first time you're going to The Hound after a case has been solved without being bandaged up,' Irina said. Klaus and Hammy led the way, eager to get to the pub. Klaus (under duress) wore a red jumper under his puffer jacket while Hammy sported a Black Watch plaid tartan coat and the green *Suck my schnauzer* bandana.

'Yeah, well. It was a close-run thing.' There was no point in confessing that my wrists and knees hadn't been this scraped up since I was a kid.

'Speaking of which, where is the handsome, if elusive, Mr Hathaway tonight?'

'He'll join us there later. As will our detective friends.'

'Huh,' she said.

Disappointed in her response, I glanced at her, and fished, 'But you knew that already, didn't you? Andy told you?'

She shrugged. 'They always turn up for a glass after we solve a case for them.'

There was the usual sound of revving engines, and we moved closer to the buildings on our right just as two sedans screamed by, the driver in the first car sucking on a yellow balloon.

'They're gonna kill someone, one of these days,' Irina muttered, pushing through the Judas gate beside the road and into the little beer garden at the front of The Hound. The outside tables were interspersed with brightly lit Christmas trees and a trio of people were huddled under the overhead heater at the end, smoking. I didn't know them, but they raised their glasses in our direction. 'Merry Christmas!'

We waved and ducked inside, divesting first the dogs then ourselves of our outerwear. 'No Christmas jumper, Louise?' Sherry, the bartender, asked from behind the bar. 'I was convinced you'd have one with little Klauses on it.'

'Nope.' I knew I didn't look cream-suit elegant but I had made an effort to dress up. My dark green cardigan had a lower-than-normal scoop neck and bell sleeves, and looked smart with my dark jeans and a pair of heeled boots. 'Everyone's in the back?'

'You're welcome to go wherever you like, love, but the dogs – and the booze – are in the function room.' Sherry rolled her eyes at the already half-lit crowd. 'For their protection.'

Klaus seemed to agree, marching us across the room, narrowly avoiding being stepped on, or kissed.

Someone had hung a sign on the door – a crazy-looking Chihuahua wearing a Santa hat saying *Feliz Navidog*. Irina scoffed, but I could tell that a smile lurked underneath the Grinch-like exterior.

The sound of barks and laughter was deafening. 'You ready?' I asked, feeling my mood lift with each step.

I unclipped Klaus from his lead and opened the door. He ran inside, tail wagging a mile a minute as he greeted his friends, canine and human, accepting treats, sniffs and pats in equal measure. The conversation paused as people turned towards me. Yaz began to clap and the others caught on. 'Three for three – way to go, Lou-eeeze!'

I blushed. 'Credit to the cops, who actually arrested the guy.'

'So, what happened?'

'We heard you were attacked last night. Are you okay?'

'Was it the same guy who attacked Meg?'

The questions came fast and furious. Kate winked at me and poured a glass of Pinot Noir, and handed it to me.

I turned to Irina, to pass it to her, but she had a barracuda sort of look in her eye. I followed her gaze to the three people holding beers in the corner: Andy, Williams and the CCTV guy, Harriman. The Family Liaison Officer we'd seen at the memorial wasn't there; I assumed she was busy updating the families on the arrest.

'They wouldn't say anything until you got here,' Yaz said.

'They probably won't say much now.' I smiled and lifted my glass to them as they approached. 'But thank you for saving my life today.'

'Thank you for keeping your cool while we apprehended the gunman,' Andy replied.

'In sub-zero weather, keeping our cool was not as much of a challenge,' Claire joked. She nudged Tank away from Nala.

'Right. So, what happened?' Yaz demanded, leaning back against her partner, Ejiro. Hercules lay at her feet, munching on something probably stolen from the table.

'Gosh, where to begin?' I mused, then answered my own question. 'We begin at the beginning. Only it isn't Eddie Morley. It was a couple of months ago, when Caren Hansen was put away for killing Jonny Tang.'

'And trying to kill you,' Jake said from the doorway. He shrugged out of the leather biker jacket, revealing a black rollneck top that made him look dangerous. And enticing.

'Yeah, that too.' I tore my gaze away and took a gulp of wine. 'She signed the shop over to Benny. Probably thought that she'd be back out in a couple of years and he'd sign it back over to her, but the problem was that Benny had a ... uhm ... boyfriend.'

'Say it for what it is, Lou. He had a steady thing with a rent-a-date,' Irina said.

'Eddie Morley. So – and I'm guessing here, but I hope our detective friends will correct me – I think there was a bit of pillow talk, Benny probably talking about his stress over having to run the salon. A salon that, incidentally, was losing money.'

'A lot of people stopped going there after Caren was arrested,' Meg said, looking glum. 'I felt bad for him. He was a good guy, trying his best ...'

'He was a psycho. But he did a great job with your hair,' Claire added, giving Meg a hug. Meg look particularly fragile and it was hard to miss the way Ethan hovered protectively over her.

'To Eddie, who'd been living on the streets, he probably thought that Benny would share the wealth,' I went on. 'Or at least take care of him a little bit. And maybe he did for a while, I don't know.' I glanced at the detectives, but they maintained their neutral poker faces. Assuming I was on the right track, I continued. 'When Benny started running into financial difficulties, or felt taken advantage of, he began to distance himself. Eddie wasn't about to miss out on a good thing, and cooked up the idea to blackmail Benny.'

'So, Benny had him bumped off?' Fi guessed. 'And what? Pete the Pusher had introduced them, maybe was in on it too, so he also had to go?'

'Sort of.'

Yaz frowned. 'I'm not gonna ask how Benny found a hitman. Or, from what you said about the different MOs, maybe even two? Did one do the up-close-and-personal for Eddie and Pete, while the other shot at you and Meg from a distance?'

I exhaled.

'For that matter, *why* go after you? *You* were not blackmailing him,' Paul said.

'That's the easier question.' I tried not to look at Meg. 'He thought we were onto him. Or maybe he hated us for our role in Caren's arrest.'

'Why me though?' Meg whispered. Her eyes were huge and full of pain. Ethan slipped an arm around her shoulder, trying to comfort her. 'He was my friend.'

'Maybe that's why,' I said as gently as I could. 'You knew him. You trusted him. He liked keeping you close because you kept him up to date with what was going on in the Pack. But maybe he was afraid that he might have said something to you to implicate himself.'

'Or because he thought the Pack was the threat, given

the way you've closed two cases so far, and he was worried that you'd all be onto him,' Jake said, and around the room people nodded. 'Maybe he went for Meg and Louise first because he wanted to send a warning.'

Andy and Williams exchanged a look but otherwise kept neutral expressions.

'I was thinking about the MOs,' Paul began. 'I believe he switched his tactics because he liked to get close to the people he *wanted* to kill. And from a distance, the people he *had* to kill.'

Ella hiccupped and put her glass of orange juice down.

'Maybe he was worried that if he got too close, you'd see his face?' Irina suggested. 'And if you managed to escape you could identify him?'

'Up close for the men,' Fi mused. 'And from a distance for the women?' Jake cleared his throat. 'And Jake. Of course. Sorry, mate. But lots of options. I don't suppose our police friends will shed a light?'

From their expressions, it looked like they wouldn't.

'I like Paul's theory,' I said. 'I'd prefer to believe that he didn't *want* to kill us. But for the timings, well. Everyone knew that Meg does kickboxing every Thursday. Maybe you told him where it was, Meg?'

She shrugged, looking miserable.

'And I had to pass the salon on the way to the DLR. He'd have seen me head out, and without Klaus, which meant that I'd be gone for a while. Maybe he just waited for me to come back late.'

'I don't think you were the original target that night, Lou,' Indy interjected. She sat in the far corner, opposite the detectives, her hand on Banjo's head as he sat quietly beside her.

'What do you mean?'

'That girl we saved, Adrian. I think she was the target. She was Eddie's friend and Benny must have thought that Eddie had told her what he was up to. You only became a target because we found her.'

'Wait a minute,' Meg wailed. 'I don't understand. Have you even *seen* Benny? He's scared of his shadow. He couldn't have done all that!'

'*Benny* is,' I agreed, and glanced at Indy, a theory forming. 'But what if he had an alter-ego. Someone who *wasn't* afraid of his shadow.'

'The one Adrian was afraid of.' Indy nodded. 'Danny. I'd bet that he circled the block and followed you home.' She glanced at Jake. 'Or followed you to Jake's but wasn't able to make his move. Hung around until you left and tried to get you then.'

Williams and Andy exchanged a glance.

'What is it?' I insisted.

Andy shrugged and looked at Williams. 'It's all right. Tell her.'

'When we got him, Benny was lying on the floor, saying "It's not me, it's Danny. It's *always* Danny",' Williams said in a falsetto. 'Willing to bet he's gonna claim some sort of split personality disorder. "Benny" was the mild hairdresser, scared of his own shadow, but who everyone loved. "Danny" was badass. The problem-solver, who got Benny out of whatever trouble he got himself into.'

'Shit,' I whispered.

'Oh, it gets better,' Williams told Harriman. 'Go ahead. This was all you.'

Harriman stood forward, looking awkward. 'I was looking at the CCTV from last night, and I saw a man fleeing in front of the Nisa. Forensics are testing the evidence on your ball to make sure it was him – Danny, Benny, whoever – but when Andy and Scott arrested him, he had a bump the size of a goose egg on the back of his head.' Harriman played with his empty beer glass, looking surprised when Ejiro pressed a bottle of San Miguel into his hand. 'Ta. When I was first looking at the CCTV, there was something about him that felt familiar. The ponytail with a buzzed undercut.'

'I never saw that. His hair was always down, around his shoulders,' Meg whispered.

'Yeah, maybe.' Harriman nodded. 'But I don't live around here. I don't know him. But I'd seen him before. On CCTV.'

'Where?'

'Two months ago. Walking down the street the night Jonny Tang was killed. He had his arm slung over the shoulders of a woman.' He glanced at Meg, and then at Claire. 'A woman wearing a fedora.'

Caren Hansen.

'Nooo.' Meg slumped in her seat, reaching for Tyrion. Ethan rested a comforting hand on her shoulder.

'It looks like he may have been involved with Jonny's murder. We included that on his arrest sheet,' Harriman went on. Claire opened her mouth and he held up his hands. 'Which will be a matter of public record. I trust the press will be diplomatic with what's being reported: you know who was arrested, because you were involved, but it cannot be put in print. Not yet. Stick with "A male in his forties", blah blah blah. Got it?'

'Of course,' she said, her eyes sparkling.

As we spoke, Irina had inched her way closer to the detectives. It was subtle, but not imperceptible, if you knew what to look for. Andy didn't seem to look alarmed. Had he noticed? Was this a sign of a rapprochement?

'What about Laura Rossi?' Claire asked.

'Who?' Harriman asked, glancing back at his colleagues.

'The woman who died in Victoria Park the Sunday before last. The original press release said the police were treating her death as suspicious. Did Benny kill her too?'

'It wasn't our case,' Andy began. 'But no. As it turned out, her death wasn't a result of taking too many drugs, but rather a lack of them. She had long-term health conditions that hadn't been managed during her time on the streets. The bruising on her body was apparently from an incident several days earlier when she'd lost her balance and hit her head on a bench as she fell.'

'My god, that's sad.'

There was a brief silence, broken by Yaz. 'Okay, let's focus on the good stuff. Two – no, wait ... *five* – cases closed with one arrest. That's not too shabby,' she said. She raised her glass to the detectives. Then to me. Then around the room. 'Good job, everyone.' Then she gave the cops a side-eye that she had to have learned from Klaus.

'And now that you have some time on your hands, can you *please* do something about those bloody boy racers?'

'Come on, even if you're not grateful to the detectives, I am,' I said, turning towards the detectives standing in the corner and raising my glass. 'Detectives Thompson, Williams and Harriman. Thank you for this. And for saving my life.'

Andy nodded, but Williams grinned and slapped him on the back. 'One other thing to celebrate. For his hard work, Andy is Detective Constable no more. As of this afternoon, he's now our DS. Let's raise a glass to Detective Sergeant Thompson!'

89

LOUISE

Partridge Bark

Gav (Violet's Dad)

Sorry all, not going to make it tonight but have a pint for me.

Claire (Tank's Mum)

Are you ok, @Gav?

Gav (Violet's Dad)

Yeah. Got rooked into helping Hazel pack up.

Fiona (Nala's Mum)

Hazel? I thought your wife was called Doris?

Gav (Violet's Dad)

Yeah, she is. But she's mates with Hazel Carstairs, what found the two dead men. She left for Spain last night. Doris told her we'd help pack up the house and get it on the market for her. Believe me, I'd rather have a beer with you lot. You know how many animal-print dog coats that woman's got?

'Good of Gav to help out. You think he'll try those jackets on Violet?' Irina said.

'She'd murder him in his sleep,' Claire replied. 'Right.

Now, who's gonna tell me the outcome of the other case? Yaz?'

'Other case?' Andy straightened to his full height, his eyes sharp. 'What other case?'

'The case of Whose Dog Shagged Sue's Shih Tzu,' Claire said with dramatic effect. 'So, you gonna tell us, Yaz?'

As Ejiro rolled his eyes, Yaz picked up her glass and moved from the wall to take centre stage. 'Okay so, remember when the Shih Tzu was in season? Anyone with an intact dog had to maintain a several-foot perimeter, right?'

Claire and I nodded. 'Yes, of course. Klaus was most definitely interested, but didn't get his shot. What happened, did the Shih Tzu – I'm sorry, I don't know her name—'

'It's Bonnie,' Yaz continued. 'Anyway, Sue's new to the neighbourhood. She might be carrying a little more weight around the waist than she needs to, but she's got a pretty face. One day she runs into—'

'Oh no,' I groaned, seeing where this was going.

'Our local welcoming committee, Tim Aziz.' Yaz took a sip of wine, her voice in full storyteller mode. 'Now, Sophie'd just given him his marching orders. Didn't mean he was alone, of course. We all know that Tim has a small stable of friends with benefits.' She shot a look at Irina, who pretended not to notice.

'But Loki's intact. Surely she wouldn't agree to seeing Tim with Loki, when Bonnie was in season,' Clare argued.

'Well, our Tim might have told a porkie-pie. He *might*

have told her that it wasn't a problem. That Loki'd been chemically castrated.'

'Utterly irresponsible! It's actually a lot of work to raise puppies.' Meg gaped. 'It's not funny. He functionally took away her consent.'

'Agreed,' Yaz said. 'And Sue could have gone to the vet to have the doggie equivalent of a morning-after pill, but she decided against it.'

'And so, the pups.'

'Go ahead,' Ejiro sighed, waving Yaz to continue. 'Go ahead and tell them.'

'Tell us what?'

'Yaz has a name for them.'

'You've met the puppies? They must be super cute!'

'They are,' Yaz agreed, scrolling through the photos on her phone. 'Now, the dad, Loki, is a handsome Jack Russell. The mum, Bonnie, is a pretty Shih Tzu.' She found an image of three adorable puppies and held it up to the group. 'May I present to you: the Jack Shihts.'

There was a split-second pause before laughter, relieved and genuine, cascaded around the room. Amidst the chaos, I exhaled louder than I'd meant to.

'You're all right?' Jake asked. I hadn't noticed him move behind me, and my skin began to tingle.

'Yeah. Just feeling a little emosh.'

'He got under your skin? That kid?'

'Eddie? Kind of. I don't condone blackmail, but I think that he must have had a horrible time to end up where he did. No one deserves that.' I leaned against the wall for a moment. 'But it's not just that. It's being here, with the

Pack. Safe, after what felt like a hellish week.' There was still so much I didn't know about him, but not only did I trust him, I felt comfortable around him.

'You stood up for a broken kid. And you stood up to a killer. That takes serious balls. You've done good.' He clinked his glass against mine. 'A force to be reckoned with.'

'Not by choice.'

'Everyone has a choice, Louise. Don't get me wrong: I'd rather you didn't put yourself in danger—'

'Hey, Louise,' Irina shouted from across the room.

'What?'

'You know you and Mr Elusive are standing under the mistletoe?'

I looked up, half shocked. Then at Jake, alarmed. The last time I'd tried to kiss him, I'd been turned down.

What was worse? Being turned down again, this time in front of a crowd of friends, or putting on a show for them?

I expected him to laugh and move away, but he smiled. Time slowed and my senses came alive as he drew nearer.

My skin tingled, and my mouth went dry. Tonight he smelled of beer and a faintly spicy cologne. I'd never noticed his cologne before. How could I have missed that?

What if it was just a show? I wanted him to kiss me, but I wanted it to *mean something*.

Heart hammering in my ears, I braced myself with one hand on his chest.

He smiled and leaned forward, and I realised I didn't care.

Acknowledgements

My greatest thanks go to my amazing editor, Katherine Armstrong, and agent, James Wills, for believing in me and my crazy idea about a bunch of people who met at the dog park solving crimes.

If it takes a village to raise a child, it takes a 'Publishing Pack' to let my *Dog Park Detectives* run free. Many thanks to Jess Barratt, Lily Searstone and the rest of the fabulous S&S team. I couldn't ask for better. Any mistakes in the book are mine alone.

It is, however, fiction. While I've slotted in a few of my favourite watering holes, I've made up the Partridge Park area and all places, people and situations are products of my overactive imagination. With two exceptions: Klaus is shamelessly based on my beloved soul dog, the Dude, and Sarah the Trainer is the iconic Sarah Kosar of Meatball Motel. She's a first-class trainer, really has been on *Britain's Got Talent*, and does use poo bags for hair ties.

The Dude and I landed on our feet when we fell in with our Pack: Kalpna Chauhan & Rolo, Cláudia Braglia Hernandez & Preta, Jen Fong Sing and Jay Ersapah and Cava, Petra Losch and Arjun Kar & the Poms, Sabrina and Neil Denman & Bella, and Sharon Galer & Otto. Although we don't see them that often, Kelly West is the reason I have the Dude, and I will be forever grateful to her, Coco and Dashie. I am so lucky to call you all my friends.

Ongoing thanks to my MoD Squad Catie Logan and Gerry Cavanagh, who were happy to trawl through the *Paw and Order* draft, rooting out plot holes and inconsistencies. I owe you wine ... a lot of wine ...

Big love to my brother and the rest of the family. Looking forward to seeing you all in good spirits and good times!

The trail from manuscript to finished book can be bumpy, and I'm fortunate to have good friends who make sure my glass is (at least) half-full. Special shoutouts to Kate Bradley, AK Turner, Steve Carter, Willow Bennett, Shaun Elyassi and Martina Tromsdorf.

As some people know, the Dude is camera-shy. Many thanks to our friend and favourite photographer, Andrew Richardson/Raven Imagery, who has the gift of capturing the Dude's spirit (and making me look presentable as well)!

Last, but never least, I am grateful for my virtual pack – my readers. I LOVE hearing from you, so please keep the lovely messages (and pics of your dogs) coming!

Blake Mara x

Murder is never just a walk in the park ...

When friends Louise and Irina find a dead body in the local park whilst walking their dogs, they are soon drawn into the mystery of who murdered local entrepreneur Phil Creasey.

Phil used to be a member of their dog walking community – nicknamed 'the Pack' – until the death of his cockapoo, and the Pack feel they owe it to Phil to investigate his death. But with Louise and Irina leading the charge, it isn't long until they're neck-deep in local gangs, stolen motorcycles and a disturbing string of poisonings.

Have the Pack bitten off more than they can chew, or can they follow their noses and solve the crime?

'A pacy and entertaining murder mystery that's a must-read for all dog-loving crime fans. Go the Dog Park Detectives!' A. K. Turner

Available in paperback, ebook and audio

SIMON & SCHUSTER

Louise and the Pack are back in another pawfully intriguing mystery…

When Yaz and her dog Hercules find a dead man on a bench along the canal with chicken bones lying around him, she immediately calls Louise – and the police.

The case is odd: a chicken bone has been forcibly rammed down the victim's throat, and the last person to see him was their friend – and Pack-mate – Claire. When the police take Claire into custody, the Pack mobilise, determined to find the real killer.

The trail leads them to Cluckin' Good Chicken shop, who not only have a gang that loiters outside, smoking weed and harassing passers-by, but have also managed to create issues with the locals. When they discover a link between the local council and organised crime, Louise and her friends find themselves in mortal danger.

Can the Pack sniff out the killer and get to the bones of the mystery?

'More good dogs than I've ever seen in a single book! Oh, and a grisly, puzzling murder to solve, with lots of twists and red herrings. But really, I'm here for the pooches, and you should be too' **Antony Johnston**

Available in paperback, ebook and audio

SIMON & SCHUSTER